Feast of Fools

NAOMI LOUD

AUTHOR'S NOTE

Please note that although every book is a different couple, this series has an overarching plot and **must be read in order.** Please read A Dance Macabre before going any further. Thank you!

These characters are **morally black.** This story is fiction and I do not condone in any way shape or form my characters' actions and behaviors throughout this story. If you do not enjoy seeing the villains win then this series is not for you.

This is a **dark romance.** It deals with heavy subject matter and may contain triggering situations such as: quick mention of a parent passing, kidnapping, forced nudity, captivity, powerlessness, hunted for sport, forcibly collared, dubious consent, coercion, murder, gore, eye gouging, gratuitous violence, maiming, nonconsensual kiss, degradation, primal play, exhibitionism, tampering with birth control, pregnancy (only in the third act), and discussions of abortion.

To my teenage crush Spike, who taught me that obsession is sometimes even more powerful than love. Having a soul is overrated.

You're not friends. You'll never be friends. You'll be in love 'til it kills you both. You'll fight, and you'll shag, and you'll hate each other until it makes you quiver, but you'll never be friends. Love isn't brains, children, it's blood—blood screaming inside you to work its will. I may be love's bitch, but at least I'm man enough to admit it.

— SPIKE

CONSTANTINE
MERCY
Agonis Territory
Crèvecoeur Territory
MANOR
BELLADONNA
LAVETA
VORE
TEA ROOM
ALEKSANDR
Carnalis Territory
Vorovsky Territory
N
W   E
S
MOUNT PRAVITIA
GEMINI
Vainglory Territory
ANIMUS
VAINGLORY TOWER
Foley Territory
PANDAEMONIUM

Vainglory

Vane-glor-ee

OMNIA VANITAS

All is vanity

Crèvecoeur

Krev-kur

MORS MIHI LUCRUM

Death is my reward

Vorovsky

Pravitia

Pra-vit-tee-a

Vor-ov-skee

MELIUS NIMIUM QUAM NON SATIS

Better too much than not enough

Foley

Folee

MUNDUS FALLI VULT, SIC FALLATUR

The world wants to be deceived, so let it be deceived

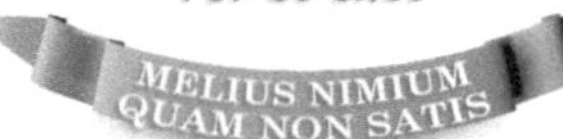

Agonis

A-gaw-nis

CAEDES EST UBIQUE

There is slaugter everywhere

Carnalis

Kar-na-lis

SINE LIBIDINE NON EST VITA

Without lust there is no life

PROLOGUE
VEIL

It was impossible to prepare for the harrowing feeling of awaiting my own sacrifice.

Naively, I always assumed I would sense when death would come to collect my soul ... like a shadow merging with my own.

Immaterial, but nonetheless there.

Waiting.

Stalking.

But nothing prepared me for today.

To gaze true evil in its eyes—one blue, one green.

I thought I knew. I thought I had a good grasp on the depravity of this city, far too similar to the one I'd left behind a month ago.

It was an incomparable feeling to have to dine in the presence of evil while pretending to be under their spell. It was as disturbing as letting a thousand spiders crawl over me without moving a single muscle or making any sound.

I feasted with those who never saw it coming. Fools. Just like myself. And feigned pleasantries, as if fear weren't dousing me in gasoline while I sat far too close to an open flame.

I watched in horror as the six heirs of Pravitia dined in

excess at the table beside us, animals gnashing on meat and bones while they spoke callously about the upcoming sacrifice. Their faces devoid of any worry lines, a psychopathic flawlessness to their dewy skin.

Now I stand in the middle of a hedge maze, lined up like cattle with the others, facing our slaughterers. A shiver crawls down my spine as I watch them leer, practically salivating at the thought of our deaths. Nausea roils in my stomach. I want to scream. I want to wail. *Something.* Instead, I do nothing but wait.

I should have fought harder when the blond with the mismatched eyes found me in the city square. But something came over me when I felt the hard tip of his knife press into my ribs.

I froze. I let fear overcome me.

Then I was shoved into a limousine, and the bearded one began his ... hypnosis? I couldn't quite tell—the one thing I *was* sure of was that it seemed to work on all the other captives but me. Their eyes became dazed, glazed over as if drugged, and a foreboding chill racked my body.

I wish the waxing moon weren't so bright as I stand here.

I wish I could stop seeing the disturbed hunger in their eyes as they continue to stare at us. As if still starving after their gluttonous meal. But I wait, caged and terrified under a forced but placid expression.

I feel the air shift. Like an invisible veil has been lifted. And by the whimpers beside me, I surmise that the one who hypnotized us has finally broken the spell the others were under. I pretend to be just as shocked as the rest of them while I furtively glance around, trying to plan a feeble attempt at an escape.

My gaze catches on my kidnapper; he's staring straight at me.

"Boo," he says with a sneer.

An unnatural sting washes over me. I realize then, somewhat late, that he's the one I'll be running from. He is the presence I should have sensed, not death—*him*.

Someone clears their throat. It's the bearded one, his gray-blue eyes as dark as the night sky.

"I suggest," he says with a slow drawl, "you run."

The words are barely out of his mouth before adrenaline surges through my body and I bolt toward one of the hedged paths, my bare feet pounding into the soft, wet grass.

I hear a laugh rise into the night. It's a hateful, wicked thing, and somehow, I know it's emanating from the man who captured me.

The one who is bound to capture me again.

THE BLOOD ROARS SO LOUDLY IN MY EARS THAT I CAN BARELY hear myself breathe. It feels like I've been running for hours, days, a lifetime. My feet are bleeding, my legs so sore that they've gone shaky and weak. I don't know how much longer I can last. I'm a rat in a maze, a lowly nothing, destined to be squashed under a shoe.

As I silently turn a corner, I slam my hand over my mouth and try to swallow a distressed scream at the sight of a body. Or at the sight of what is left of it ...

The only thing I can properly discern is black hair, sticky with blood, but the face is indistinguishable, cruelly pummeled and macerated—bludgeoned to its very last breath.

I bite down into my palm as tears burn my cheeks, anguish pulsing through my veins as I imagine my own agonizing fate at the hands of one of the ruling families.

They are hardly human. Just a sick, animated rendering of the gods controlling this city.

My mouth fills up with saliva. I'm about to be sick, but I

swallow it back down and run as far away as I can from the massacred corpse.

I turn right, then left, the air burning my lungs, my hair matted with sweat. I slow down. Listen. There's no sign of life, but my body buzzes with the maddening knowledge that I am not alone in this maze. I stumble over a raised root and can't help but swear under my breath, blindly grasping at the small branches of the hedge as I turn another corner. The hard bark digs into my palms, but I pay it no mind. Not when my mind is racing with all the tormenting possibilities of my eventual capture.

I barely have time to lift my gaze before a hand flies out from the darkness and catches me by the throat. Those mismatched eyes glow like blazing coal.

He found me.

My scream is visceral, the fear unholy, and my first instinct is to try to turn my body away from him. My impulse backfires, and I pitch backward, bringing us both down to the ground with him landing on top of me.

I react like a trapped animal. Thrashing under him, bleating like a dying goat, avoiding his eyes as if they would hold power over me.

His laugh is dark and twisted, a strand of blond hair falling over his forehead, followed by a few *tsks*. "Don't think you can escape me now," he says, and his voice feels like being dunked into an icy bath.

"Get off me, you monster!" I shriek.

I'm still trying to fight him, even after he's managed to pin my legs under him and slam my wrists over my head.

His body grows still, and mine does too. My eyes land on him as he tilts his head to the side, sniffing the air before his piercing gaze returns to mine.

"Say that again," he orders.

I'm momentarily confused, surprised by the change in his

demeanor. It's a fleeting feeling, and soon enough, I renew my attempt to fight him off. "Let me go!" I yell.

His eyes narrow as he lifts a manicured brow while his fingers tighten around my wrists, his many rings digging grooves into my skin. "Who are you?" he says slowly.

My fighting wanes, the confusion returning.

Who am I?

"I — I'm—" I stop, feeling ridiculous that I even considered answering his question, and I begin to struggle under his grasp again. "Let me go!"

His expression falters, and I'm convinced my mind is playing tricks on me—some desperate last wish before he kills me—because he appears to be deliberating.

Then he lets me go. Pushing himself off the ground, he jumps back up onto his feet.

I immediately skitter backward, stunned but nonetheless fearful.

This is a trap. It must be a trap.

For a long pregnant pause, we stare at each other. The sweat beading my forehead turns cold against the night chill. Under his ripped linen shirt, his tattooed chest heaves with rapid breaths. Then, finally, he speaks again, resolve in his tone. "Two rights, one left, and another right."

I'm stunned, the words taking far too long to sink in.

Is he—is he telling me how to escape?

Impossible. I don't dare move.

He pouts; it's mocking but playful, and my terror only intensifies.

With one hand on his hip, he leans closer and flicks his other hand my way. "Run, run, run, little rabbit, before I change my mind," he singsongs, his lips curling into a bloodcurdling grin.

This can't be real.

This can't be real.

I scramble to my feet and run for my life.

It's much too literal, my legs pumping as hard as they can, and I can't bear looking behind me, for fear of seeing him prowling after me. I expect him to follow but I at least need to try.

Then I see it—a small opening in the maze.

My laugh is crazed. I don't dare slow down.

He let me go.

He let me go.

I repeat the words over and over again as I run and run and run, successfully escaping my fate.

1

VEIL

One Month Later

I've been waiting for over an hour for the proper mark. My stomach is growling, tight with hunger, but I don't dare leave my spot. Tucked into the mouth of a small alleyway, I have the perfect vantage point to study the outside market.

It's late afternoon, and the area is bustling with people, the kiosks bursting with bright colors and titillating flavors.

The market only opens on weekends, and I've been waiting all week for the chance to snatch some unlucky elite's wallet. No one else from the city can afford to shop here anyhow. Luxurious furs, garish jewels, and mouthwatering food that I myself could only ever imagine purchasing.

I would leave this city if I godsdamned could.

It was the first thing I tried to do after the night of the Feast of Fools. But I realized very quickly that I was unable to.

Physically, I couldn't escape, as if something was keeping me bound to the city of Pravitia. Try as I might, I could never reach the city borders. Streets would become endless, or I would find myself walking in circles. The city limits no longer existed. I could never pierce whatever—*force?*—keeping me locked inside.

When my fate finally dawned on me, just as comforting as cellophane wrapped tightly around my face, I nearly went into a catatonic state.

I might have escaped the maze, but I was imprisoned nonetheless. Since then, I've wondered if the force keeping me here is the same one that pulled me to Pravitia in the first place.

My gaze continues to sweep the market, the crowd of oblivious upper crust taking leisurely strolls from one kiosk to the next, enjoying the rarity of a sunny winter day.

I'm growing impatient, chewing on the inside of my cheek as I track them one by one, my simmering repulsion for them burning incessantly inside of me.

I hate them.

I hate them all.

The ruling families especially.

Even though I'm rather new to the city, the social order of Pravitia is all too familiar to me.

The city I left behind was disturbingly similar.

Ruling families.

Gods.

The mad elite.

Although I don't recall anything as ruthless as the maze hunt. Then again, I never had the *pleasure* of being as close to the inner circle as I was that night.

I haven't since either.

I can't even fathom the depths of their depravity ...

I only know the rumors and what I've seen with my own eyes. Like the blond one with the mismatched eyes, whose name I learned later is Gemini Foley, servant to the god of trickery.

A month has passed since he chased me through the maze, and still, I dream of him. Every night, I wake up in a cold sweat, cursed to relive those terrifying moments when he had me trapped under him. A cold shiver travels down my spine at the memory, and I let out a small sigh, my lungs feeling tight.

My eyes *finally* land on a suitable mark, and I straighten, now on full alert.

Middle-aged man with a haughty expression under his salt-and-pepper beard. I could make a fortune selling his suit alone. I watch him slip his money clip into the left inner pocket of his suit jacket, and I grin.

Perfect.

Pushing off the wall I was leaning against, I begin to trail him, weaving between bodies effortlessly while keeping my attention fixed on him. After slipping on my red-rimmed sunglasses, I slide my hands into the pockets of the long tweed coat I lifted a few weeks ago. It's two sizes too big, and I swim in it, but beggars can't be choosers. Or more accurately, muggers can't be choosers. The quality is luxurious enough to masquerade me as being part of the wealthy for a few minutes, just long enough for me to accomplish what I came here to do and disappear back into the crowd.

I track my mark with the same relish as someone who's been promised a warm meal and a cozy place to sleep after weathering a cold winter day.

My urges are similar in nature.

The desperate will to survive.

To fight for a rightful place at the table.

I study the man as he stops. Picking up a cigar from a display case, he runs it along his nose, closing his eyes as he inhales the smell of tobacco.

My intuition tickles the back of my neck, like a careful whisper nudging me along, urging me to act. I've never doubted it before—and never been caught before either.

Pickpocketing is in my blood.

Taking advantage of the man's distraction, I head straight for him.

Pretending to trip, I land directly into his chest, my hand inconspicuously slipping under his jacket, my fingers curling around his money clip before he even notices the weight of my body on his.

"Oh my!" I say breathlessly, acting like a damsel in distress to lull this idiot into a false sense of security. "Clumsy me."

His money clip is already safely in my coat pocket before his hands smooth down my arms, helping me back onto my feet. My eyes dip to his gold watch, and I quickly run through the possible scenarios where I could add it to my collection, but decide against it.

"Never be too greedy," I hear my father remind me from beyond the grave. *"That's when the risk of getting caught is at its highest."*

I pretend not to notice how the man's gaze travels hungrily down my body, my coat open, revealing my favorite leopard-print shift dress underneath.

"Lucky I was there to catch you," he says, his eyes now stuck on my breasts.

I hide my disgust under a shrill, forced laugh. "Lucky indeed."

The same intuition signals to me that it's time to leave. I listen, not giving the man the chance to react before I zigzag my way through the crowd. I vanish into a small side street on the north end of the market.

The high I experience after a successful pickpocket is unmatched. Like a pleasurable thrill thrumming throughout my body. And for those small, fleeting moments, I feel invincible.

I don't remember a time when I wasn't addicted to the feeling. A time before the compulsion to steal didn't pulse under my skin like an itch I could never quite scratch.

When I'm a ways away from the market and prying eyes, I take the money clip out of my pocket and grin victoriously when I find a few thousand dollars neatly folded inside of it. Stuffing the money into my coat pocket, I throw the clip into a garbage can nearby and make my way back to my apartment to change.

This calls for a celebration.

2

VEIL

The pub is relatively busy when I walk in, considering it's late afternoon—if a bare-bones room with no liquor license and the heavy scent of urine can even be called that. This place doesn't even have a name; the locals just call it *the pub* for convenience's sake.

The lights are dim as I sweep my gaze across the cramped space. There isn't a single window in here, and after a few pints, it's easy to forget what time it is. It's always the middle of the night here—the witching hour, where anything can happen and nothing is off-limits.

I find my roommates near the makeshift bar. Zazel stands in front of Antoinette and Madeline, who are perched on a couple of stools. Zazel waves their hands around animatedly, most likely entertaining the other two with another one of their stories from Animus, the circus where they perform as a sword-swallower.

Antoinette's mouth has fallen slightly open, her gaze fixed on Zazel, her shaved head dyed a similar hue to her sparkling blue eyes. Pursing her black-painted lips, Madeline seems much less interested, her attention anywhere but on our friend.

She's even hungrier than I am, always looking for her next target, even in a place as desolate as this. She's never been deterred by the fact that everyone in here is a grifter, just like us. She believes there's always *something* to take from anyone she encounters.

Sidestepping a table that's been knocked over, along with a drunk slumped on the floor beside it, I make my way toward my crew.

"You should have heard the moan she let out," Zazel declares with a wolfish grin.

"Not again," I say with an exaggerated sigh as I sit on the empty stool next to Madeline.

Antoinette shushes me, taking the cigarette tucked behind her ear and lighting it. "Zazel was just getting to the good part," she mutters while smoke slips lazily out of her lips.

"Let me guess ... they impressed a bored toff with their sword-swallowing skills and ended up with their hands up her skirt backstage."

Zazel barks a laugh. "You're no fun."

"Am I wrong?" I drolly ask with a raise of my brow.

Zazel falls silent, struggling to hide their smirk, a few strands of their short strawberry-blond hair falling over their gray eyes. "It was beneath the stands," they finally let out slowly, tongue pushing against their freckled cheek.

"Semantics," I volley back.

We stare at each other for a beat, then burst into a laugh before Madeline interrupts us.

"You have that look in your eye." She cocks her head to the side, her short black bob swishing over her shoulder as she studies me. She lifts a half-shaved eyebrow. "Had a nice stroll through the market?"

I don't bother concealing my triumphant grin, swinging around on my seat to order a pint and a round of shots to celebrate.

"Two months' rent at least."

The four of us have been roommates since I arrived in Pravitia two months ago. Friendships forged from convenience more than anything. Our dismal apartment is located above a fish market a couple of streets away from the pub. The stench alone must have driven down the cost of rent.

Zazel whoops loudly behind me and grabs my shoulder before shaking it. "That's why you're the best."

"Please," I say with a chuckle, trying to sound humble. I turn back around to face Zazel before adding, "We all have our strengths."

"We should go to the casino to celebrate," Antoinette says with her large, beaming smile. "Try our luck at the tables," she adds as she stubs her cigarette with a chipped, painted nail.

The two others agree cheerfully while I try to conceal the dread dripping down my throat, sour and bitter.

Since I survived an attempted sacrifice, I've learned quite a few things about the city I'm trapped in. First was the cold realization that I was living in the very neighborhood of the man who had tried to kill me. The Foley territory encompasses all of Pravitia's harbor, including Pandaemonium—the casino—owned by my tormentor.

When I found out, I considered moving, considered gathering my things and slithering into a different neighborhood to hide.

But what was the point when I couldn't even escape the city in the first place?

I wasn't naive enough to believe that any other neighborhood, ruled by one of the other five families, would be any better.

I know the extent of their evil. I attended the public execution two weeks ago after all. Unlike the majority of the city, I haven't been brainwashed to believe that the troupe of actors deserved to die.

The ruling families are vile, ruthless creatures. Their thirst for blood makes my stomach churn, and the image of severed heads and bludgeoned bodies has stuck to me like boiling tar to burned skin.

"I don't — uh ..." I stutter over whatever excuse I'll conjure up today as to why I won't accompany my friends to the casino. "I'm busy."

Madeline shoots me a deadpan look, but doesn't say anything while I purposely avoid Zazel's inquiring gaze.

"Busy with?" Zazel presses, their thumbs hooked in the loops of their baggy jeans.

"Things," I reply dumbly.

I'm hoping they'll drop the subject, but I know better than to hold my breath. No one in this city, including my friends, seems as disturbed as I am by what goes on here. I seem to be cursed to see the perturbing reality as it is when everyone else doesn't. At least back home, my father seemed to see things as clearly as me.

The perversity of Pravitia is intangible, a reality that thins out and disappears quickly in the resident's mind. It's then eagerly replaced with the gluttony of excess, found within the Vorovsky territory or the countless mind-numbing orgies in the Carnalis neighborhood. Whereas here, in the Foley neighborhood, mischief and chaos seem to rule the streets. It's harder to fully capture the essence into a singular image or situation.

The one thing I do know is that, even in a city like this one, there are *always* outliers. Outsiders who seek to escape the shackles of polite society. When I linger on the thought, I find it ironic, like a crude mirror reflecting back the same dark urges as the six families ruling Pravitia. The very top and the very bottom, unwilling to conform or submit. However, the glaring difference between us and them is that we run the fatal risk of getting caught—for *them*, there's no such thing as consequences.

"Veil, the hermit," Antoinette mutters as she stands. "You're so boring."

A guilty twinge squeezes my stomach knowing I've refused most of their invitations since the Feast of Fools, avoiding all bars and clubs owned by the ruling families, *especially* in the Foley neighborhood. The money I scored burns my thigh through my pocket as I chew on Antoinette's comment, and I'm suddenly sick of it all.

Sick of hiding. Sick of operating under the paralyzing fear that I will encounter Gemini Foley in the flesh—again.

I can't live the rest of my life looking over my shoulder, living in fear, waiting for him to finish what he started.

"Fine," I relent. "Let's go to the casino."

3

GEMINI

No matter the time of day, Pandaemonium is always filled with liars, cheats, and gamblers. The citizens of Pravitia are riddled with vices, desperate to have them seep out inside one of our establishments, like stale sweat from their pores.

But the word *vice* holds no real meaning in a city like Pravitia, when our gods consume the essence of the word greedily from the hearts of its people, like ambrosia as sweet as an overripe fruit.

I let out a bored sigh, leaning my elbow and upper body on the head and neck of the carousel horse I'm sitting atop. My legs are crossed, swung to one side of the dark-winged horse as it gently gallops up and down. Round and round and round the carousel it goes.

Balancing a full coupe of champagne in my free hand, I idly observe Constantine hang her body halfway off her horse. She's holding on by only her hands, her blonde ponytails grazing the floor as her crazed giggles drift up and merge with the fanfare of the carousel. Flinging one of her legs straight up, she reveals the hot-pink thong underneath her short, pleated skirt, unbothered and most likely hoping someone is enjoying the free show.

Some might say Constantine is an acquired taste, but at least she doesn't carry herself like the other heirs. Most of whom have always taken themselves *much* too seriously, dreadfully focused on acquiring as much power and notoriety as possible inside the walls of our dear city.

I've never been interested in that kind of power.

I find it quite a bore actually.

Then again …

Being the gods' plaything comes with a lot of perks. The ability to manipulate chaos as I please, for one. Collecting everyone's secrets is another.

It's the only kind of influence I care for.

Because who are people without their secrets?

There's a thrill to finding people's vulnerabilities. A loose thread in their perfectly tailored facade. And after they so freely offer up their secrets, I just need to *pull* as they unravel, naked before me.

Finally having had enough of the carousel, I hold on to my coupe and jump down, the two long chains hanging on the side of my plaid pants rattling with the force of the movement. Strutting over to an empty poker table, I push the red gossamer hanging from the ceiling to the side and sit down.

The fabric flutters back into place, creating a fleeting sense of privacy and dividing the tables from one another. I have no interest in playing tonight, but I reach for the discarded pack of cards anyhow, snaking a single card over and around my fingers as I take a long sip of champagne with the other hand.

Constantine joins me not long after—Albert, her sentinel, trailing close behind, as usual. She jumps into the velvet seat beside me with a small *Oomph*. A mojito appears in front of her, brought by one of the staff before her derriere has time to fully connect with the cushion.

"Do you think they've fucked yet?" she says out of the blue while signaling Albert to approach.

He steps up to her seat, his square face severe and glowering as he towers over her. Opening his suit jacket, he pulls out a small hunting knife from the inside and hands it to Constantine.

I don't need her to clarify who *they* are—she's obviously referring to our two new co-rulers.

I grin, still fiddling with the one playing card as I shoot her a sideways look, recalling the loaded stare I witnessed between Mercy and Wolfgang at the public execution. "I think they've been enjoying their foreplay far too much to have indulged in anything yet."

Constantine bursts out laughing, her gaze cast down on the table as she repeatedly stabs the knife into the open spaces between her outstretched fingers. "Silly rabbits."

I let out an amused hum, my eyes sweeping over the casino floor while I take a sip of champagne.

My body grows unnaturally still, like a predator finally catching sight of their prey, when I land on a familiar face across the room. My nape tingles, and I almost laugh in delight.

It's *her*.

Waves of brown hair tumble over the back of her gray knitted sweater, the rolled sleeves revealing countless tattoos on her fair skin. By the look of how her jeans hang loosely from her hips, she hasn't had a decent meal in weeks. I wrinkle my nose at the sight.

My imagination quickly fights to replace the unsavory sight. Of her restrained and me feeding her, like my very own pet. Her curves would fill in nicely if I were the one caring for her. My body heats at the thought, my tongue smoothing over my teeth as I continue to study her from my vantage point.

She's infested my thoughts ever since I let her escape the

maze, unscathed. Naively, I thought the gods would soon lead me back to her. But a month has passed since then, and this is my first sighting of the waif. Luckily, a small inkling told me Pravitia had kept her nice and safe for me. I'm usually not a patient person—but who am I to twist the timing of fate?

She's here now, isn't she?

Constantine continues to babble beside me, but I'm no longer listening. Instead, my gaze burns into the profile of the brunette's heart-shaped face as she settles into a chair at a roulette table. She bends over to speak to whoever is sitting beside her, and I recognize them as Zazel, one of my performers at Animus.

Hearing Constantine chirp a breathy *Oops!* beside me, I snap my attention back to our table, only to find the blade of the knife jutting out of the thick of her palm.

"Gods be damned," I mutter as I reach over and yank the knife out of her hand, blood gushing out of the wound as soon as it slides out.

"I could have done that myself," Constantine says with a pout.

Typical, coming from the servant of the god of torture. She can't feel pain and has a knack for self-inflicted wounds.

The blood is pooling on the green felt of the table, and I let out a theatrical sigh as I tug on the pink ribbon tied around one of her ponytails and impatiently wrap it around her palm to staunch the bleed.

"Go fix yourself," I say with a flick of a hand.

Constantine rolls her eyes. "Party pooper." She slides out of her seat, and with her uninjured hand, snaps her fingers to Albert, who follows her into the back of the casino like a large, bulky shadow.

Quickly swiveling my attention back to the roulette table, I suck in a breath when I realize my sacrifice is gone. I deliberate if I should go find her; she's most likely still somewhere inside the walls of my casino. I decide to bide my time instead.

I've been known to play with my dinner before. I'm sure toying with her will be as delectable as when I finally sink my teeth into her ripe flesh. Sipping from my coupe, I lean into the back of my chair as I continue to flip the playing card between my fingers and slowly devise a plan.

At least now I know how to find her again.

4

GEMINI

*I*dly kick an empty can with my boot as I stroll down the alleyway, my hands tucked into my pants pockets. The rank stench of garbage fills my nostrils and makes my stomach twist, but I ignore it, stepping into a run-down archway, leading into an even more dilapidated corridor.

It only takes a few quick strides before I reach the end. The gentleman manning the door straightens his shoulders when he sees me, seeming nervous, but still flashes me a warm smile. Unlike most of my ruling counterparts, I'm not particularly interested in having my followers or staff fear me.

Intentional fear, that is.

It's unimaginative and lacks subtlety.

I would rather lull them into false safety—false friendship even—before killing them with a smile. Unfortunately, I've spilled enough blood in my twenty-seven years to have my reputation precede me. Being best friends with the most ruthless of them all—Mercy and Constantine—hasn't helped my image either.

Fear is the static behind the noise in Pravitia. We all feed on it. Served differently, depending on our personal whims. I like mine wrapped in apprehensive trust. And when I finally break that facade, the betrayal tastes even sweeter.

Besides, the constant charade makes it all the more interesting.

Entertainment is key when everything has come so easily for me. Therefore, boredom must be avoided at all costs. I like to play the role of a benevolent god with my followers. My wrath is just as grandiose. I paw at the citizens of Pravitia like a cat playing with a dying mouse.

The man greets me with a respectful nod. "Mr. Foley," he says while opening the door for me. "Welcome back."

A code word is required to enter. But I breeze past without it, and even *if* I wasn't the owner of Animus, no one would ever dare ask me for one.

I give the man a soft tap on his cheek as I pass him. "Mr. Foley was my father, love. He was a bore — I'm not. Best remember that next time."

"Of course, sir — I mean, Gemini. I — I apologize for the slip," I hear him stutter behind me.

I give him a curt wave of the hand, dismissing him without looking back as I walk down another corridor. This one isn't as run-down, the walls painted plain black with dim golden sconces lighting a path to the red velvet curtains at the very end.

When I push them to the side, the circus finally appears in all its glory. There's an irony to my casino resembling a circus tent on the outside while Animus is hidden in an abandoned factory near the harbor. It's all part of the charmed illusion attached to the Foley name.

No one should ever trust what's right in front of them—especially if it's me.

The sweet and salty aroma of popcorn and cotton candy is the first thing to tickle my senses. I've arrived in the middle of an act. My eyes slide up to the performer, walking steadily across a tightrope near the high ceiling. Large swaths of gold, red, and black gossamer are pinned to the center of the ceiling, hanging loosely and connecting to the edges of the walls, re-creating the peaked interior of a circus tent.

The crowd, who has gathered on the metal stands surrounding the circular stage, seems to be holding their breaths, waiting to see if the funambulist will fall or if they will traverse the tightrope successfully.

I don't care either way.

I head backstage, knowing I'll find Zazel in their dressing room. Their sword-swallowing skills are a crowd favorite. Entering without knocking first, I find them in a state of undress, wearing nothing but a binder and black boxer briefs.

They startle, but don't rush to cover themselves, flashing me a grin and a quick salute before leaning over to pick up a black linen shirt from the vanity chair.

"What brings you in tonight, boss?" they ask, tugging the shirt over their head before running a hand through their cropped strawberry-blond hair.

I close the door behind me and perch on the edge of the small couch, facing Zazel, casually crossing a leg over the other as I steeple my hands over one knee.

My body language is calculated—friendly.

I could easily force the truth out of their mouth like a pair of pliers extracting a rotting tooth. I would much rather they give it away willingly; I'd sniff out their lies eventually. This way, no one gets hurt, and we can all continue to uphold the illusion of security.

"A little birdie told me you've made a new friend," I drawl with an inquiring smile.

Zazel's eyes narrow. "A new friend?" they repeat as they slip into a pair of black trousers, still barefoot.

"You were both at Pandaemonium yesterday. Brown hair,

tattoos," I rattle off before pausing, recalling the ill-state of her. "Rail thin."

"You mean Veil?" Turning their back to me, they sit in front of the vanity mirror, brightly illuminated with light bulbs around the edges, their gaze meeting mine through the reflection. "My roommate?"

"Veil," I say quietly, smoothing every letter of her name over my tongue before swallowing them down with relish. "Last name?"

"Vulturine," Zazel mutters as they apply some mascara, their mouth slightly open with concentration.

"Do you still live down on Crescent Street?" I probe further.

I know where Zazel resides, just as I know where all my employees live. I make every detail about them my business. When used properly and efficiently, controlling them with information is just as powerful as governing them with fear.

Zazel's answer is laced with suspicion. "Yes ..." they answer slowly, now raking gel through their hair, still studying me through the mirror. "Why the sudden interest, boss?"

I can tell they're being careful not to cross an invisible line between us, and I can appreciate their survival instinct while still being curious enough to ask the question.

I jump to my feet, acting disinterested while straightening the rings on my fingers and inspecting my black nail polish. After a loaded beat, I find their gaze and shoot them a wink, followed by a cocky grin. "Wouldn't you like to know, love?"

5

VEIL

I try to ignore the stale scent of day-old fish wafting through the open window as I sit, bored to death, reading a book in the living room of our shared apartment. Tucked into the corner of the ratty couch, I sigh loudly, listening to the intermittent *swat* of darts hitting the drywall behind me, Madeline just as bored as I am.

Antoinette plops beside me on the couch, chewing on a mouthful of the sandwich she just made herself, the bread most likely stale and expired.

None of us have spoken in over an hour, wordlessly waiting for Zazel to come home from their shift at Animus. They're the only one in the group that has a real job, the rest of us choosing to stick to the shadows and prey on the rich to support ourselves.

Petty theft is not for the weak.

Especially when the fridge has been empty for the past few days and there seem to be holes in every item of clothing I own.

It's not like I've never been legally employed. I could be if I wanted to, but the thought of a boss overseeing my every move has my teeth clenching in aggravation. But I could never deny my nature. Pickpocketing is simply a part of who I am. I couldn't suppress it even if I tried.

The front door finally flies open, and Zazel appears, ushering with them a refreshing burst of life into the vat of boredom we were all drowning in. I slam my book closed and twist my body to face Zazel as Madeline gives them a distracted wave, still focused on her dart game.

"Finally!" Antoinette chirps as she leaps up to greet Zazel, following them into the open kitchen. Hopping up and sitting on the counter beside the dirty sink, Antoinette peppers Zazel with leading questions about their night at the circus as they reach into the fridge for a stray beer.

Cracking the can open, Zazel rests their hip on the counter next to Antoinette and takes a large sip, eyeing her with a smirk. Their eyes are still lined in black, a rouge tint to their cheeks, but they've changed into a loose crop top and jeans.

"Bored, are we?" they quip.

Antoinette bursts out laughing and leans into her palms, which are resting on either side of her swinging legs. "It's just not as fun when you're not around."

Madeline shoots Antoinette a deadpan look while blindly throwing a dart straight into the bullseye. "Thanks a lot."

Antoinette snorts. "You know what I mean, Maddie. Veil, back me up."

I quirk a smirk. "Actually, what *do* you mean?"

She puffs a breath and rolls her eyes. "Everyone is so sensitive," she mutters.

And it's my turn to bark a laugh. My attention snags on Zazel, who seems to be observing me, lost in thought.

Something in their pensive expression makes the hair on my arms stand on end.

"What?" I ask.

They blink, as if focusing back on the three of us, and shrug a shoulder, trying to conceal a grin behind their beer can.

"What is it?" I press, saying the words slowly.

"You might have found yourself a secret admirer," they say with levity.

But as they break eye contact and look away, I catch something much heavier lingering behind their gray eyes. Wariness? Uncertainty? It only lasts a split second, and it's gone when they find my gaze again.

Dread trickles through my veins, an ominous chill sweeping over my skin, and I fight against a full-body shiver before asking, "What do you mean, a secret admirer?" My mind has latched on to the worrisome improbability that they're referring to the monster in my nightmares, but I keep my tone light.

Impossible. Why would it be—

"My boss came by tonight, asking about you."

My heart pitches out of my chest, and my breathing slows, my vision blurring while I try to process what they just said.

He found me. He found me, and now he's going to kill me.

"Gemini Foley?" I ask dumbly, already knowing the answer but needing Zazel to spell it out for me before I lose all sense of composure.

"The one and only," they answer casually before taking another sip of their beer.

Antoinette hums in delight. "Oh, to marry into the ruling class," she says, stars in her eyes, as if everyone in this damn city would be over the moon to discover that one of the heirs had their eye on them.

Even Madeline has stopped her game of darts, turning her attention to Zazel, her brown eyes widening.

I swipe a hand over my face, visibly shaking, and clear my throat. "What did he say exactly?"

"Not much." They push themselves off the counter and walk over to the couch, propping themselves on the armrest opposite me. "He just asked a few questions about the tattooed brunette he saw with me at the casino yesterday. Told him we were roommates."

I feel the blood drain from my face as I chew on my bottom lip, restraining myself from grilling Zazel with the exact details of the conversation.

What's the point?

He found me.

Zazel furrows their eyebrows in worry, sitting closer to me. "Veil?" Their hand reaches out to touch my arm. "Are you okay? You just got really pale."

"I'm just ..." I stumble over my words, knowing I can't possibly explain what happened during the Feast of Fools. Something tells me they wouldn't believe me, as if deliberately blind to the heirs' truest nature. Amoral creatures brimming with bloodlust. I choose the one thing that feels closest to the truth. "He scares me — they all do."

Antoinette walks up to the couch and leans her hands against the back, peering down at me. "Gemini isn't like the others." Her tone is reassuring, and I can tell she believes every word she says. "He actually cares about his followers."

Madeline agrees as she resumes her game of darts and Zazel smiles warmly and nods.

"I don't think you have anything to worry about," they say. "He's probably forgotten all about you already. I've never seen him with the same person twice under his arm in the three years I've worked for him."

If they only knew ...

Eager to change the subject, I shove their thigh with my foot. "Reminds me of someone," I say with a grin that I hope looks real. Inside, I'm reeling.

Zazel bursts out laughing, shoving me right back, and gradually, the conversation shifts as we prepare to leave the house for a drink at the pub.

For the rest of the night, I pretend I'm not fixated on the thought of Gemini Foley and how he once let me go.

I don't think I'll manage to escape death twice.

6

GEMINI

There's a chill in the air tonight. The rain has ceased at least, but it's left large puddles throughout the streets. My clothes are damp, my knitted shirt sticking to my stomach, but I pay it no mind while I play with a silver coin, threading it through my fingers.

Standing at the mouth of the alleyway, I lean back into the shadows, my gaze fixed on the two windows above the fish market across the street.

I've been fighting a mild disgust from the smell ever since I arrived twenty minutes ago. I hope Veil's wardrobe doesn't carry the same odor or else I'll need to strip her naked and burn all her clothes.

Who am I kidding? I'll do that in any case.

She's *my* puppet. A nimble little doll, gifted to me by my god. I've been a patient boy, and I now itch to have her returned to me.

From my vantage point, I can't see much inside, and I consider killing the tenant who lives in the apartment facing her bedroom window just so I can get a closer, more intimate look. I mull it over, the idea quite enticing, but decide against it. I just had these trousers dry-cleaned.

The building door opens, and Veil and her ragtag crew spill out onto the streets. I press myself further into the shadows, my body humming to snatch her and drag her away. I somehow manage to fight my impulsive nature, wrestling it into compliance, and ignore its snarling protests while I watch her stroll down the street with her friends.

For now, I'm curious enough just to observe her. To get to know her without my presence influencing her behavior. I can't believe she's been right under my nose this entire time—in my territory, of all places. She must lack some crucial survival instincts to have stayed so close.

Or ...

She's not from Pravitia and doesn't know any better. It would explain why I'd never seen her before I caught her in the maze. It's a rare occurrence to have wayward visitors from outside Pravitia. The city acts like a shield to keep the unwanted out—and the wanted in. Must be our gods' influence, as always.

Before the small group disappears around the corner, I step out from the cloaked alley and follow them down the street.

I feel a vague embarrassment just *looking* at Veil's ill-fitting coat. It swallows her whole and is clearly meant for someone much bigger than her.

"Unacceptable," I mutter under my breath.

I yearn to dress her in custom-made outfits, to brush her wavy brown hair until the strands turn to silk under my touch. She appears skittish, looking over her shoulder, her gaze shifty as it sweeps over the crowded street behind her.

Her friends seem unaware of her discomfort, but to me, it's as glaring as the morning sun. I'm sure Zazel told her about my little visit earlier, and a thrill of excitement runs up my spine at the thought of Veil now being on edge because of me.

I smile, my eyes narrowing with delight.

As long as I'm in her head.

Her little crew continues down one of the main avenues leading to the harbor when I witness Veil slam straight into a woman walking in the opposite direction. I chuckle at Veil's shocked reaction, fumbling to apologize, her body language frazzled and alarmed.

My steady gait slows to a stop while Veil continues to apologize. Until my attention zeroes in on her tucking a wallet into the deep pocket of her coat.

I can't believe it. My heart squeezes, and glee swarms my chest at the sight.

Oh, my pretty, pretty, petty thief.

You're not as sinless as I thought.

I turn ravenous. Needing to peel the layers of this little enigma.

Maybe she does belong in my neighborhood after all.

Eventually, the four of them disappear into a building, which I recognize immediately as one of those illegal bars that I turn a blind eye to. I should care. But I don't. As a slave to the god of trickery, who would I be if I didn't allow my followers to emulate my cunning nature?

They can do as they so please, as long as they worship me.

Knowing I'll immediately be recognized if I stroll inside without *something* to conceal my identity, I look around the busy street for anything that might help my current conundrum.

I snap my fingers at a random passerby. "You," I order, "hand me your hoodie."

They startle, eyes widening when they realize who I am, but promptly do as I said, nervously unzipping their hoodie and handing it over.

I smile. "Much appreciated, love." My voice is sickly-sweet, like a mouthful of honey. I flick my fingers in their direction. "Now off you go."

Typically, I'd never be caught dead in something as uncivilized as a zip-up hoodie, but alas, desperate times call for desperate measures. I shrug the damn thing on, still warm from its previous owner, and I curl my lips in disdain, disliking the feeling.

I pull the hood up, ensuring my face is at least half concealed before stepping into the dive. My appraisal is quick, and I locate my petty thief near the bar, drinking a pint with the other three.

Luckily, there's a crowd tonight. I snake my way through the throngs of bodies, finding a table in the dark corner, facing the bar.

I order a gin on ice from a passing server and turn to face my prize, my heart racing as I gobble up every little piece of her I can.

Like the way she presses her fingers to her mouth after taking a big gulp of beer. Or how her pointed nose crinkles when she laughs. The idle twirl of a strand of hair around her finger as she listens to her friends speak.

I grip my glass, knuckles whitening.

I need it all.

For the rest of the night, I study her—*consume* her.

Even hours later, it's not nearly enough.

I can't ignore the growing lust surging through my veins as I watch her. My gaze is fixed on the flush on her cheeks, and I'm overwhelmed by the sudden desire to be the reason behind her skin burning up. My train of thought turns desperate; needing to know how warm her skin feels under my possessive touch.

As time passes, my impatience grows and grows and grows until I can barely contain it.

I thought I could bide my time.

Let myself enjoy the hunt as much as the catch.

I should have known better—should have known I could never follow such *dull* plans before falling victim to my impulsive temperament.

I leave before the urge to throw her over my shoulder and carry her out, kicking and screaming, overtakes me.

Soon.

7

GEMINI

I might not sense my dear god of trickery as intimately as Mercy senses her god of death, but in a crowd as considerable as this, I believe we feel all our gods' powers pulsing through the mob of Pravitians.

Today, we celebrate our two co-rulers, Mercy and Wolfgang —the first double inauguration in our city's written history. I watch them now, cloaked in glimmering gold as they stand front and center before our febrile citizens. The rest of us sit behind the powerful duo in thrones made of carved wood, our parents at our sides.

Even at a time like this—while the moon eclipses the sun in its totality for the first time in nineteen years, the day gradually turning into night—I can't help the faint hum of boredom buzzing under my skin, like the constant static of an off-tune radio.

My attention wanders. I lazily sweep my gaze over the crowd as the moon begins to cast its shadow over Pravitia. My dormant adrenaline spikes when I serendipitously find my petty thief among the countless faces. Her attention is fixed on her two rulers spilling their blood in small ceremonial vials. I

36

jump to my feet without much thought and sneak offstage, ignoring my mother's low hiss of disapproval behind me.

According to the Oracle, the eclipse is an important and reverent moment, imbued with auspicious power.

So why not utilize it for myself?

I can't think of a better time to divert Veil's fate, to snatch it from thin air and claim her all to myself.

At first, I'm quick enough to slither through bodies, unnoticed, but my gold three-piece suit practically glows, even with the dying sun above us. Soon enough, citizens recognize me and give me a wide berth, the crowd parting as if a force field were propelling them backward.

Distracted, it takes Veil a few crucial seconds to notice the disturbance in the status quo, and by the time her curious gaze lands on me, I'm heading straight for her.

I would laugh at how her brown eyes widen in alarm if I wasn't already salivating like a rabid dog. Her body freezes, then jolts into action as she turns her back to me and *runs*.

My smile turns wicked, and my heart pumps wildly in anticipation as I chase her through the mass of bodies. My eyes track her effortlessly, as if programmed to always find her, wherever she may go.

I watch with gleeful amusement as Veil shoves people out of her way while the sun slowly reappears from its trip behind the moon. The sunlight illuminates her terror-streaked face each time she glances back while I gracefully make my advance. I haven't even broken a sweat—I could never tire of chasing my obsession.

I wouldn't have been willing to let her go in the maze if I'd been blessed with such an entertaining chase. There was too much hiding then, but today? I witness every little reaction she makes. She's delicious, and I long to lick the glistening sweat on her forehead and taste the fear there.

Because that fear is *me*.

I already exist inside of her, her pores familiar to the flavors of Gemini Foley.

Reaching the end of the crowd, she ducks out onto a deserted street off the side of the city square. I follow her, exhilaration stoking the flames of adrenaline in my veins, knowing I'm close to catching her.

She's fast. Swift in her escape, as if she's done this countless times before. But Pravitia is my city; I know every street, every dip in the sidewalks and every alleyway.

Which gives me an idea.

I chuckle, delighted, as I anticipate her next move and turn into an alley. Just when she thinks she's finally escaped me, she will be led directly to me.

Silly rabbit.

I will always catch you.

I jog through the alley until I reach the other side, the street deserted as I take a quick peek. Her strained breaths reveal her location before she even turns the corner, and I press myself into the wall, waiting for the perfect moment to step out from my hiding spot.

Three ...

Two ...

One ...

Her distressed scream is fabulously intoxicating as she tries to sidestep me, but realizes she has nowhere left to run, her eyes widening in terror, her breathing turning panicked. I give her a playful frown just to further antagonize her.

She makes one last attempt to escape, but I'm faster, grabbing her wrist and twisting her around. Wrapping my arms around her torso, I pin her hands to her sides as I push her back to my chest. I get a lungful of her shampoo as she struggles against me. Luckily, she doesn't smell like the fish market, but of sweet, ripe mangoes.

She shrieks, and I laugh.

Her legs thrash up in the air like a savage alley cat, which causes my laughter to swell. I attempt to press her to the wall to temper her violent objections, but she plants her feet flat against the bricks and pushes off with all the force she has in her thighs.

"Let me go!" she shrieks again as I stumble backward while trying to keep her tight to my chest, her legs still flailing this way and that.

When my back hits the brick wall behind me, I keep us pinned there, shushing into her ear as she continues to scream.

I can feel that strange absence, even now.

Her words stripped naked, so similar to—

A thunderous boom wrenches me out of my thoughts; it startles me enough that I almost let Veil slip out of my grip. I hear distant screams, some fast approaching, like a mob is running toward us. I cock my ear, trying to pick up more clues. Was that an explosion? The disturbance sounded like it came from the city square. My mind flashes to my friends and family onstage. Shocked by the noise, Veil bellows with renewed vengeance, still fighting me.

"*Please*," she says, her tone turning mournful, then chokes on a sob. "I don't want to die."

She continues to struggle, but she's losing momentum, her feet finally making contact with the ground.

Unmoved by her small show of weakness, I still take a few moments to deliberate.

I could let her go, assuage my worry, and find out if my loved ones are safe.

Or …

Making up my mind, I tighten my grip around her chest. "Die?" I rasp into the shell of her ear. "Why would I *ever* kill my new favorite pet?"

GEMINI

My new doll fought me all the way home. Luckily for me, she's underfed and underweight, and my dragging her to the dock was a facile feat, if not slightly grating with her constant flailing of limbs.

We zipped across the harbor on a speedboat to reach the other side, where my house is perched atop a cliff facing Pandaemonium.

My driver didn't bat an eye—didn't dare question why I was abducting a little twig-like thief—even when I tried to silence her protest with a hand over her mouth. She bit down into my palm and broke the skin.

I must say, I rather enjoyed that.

My delighted laugh seemed to unnerve her more than the actual kidnapping. She grew quiet for the second half of the ride, but I didn't risk letting her go, even after she calmed down. She seemed like the type who would fling herself off the boat in an attempt to escape.

Now here we are, in my living room, staring at one another as she sits on my red leather couch and I stand in front of her. Her long, wavy hair is wild from the windy boat ride. She's wrapped her arms around her waist, her fingers nervously toying with the sleeve of her ratty sweatshirt.

No, no, no, that won't do.

I'll need to rectify her hideous wardrobe immediately.

She hasn't made a peep since we stepped onto my property. The sun has had time to set somewhere in the distance, the shadows gradually crawling up the living room walls like vines.

Finally having had enough of our silly staring game, I let out a bored sigh and break eye contact. I turn to the wet bar, next to my vinyl collection near the floor-to-ceiling windows.

"In the mood for a drink, love?" I ask over my shoulder as I lean down and open a small wine fridge, stocked with my favorite champagne. I pull out a bottle and uncork it while I wait for an answer, but I'm met with icy silence instead.

Unbothered by her lack of participation, I pour us two glasses and set hers on the coffee table before sitting on the couch a few seats away, sitting diagonally from her on the sectional. Her coupe is left untouched in front of her.

I give her a small tut, waving at her champagne. "Don't be shy now, you've come such a long way to visit me."

I take a refreshing sip of champagne while I wait for her to speak. Although I'm unsure if I have the patience, especially when there's the pressing matter of the bombing and its aftermath.

I made a few quick calls when we first arrived at the house, making sure my mother was safe, but grew worried when Mercy and Constantine didn't answer my call. I managed to reach Aleksandr, who informed me Mercy was in hiding with Wolfgang and Constantine was in the hospital after a large beam fell on her.

I plan to visit later this evening, after I've dealt with my new favorite acquisition

Veil's stormy brown eyes slowly slide to mine, her arms still tightly tucked across her body.

"Why did you let me go in the first place if it was to just kidnap me again?" she mutters, her tone flat and defeated.

I let the silence percolate between us before I smile, flashing her my roguish charm.

"You are mistaken, pet." I lean forward, placing my glass on the table before settling back into the couch. I tilt my head to lean into my outstretched index and thumb, crossing my legs in her direction. "I never said *anything* about letting you go."

Her thick brows furrow in confusion as her mouth presses into a thin line. "You *did* let me go," she repeats, as if I didn't quite understand her the first time.

I chuckle. "Don't mistake my mercy with selflessness, love. I always intended to find you again." I narrow my eyes in mischief. "The gods specifically chose you for me; it would be a slight against them if I *ever* let you go."

Her gaze turns hard, and her laugh is dry and derisive. "The gods," she repeats in disgust.

"Careful," I respond with a tsk. "Our gods do not respond kindly to heresy. Especially in the presence of one of their humble servants."

I reach for the champagne again and finish it in one big, undignified gulp, the bubbles tickling the back of my nose. "Now," I declare as I spring up from the couch, "if you'll excuse me, I must visit a dear friend."

I snatch Veil's elbow with a strong hand and pull her onto her feet.

"Wait," she splutters as I drag her out of the living room and into the hallway. "You're just going to leave me here?"

"Cunning little creature," I mumble, my hand still firmly latched around her arm.

Opening the door to one of my guest bedrooms, I shove her inside. She stumbles in, eyes wide.

I pull out the handcuffs I previously tucked into the back of my pants and guide her to sit near the top of the bed.

"Please," she continues to protest, but doesn't try to fight me. "You don't need to do that; I'll be good, I promise." There's a small quiver in her voice, and it sends a delicious shiver down my body.

"Oh, I'm sure you will be, love," I reply drolly as I latch her wrist with one of the cuffs and attach the other to one of the bars on the wired bed frame. "Now sit tight," I say with a smile. Staying eye to eye with her, I give her nose a light tap with my finger and wink. "I'll be back soon."

I catch a flash of fury behind her irises before standing back up to my full height.

And, *oh*, that pleases me even more than her delectable fear.

"Gemmie!" Constantine chirps loudly when I enter her hospital room.

The place, decorated in soft florals and pale yellows, is spacious but dimly lit due to the pulled curtains, concealing the Pravitian cityscape behind it.

Constantine is propped on a mountain of pillows, her leg raised and set in a pink cast. She pushes herself up and looks like she's planning to stand, but Aleksandr jumps to his feet and fusses over her like a startled mother bird trying to protect the nest.

"Tinny," he scolds, pushing her back down by a palm to the forehead, "you're *injured*."

She puffs out a short but shrill shriek, her blue eyes rolling upward dramatically, and I laugh as I bend down to kiss her on the cheek. I can't help but antagonize her by patting the top of her head.

"There, there, my love. How are you feeling?"

"Never better," she answers glibly with a wide smile.

We both ignore Aleksandr grumbling under his breath. He's changed into a black velour tracksuit, his brown hair disheveled, as if he's been continuously raking his fingers through it.

"Where were you?" Constantine asks, a curious twinkle in her eye, as I pull a chair closer to her bedside.

The room falls silent. My eyes jump to Aleksandr, pacing near the window, then back to Constantine. She shoots me an understanding look.

"Sasha," she says, her tone warm, turning her attention to her childhood best friend. "Can we ..." She doesn't finish her sentence and simply signals to the door with a small jerk of her head.

Aleksandr sighs but mutters, "Sure." Taking his phone out of his pocket, he adds, "I need to make some calls anyway."

I watch his shoulders slump while he steps out of the room, before I look back to Constantine.

She answers my question before I ask it. "Alina died in the bombing." Her tone holds as much empathy as she can muster for someone who has never experienced emotional pain before.

Aleksandr losing his mother certainly explains his morose attitude.

I nod solemnly, leaning my elbows on her bed. "Anyone else?"

"Not of importance."

We stay silent for a few seconds until she swats my arm, shifting the mood. "Where were you? Your mother says you left in the middle of the ceremony."

I quirk a conspiratorial smile. Slowly walking two fingers up the length of her cast, I consider how much I want to tell Constantine.

"I've caught myself a little rabbit," I finally say. "I was busy chasing it when the bombing occurred."

Constantine's eyes grow wide as her mouth drops open in an excited gasp.

I cut her off before she even utters a word. "Hands off, Tinny. This one is mine."

She pouts, crossing her arms petulantly. "You're no fun."

I chuckle softly at her spoiled attitude.

"What's so special about this one?"

I lean back in my chair, grinning from ear to ear as a buzz of reckless anticipation hums in my chest. "I'm not sure yet, but I'm desperate to find out."

9

VEIL

I've lost track of how long I've been handcuffed to a bed in *Gemini Foley's* house.

It must have been hours by now. And yet here I sit. I fight the exhaustion and struggle to keep my droopy eyelids open and alert. My wrist is raw from the vain efforts to try to break out of the handcuffs, and the now-sensitive skin smarts at just the thought of trying again.

There's not much to look at to pass the time either. The bed is under large windows in the corner of the bedroom, and a redwood armoire sits on the opposite wall of the bed.

Although my vision has grown used to the dark, the furniture, cloaked in shadow, plays tricks on my mind. Everywhere I look, I feel threatened, as if even inanimate objects were willing actors to my ultimate demise.

I stare at an empty wall instead.

The door bursts open, and the sudden flick of the lights has my heart jumping into my throat from the shock. I squint, my hand attempting to shelter my eyes.

"Apologies for my tardiness, pet. I came back as soon as I

could," Gemini says with a flurry of theatrical movements, his tone light and jovial.

I say nothing as I scamper back up the bed, pulling my knees up to my chest, my heart pounding wildly against my rib cage.

He's changed out of his gold suit and into a red mesh tank top, tucked into tight black jeans. His bared skin reveals a sporadic collection of tattoos, including playing cards and a carousel horse on his chest. My gaze snags on a tattoo of two snakes that appear to be coiling around his collarbone, near where a set of silver chains adorn his neck.

With a small furrow to his brow, he pins me with his stare, his eyes shimmering as they inspect me. A thin line of black eyeliner is smudged under his lower lashes.

He points a finger at me, making it twirl in tight circles. "You need to shower," he states, wrinkling his nose at me. "I can smell the appalling stench of fish on your clothes."

Pulling the key out of the front pocket of his jeans, he walks up to the bed and unlocks the cuff from my wrist.

"What time is it?" is all I can muster to ask.

Gemini hums, as if everything I say somehow delights him. "Time is but an illusion, love."

While I'm still sitting on the bed, he lifts my wrist and inspects it, seeming displeased by the swollen red skin. He slowly drags his thumb over it, and a confusing shiver dances down my spine.

Letting out a small tsk, he mutters, "Unacceptable." His piercing eyes lift to meet mine. "No doll of mine will defile their skin in this manner — understood?"

A warring of emotions pulses through me—horrified dread by being referred to as his doll, but also irritation that he would blame this on *me*.

"I'm not the one who handcuffed me to the bed." The words

fly out of my mouth before I can swallow them back down. I shrink, fearing his reaction.

But all he does is chuckle. It's warm, amused even, and it leaves me deeply unnerved.

"Then I suggest you stop struggling like a caught butterfly and accept your fate, pet."

"WELL? WHAT ARE YOU WAITING FOR, LOVE?" GEMINI LEANS casually against the wide bathroom sink, arms crossed as he lazily inspects his nail polish.

After he uncuffed me, he led me to his bedroom and into his vast en suite.

I couldn't help but note that his room was right next door to the one he'd locked me in.

Even with the terror muddling my thoughts, I'm taken by the charm of his bathroom, especially the two claw-foot bathtubs sitting under large stained-glass windows. The floor is an intricate mosaic of colorful tiles while the shower takes up most of the wall opposite to where Gemini now stands.

He hasn't glanced my way since he last spoke, but I can tell he's waiting for an answer.

"Privacy," I finally say with as much assertiveness as I can muster.

"This *is* private," he responds, his attention elsewhere.

"You're still here."

His roguish eyes finally slide to mine. "I don't count." Pushing himself off the sink, he strides toward me. "Now take this off," he orders, pinching my sweatshirt with two dainty fingers, "before I rip it off myself with my teeth."

I swallow hard, holding his piercing gaze. I should scream, protest, run even, but my intuition tells me I wouldn't make it far.

He claims he doesn't intend to kill me, but why would I trust a word he says?

I decide on compliance for now. I'll bide my time until I find a better way to escape. Still, I can't help but jut my chin out in defiance before muttering an angry, "Fine."

With a huff, I take my clothes off, my movements rushed and aggrieved.

Until I'm naked.

Painfully vulnerable in front of my captor.

Gemini gives my naked body a quick, cursory glance. But seems more interested in kicking my pile of clothes into a corner of the bathroom with the tip of his boot, as if he can't wait to distance himself from them. The shame of standing naked in front of Gemini morphs into an even more complex version of the emotion as he handles my clothes with such disgust. As if I'd ever had any real choice in the matter.

I feel as insignificant as grime under his overpriced shoe.

My bitterness tastes like ash on my tongue, and I don't wait for another command before stepping into the shower. Now, only a pristinely clean windowpane stands between us.

The faster I do this, the faster it's over.

Giving him my back, I turn on the hot water. Even while I'm racked with nerves, the impressive showerhead leaves me breathless as I step under the soothing rainfall. I stifle my positive reaction. I would never want to admit to a single ounce of pleasure while that monster is watching me.

While I'm lathering my body with luxurious soaps, with even more luxurious names, I hear Gemini behind me. "Make sure to use the exfoliator."

I peek over my shoulder and realize that he's barely paying attention to me. Too busy doing a handstand in the middle of the bathroom, necklaces dangling in his face while he balances on one hand, then the next.

I can't control the small ripple of relief that washes over me at the lack of attention.

When I'm all washed up—and exfoliated—it takes me longer than it should to turn off the water, having fallen into a feeble sense of safety behind the confines of the foggy glass.

I don't know what awaits me after this.

Regretfully, I turn off the shower and slowly turn to face him, not bothering to cover my naked body with my arms and hands. I might feel weak and powerless, but I refuse to let it show.

Gemini has resumed an upright position and holds up a fluffy, large towel toward me. I step onto the plush bathroom rug and reach for it, but he pulls away with a taunting smirk and gives me a few tuts while slowly shaking his head.

My throat tightens, and I swallow hard, but again, I say nothing, except for a small, defeated sigh escaping my lips. I break out into full-body goose bumps when Gemini wraps the warm towel around my body and begins to dry me off. But even when his hands come *far* too close to the middle of my legs, his touch doesn't convey anything sexual.

I'm left relieved yet confused—unsure of what to make of his intentions.

"There," he says softly after carefully patting down my hair and tucking the towel around my chest, his fingers delicate against my skin.

His expression is far too innocent for the monster I know lies inside. He might *appear* as a debonair aristocrat, but I will never forget who he is and what true evil hides behind the jester persona.

Coaxing me to stand in front of the mirror, he reaches for a hairbrush.

"I can do that myself," I state, knowing full well that my protest will have no sway whatsoever.

"Now why would I let you do that?" he says, his toothy grin

lighting up his eyes as he watches me in the mirror. "Be a well-behaved doll and stay still."

Unease crawls all over my skin again from him referring to me as his doll, but I remind myself to stay docile—for now.

I press my lips together and say nothing more as he gently brushes my hair, careful stroke after careful stroke.

Having nowhere else to look, I study him through the glass. I linger on the small silver loops around his earlobes, then on the short strand of blond hair falling over his forehead. A thin scar cuts through his left eyebrow; it's more prominent now that his brow is furrowed as he meticulously works on a knot in my hair.

"What kind of rube doesn't use conditioner?" he mutters under his breath.

He then falls back in silent concentration.

After successfully detangling my hair, he plaits it with deft fingers into one long braid before stepping back with a pleased sigh and inspecting me.

"Wait here," he says before disappearing into his bedroom and returning after a few short moments. He hands me a pair of cotton shorts and a loose T-shirt. "You can wear this to bed." Then winks. "Tomorrow, I'll show you to your new wardrobe."

Something about his wink makes my nape prickle, but I take the clothes without balking. I pause, hoping that he'll turn around while I get dressed.

He does nothing of the sort.

How silly of me.

I drop the towel, and this time, his gaze lingers.

"I can't wait to feed you," he says distractedly, falling silent again while he continues to observe me.

My heart squeezes with apprehension, but I ignore him while I step into the shorts first, then quickly pull the shirt over my head. The bright scent of blood orange and cloves lingering in the fabric overwhelms my senses. I recognize Gemini's scent from the multiple times he's pinned me to him, and I grow weary, realizing I won't be able to escape him, even while I sleep.

Considering I've had the same nightmare of the maze chase for weeks now, I never did escape him in the first place.

Taking my hand in his, he leads me back to the guest room. Cold sweat prickles my forehead when I realize he'll most likely handcuff me to the bed again. Instead, he pulls down the duvet and pats the mattress for me to climb in. I eye him with suspicion, but do as he instructed, apprehensively sliding under the covers, my gaze locked on his.

His charming expression is but a derisive facade, and anxiety roils in my stomach as he pulls the covers up to my chin.

Bending over so that his lips are close to my ear, he whispers, "If you try to escape, you'll never make it off the property." He presses a chaste kiss on my forehead. "Sweet dreams."

My eyes sting with unshed tears as he strolls to the door and turns off the lights, plunging me back into darkness. I hear the lock turn, and I fight against the claustrophobia clawing behind my chest. Rolling to my side, I bring my knees up to my chest, squeezing my eyes tightly shut.

Why did I ever come to Pravitia?

10

VEIL

I hear the key turn in the lock before my mind is fully conscious. My body, on the other hand, instantly propels me out of sleep and into a state of high alert. I scramble to sit up in bed before Gemini opens the door.

The first thing I notice when he pokes his head inside is that his blond hair is now dyed pink.

"Oh good!" he declares, his tone bright and chipper. "You're awake."

I have the reflex to contradict him and tell him I was sleeping, but decide against it, choosing pointed silence instead.

He takes one large step inside and sweeps his appraising gaze around the room. He's dressed in a tweed vest, his chest bare underneath, and matching trousers. A white measuring tape, draped around his neck, hangs loosely over the vest.

It appears he's surveying the room, as if making sure everything is to his liking—as in no signs of a failed escape, I'm sure.

I didn't bother checking if the windows were locked when he left last night.

And if they weren't? Where would I go? Where would I hide?

The city is his. I don't belong here, and yet I can't leave. Maybe he's right, and I should accept my fate.

Destined to become Gemini Foley's plaything.

My free will clasped tightly in the palm of his hand.

"We are having breakfast on the terrace," he declares, his hands giving two short claps, shoulders and neck straightening. He flashes me an impatient look, followed by a dazzling smile. "Come, come. Time to get dressed. The morning birds are singing a new song."

His words from last night drift back like an ominous whisper.

"Tomorrow, I'll show you to your new wardrobe."

His turn of phrase and the way he's waiting for me to follow him makes me think that wherever this new wardrobe is, it's not in this room.

I cautiously climb out of bed, my gaze serious and suspicious, the scent of him still faintly clinging to the clothes he had me wear last night.

"Can I—"

"Wash up first? Yes, yes," he answers abruptly with a curt nod, flicking his hand toward the small en suite connected to the guest room. "Go on now, quickly."

The impatience in his tone and body language has me scurrying into the bathroom, splashing some water onto my face and freshening up as fast as I can before returning to the bedroom, my hair now twisted into a high bun.

His smile is beatific, per usual, as he takes my hand. The metal of his rings is warm on my cold skin, and his fingers are slender, his skin as soft as a newborn—further proof that he's never had to work a real day in his life. Walking out of the hallway, I'm struck by the view welcoming me beyond the living room windows.

The sun is low on the horizon. It must be early morning

with the way the rays shine over the Pravitian skyline. From this vantage point, with the harbor between us, it's ... it's beautiful.

I've never seen the city of Pravitia like this before.

A bizarre sense of shame smothers the feeling when I consider how mistreated I've felt by the city since I arrived. Perversity, cloaked in beauty. It strangely reminds me of the one whose hand is currently squeezing mine as we pass the living room and head into another vast hallway.

"Here we are," he announces after passing a handful of closed doors. Letting go of my hand, he fishes out a key hanging on a thin leather string from inside his vest.

His eyes glimmer with excitement as he unlocks the door, and my curiosity gets the better of me. Anticipation begins to tickle my stomach as I wonder what kind of wardrobe is waiting for me behind the closed door.

Placing a hand on the small of my back, he coaxes me inside first, but the room is pitch-black, and I can't see a single thing.

Behind me, Gemini flicks the lights on, and I stifle a scream.

Taking a shaky step backward, I'm stopped by a hard chest.

Gemini's hands curl around my arms as his breath fans over my cheek before he speaks. "Do you like them?" he rasps, his voice low and much darker than usual.

An unnerving shiver tingles up my nape. I'm still having trouble understanding what my eyes are seeing.

The space is much bigger than I expected, more like a windowless warehouse than a room in the middle of his house.

Rows and rows and rows of mannequins face us, all dressed in different outfits.

And they all ... look like ... *me.*

They resemble wax dolls more than mannequins. My features and likeness have been captured in the most unsettling of ways; the only things missing are the tattoos covering most of my body.

I swallow hard, my heart beating at an alarming rate, but I try my hardest to stay calm and look unperturbed.

"How did you even have time to ... do all of this?" I finally ask, relieved Gemini is still behind me and can't see the horror in my eyes.

He chuckles, his mouth still close to my ear. My body breaks out in goose bumps.

"I told you, I never let you go." He drags his nose down my neck, and my breath hitches. "It was just a matter of time before you were back where you belonged."

"Which is?" I find myself asking, although I already know the answer. I clench my jaw, teeth gnashing together while I wait for him to respond.

Letting go of my arms, he circles to face me, his gaze hooded and predatory. "By my side."

"Like your trophy?" I bite back.

"Precisely," he drawls.

With a quick twist of his heels, he struts farther into the drafty room, hands clasped behind his back until he twirls back to face me. He snaps his fingers and points to the spot next to him. "Come stand here."

My survival instincts are begging me to run, and my eyes flit to the open door.

Gemini catches my movement. "Don't you dare, pet," he says, carefully enunciating every word.

Fear tightens my throat, but I keep my head up as I slowly walk to where he's pointing while trying my best to ignore the mannequins surrounding me.

He snaps his fingers again. "Clothes off."

I balk at his words, and his eyes narrow menacingly. His smirk slowly tugs at his lips, as if he expects me to defy him again. Instead, I match the intensity of his gaze and take off my clothes without any protest. There's a small chill in the room, and I feel my nipples tightening into peaks. I keep my chin raised and my back straight, attempting to clutch on to the last of my dignity.

His chest rumbles with a pleased hum as I stand naked in front of him once again. The vulnerability of the act has not become easier, still as raw as last night. Except his gaze is a lot less clinical this time, as if he's letting me see past the illusion, to the real him and his real intentions.

Tugging the measuring tape off his neck with a flick of the wrist, he circles around me. "What should I dress my doll up in today?" he says under his breath, holding up the tape to my shoulders and then the length of my arm.

I feel his fingers graze my body with every phony measurement he makes—it's clearly all an act, as the clothes are ready to wear—and the realization of who has me captive sinks deeper and deeper into my skin.

Does he even see me as human?

I am but a shiny new toy for him to play with.

And what happens when he grows bored of me?

My stomach churns at the thought, but I try to regulate my breathing and keep a smooth expression on my face while Gemini continues to circle me like a starving vulture.

Finally, he steps away, discarding the measuring tape with a flick of his wrist. I watch it flutter to the floor as he begins to wind his way around the mannequins. He stops in front of one, gives it a long once-over, and shakes his head before continuing on.

"Ah!" I hear him say, now much farther away.

I can't see him from where I'm standing, and I remain still, crossing my arms around my chest in a vain attempt to stay warm.

There's a rustle of sounds, then more silence before he reappears with what I can only make out as black clothing.

As he strolls back up to me, his grin widens, as if every moment of this bizarre game has him tickled with amusement.

He's psychotic. Out of his mind.

"Arms up," he orders.

My lips thin into a line, and I hope my stare conveys every horrible thing I want to yell at him, but I slowly raise my arms anyhow.

"Hold still," he says before tugging a tight, long-sleeved maxi dress over my head.

His hands smooth over the curves of my breasts, over my stomach, then hips while slipping the dress down my body. I note the lack of underwear.

I tremble under his touch. A maddening cognitive dissonance muddling my thoughts. His seemingly harmless behavior is at war with the countless mannequins staring back at me, their faces expressionless and frighteningly uncanny.

Gemini circles me once again. The dress is backless, and I jump when I feel a finger smooth down my naked spine.

"So many tattoos, and yet you've left your back unmarked," he muses, his finger idly drawing spirals over my exposed skin.

I expect him to ask me why.

But the question never comes.

Instead, he faces me, holding up his finger as if to tell me to wait there, and heads to the left-facing wall, where a large collection of shoes and jewelry are displayed.

Shortly after, he returns, holding a pair of black platform boots and a thin pair of socks.

Beginning to learn his quirks, I'm not surprised when he drops down on one knee and asks me to hold up my foot. One after the other, he slips the socks on my feet and then fastens the boots. By the time he's done, I'm ready to implode, his careful and meticulous ministrations starting to burn a hole in my chest.

I'm beginning to wish for his violence. It's upsetting and so illogical, but at least I would know the extent of his evil. His current behavior feels a lot more insidious. Like the feathery touch of his fingers when he clasps a necklace around my neck, the pendant falling just above my cleavage. I don't look down to see what it is, only knowing that it feels heavy against my chest.

BREAKFAST IS SERVED ON THE TERRACE. IT'S A MILD WINTER DAY, and my long-sleeved dress is enough to keep me warm when paired with the strong morning rays. The terrace overlooks the harbor and is built so close to the edge of the cliff that it appears we're floating in midair.

On the table sits a wide array of food—from mountains of fresh-cut fruits to eggs, bacon, and toasted bread. My mouth waters, and my stomach rumbles loudly. I know Gemini hears it by the entertained look I catch from the corner of my eye, but I ignore him.

I suspect he wasn't the one who cooked all this food, but I haven't seen or heard a single soul aside from Gemini since he dragged me here yesterday.

Yesterday ...

How time has morphed into anything but. My existence feels much different now, not even twenty-four hours later.

Gemini pulls out a chair for me, and I give him a small nod before I sit.

"Hands on your lap, my pet," he casually announces as he drags a chair as close to mine as he possibly can.

"But ..." I begin to say, but never finish my sentence.

He intends to feed me.

An intense burst of hysteria overcomes me momentarily. I feel like I'm losing all sense of control, even the ability to feed myself.

Gemini pops a raspberry into his mouth, unbothered by my current state of crisis, before sticking a fork into the juiciest strawberry I've ever seen. He offers it to me, and my reservations crumble with the need to have a taste.

When I lean over to catch the fruit with my teeth, Gemini pulls the fork back with a smirk, and my stomach sinks, feeling like a toy—yet again. We don't exchange any words as he smiles and I glare. He offers the strawberry again with mock innocence, but I stare at him for a long, tense breath before leaning over again. Because, deep down, I want that godsdamned strawberry even if my dignity is slipping further away from me with each passing second.

It's as delicious as I expected, and I immediately hunger for more, but keep my hands on my lap, back straight, while I watch Gemini butter some toast, humming idly.

"You will eat everything I give you — understood?" he says, his gaze lifting to mine as he pushes the buttered toast to my lips. His eyes turn hard, but it's gone in a flash as he repeats, "Understood?"

I nod, my nervous gaze fixed on his. "Understood," I mutter before taking a bite of the bread, chewing slowly.

We continue this charade until the toast is all gone, and he moves on to a piece of bacon, then a small sip of orange juice, followed by some eggs.

Unrolling a cloth napkin, he dabs the corner of my mouth, his attention oddly focused, as if he were performing the most serious of tasks.

"What happens when you tire of me?" The words slip out without much thought.

He quirks his eyebrow up, his hand still hovering near my lips, while he cants his head to the side, studying me, as if trying to decipher a riddle.

"Where are you from, Veil Vulturine?" he finally says.

Hearing my full name coming out of his lips has my skin

tingle with a mystifying shiver. As if he's looking at me, the real Veil, for the first time since he kidnapped me and not the doll he wishes to play with.

"Does it matter?" I ask, somehow wanting to avoid the subject.

Gemini leans back in his chair, discarding the napkin, and smirks. "Oh, that it does, pet. That it does." He crosses one leg over the other and then does the same with his arms, his wrists hanging loosely atop his knee.

I allow myself the liberty of a sigh before replying, "I'm from Corutio. It's a city north—"

"Oh, I know of it," he says with a dismissive wave of his hand.

His expression turns far too serious for my liking, as if this small piece of information confused him even further.

Silence lingers.

His eyes narrow.

I swallow hard.

Breaking eye contact, he sighs. "Our gods favor more than just our dear Pravitia, I fear," he declares, as if miffed that his beloved city isn't one of a kind.

"Have you been?" I ask warily.

"Nonsense," he says, his gaze landing back on me.

His grin turns wicked, and my heart squeezes in apprehension at the sight.

"Why would I leave this city when I have everything I would ever desire"—he taps a finger on the table with the cadence of his two last words—"right here?"

11

GEMINI

"**K**illed your little rabbit yet?"

Leaning over Constantine's pink cast, black marker in hand, I lift my eyes to hers and grin.

"Why would I *ever* do such a thing, love?" I drawl mockingly.

We are the first to arrive at the meeting. The boardroom is quiet as we sit around the large quartz table, waiting for the others to finally make an appearance.

Constantine tries to swat my head but misses, and I chuckle as I return to my doodle of a crying clown.

"Don't be absurd, Gemmie. Killing is the best part," she muses, stars in her eyes. Then her expression falls, and she pouts. "I miss it."

I shoot her an amused glance. "Poor little Tin-Tin," I quip. "Too injured to maim others. How long has it been?"

She crosses her arms and sighs. "At least a week."

I bark out a laugh, my eyes trained on her cast as I start on a doodle of a snake coiling around a key.

"You don't usually hold on to them for this long," Constantine notes, returning to her previous question.

62

"It's only been four days, Tinny."

"And? Your proclivities to boredom are legendary."

Focusing on drawing the snake's tongue, I grin. "Touché." I chuckle softly. "But this one ..." I'm not sure how to continue. There's so much to Veil I can't explain. She's like attempting to grab handfuls of mist, and I'm left with nothing but an impression of who she might be. "She's quite the unexpected enigma, I must admit."

"Oh?" Constantine replies, curiosity brightening her blue eyes.

I don't have the chance to elaborate. The echo of footsteps approaching has us both falling silent, our attention now on the entrance. A few seconds later, our most powerful little duo appears. As usual, Mercy is dressed all in black, her dagger peeking from between the slit in her skirt, and Wolfgang has donned a wine-red three-piece suit.

I flash them a jovial smile. "Their magnificences have arrived."

"There you are!" I announce after unlocking the door of her bedroom.

I find Veil staring out the window. She's pulled her legs up, her feet tucked under her on the reading chair.

Her shoulders tighten, nervous gaze flitting to mine. My doll has grown less flighty now that a few days have passed, but the fear lingers. The taste still so sweet.

"What were you up to while I was gone?" I ask while I fall onto her bed, facing her. I lean back onto my palms, perching the heel of my boot on the tip of the other.

She gives me a strange look. "Nothing." She worries her bottom lip before adding, "Maybe I could have a few books to read?

My eyebrows jump in surprise. "Right," I reply distractedly. "Books."

Leaping to my feet, I don't miss the small wince Veil makes due to my sudden movement. I pretend not to notice as I prance up to her chair and offer my hand with a coy smile.

I might not be known for my patience, but for my favorite doll? I'm prepared to wait lifetimes for her to turn malleable under my touch.

"Let's have a picnic by the water."

"I'm not hungry," she says softly, avoiding my gaze.

"Did I ask?" I spit back, my tone slightly harsher than I intended.

Her brown eyes crash into mine, pupils widening as her mouth falls slightly agape. Whatever she sees in my expression has her pinching her lips and delicately placing her palm in mine. With my gaze still on hers, I smile sweetly and press my lips to her hand before pulling her up to her feet.

***

"Tell me about yourself, pet."

We're settled on a quilted blanket under a large oak tree, its leaves shading us from the afternoon sun.

A few pieces of cheese and half-eaten grapes lie abandoned beside us, along with the empty champagne bottle, flipped over in the ice bucket. I carefully paint Veil's nails a light shade of yellow as she peers at me from under her long eyelashes.

It's warmer than expected for mid-December, and Veil's coat has been discarded, pooling around her. Today's outfit is a cream knit dress, paired with knee-high boots, my family sigil —a snake coiling around a hand—hanging from a thin silver chain from her neck.

"What is there to say?" she finally mutters glumly.

I drag my tongue over my teeth, annoyed at her lack of

participation, but keep my expression casual. "Tell me," I say as I blow on the wet nail polish, "is there any point in keeping you alive if you cannot manage to find *one* meaningful thing to say about yourself?"

I lift my gaze just in time to catch the fear splashed in her eyes. She tries to take her hand away, but my hold only tightens, careful not to smudge her fresh coat of nail polish.

I smile sweetly. "Now," I say, "let's try this again. Tell me about yourself, pet."

She falls silent, her head turning to the water. Her brown hair tumbles over her shoulder, and I take a moment to count the freckles on her cheeks and nose that have appeared since we've been in the sun. Finally, her careful gaze returns to mine while I place her palm on her knee and start on the other hand.

"I was a gymnast and a dancer back in Corutio," she offers.

I don't speak for longer than I need to, rolling her answer in my mouth as if I could somehow catch the taste of it. She could be lying. I can't tell. And a thrill tickles through my veins at that exact fact. It's partly why she's my very own puzzle with *quite* the valuable missing piece.

I might not know much about my Veil Vulturine, but one thing I do know is that she was a gift to me from the gods. Our fates are somehow conjoined, and eventually, the truth will reveal itself to me. It always does.

I let out a small hum before saying, "A petty thief *and* a dancer? Quite the combination."

"How would you know that?" she asks quickly.

"What? That you're a thief? I have eyes, pet," I answer with a snort.

She stays quiet for a beat. "You watched me."

"Surprised?" I ask, blowing on her freshly manicured nails.

From the corner of my eye, I see Veil's gaze turn distant until she speaks again.

"One was for pleasure," she says. "The other is a compul—" She stops abruptly, as if catching herself. "Necessity."

Compulsion?

Oh ... what is my petty little thief hiding?

I ignore her stumble and finish painting the last nail before looking up. "What else do you do for pleasure, Veil Vulturine?"

I watch her throat work around a hard swallow, her cheeks turning a light shade of pink.

My, my, my, what a pretty doll I have.

Something about me saying her full name flusters her. I noticed it the first time we had breakfast on the terrace. I now use it sparingly, wanting whatever effect it has over her to last for as long as I can control it.

"Pleasure is a luxury," she finally answers.

I blow on her nails one final time, but keep her hand in mine while I pin her with my stare.

"Is that so?" I say darkly.

Her chest rises, then falls before she nods. "It is."

"Who then can afford such a luxury?"

She studies me, a small crease between her brows on her otherwise smooth face. There's a small tremble in her voice when she answers, "People like you."

"People like me?" I repeat with a teasing laugh. "Well then," I say, my smile turning wolfish as my thumb smooths over her knuckles, "lucky for you, I like to share."

12

VEIL

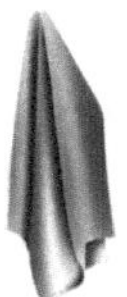

It's been six days since the heir of the Foley family ripped me from the crowd in the Pravitia city square. Sometimes, I worry that I'm mistaken and that I've lost track of time. Has it been longer than six days? I wonder if Zazel has dared to ask Gemini about me.

Would he even care to lie?

Why would he bother when he is so clearly above the law?

I try to seek hope in my small silver linings. Like how after my timid mention of boredom, Gemini brought in a large bookcase, then stocked it full of books. I'm still confined to the guest bedroom—except when he wants my company, which has been quite limited in the past few days. Though when he demands my attention, dresses me like his doll, and asks me a never-ending parade of asinine questions, he appears distracted.

I find solace in my time alone. Sometimes, I even catch myself feeling somewhat relieved for the small interruption of not having to fend for myself. Here, as his captive, I'm no longer burdened with struggling to lift a few dollars out of strangers' pockets just so I can eat that night.

I fear that humans are far too adaptable, and now that my

initial shock of being kidnapped has worn away, Gemini is slowly lulling me into a false sense of security.

But he's a snake.

And any day now, he will devour me whole.

If I needed a reminder of my fate, Gemini certainly succeeded tonight.

I pretend not to feel his scorching gaze against my cheek. He's facing me, sitting on the seat across from me in the town car, while I stare out the window as we head deeper into the city.

When he announced that we were to go out tonight to celebrate the beginning of Tithe Season—a weeklong festivity honoring the six heirs—my heart fluttered with excitement. I was relieved to know there was no way he could have witnessed my body's reaction to the news.

I shouldn't be this delighted just to leave his property.

He carefully chose my outfit before we left, picking out a black pleated skirt, white knit thigh-high socks with delicate black bows at the thighs, and a black buttoned shirt so tight that it can barely contain my small breasts. My initial excitement, however, quickly evaporated when he added the last touch to my outfit—a black leather collar, connected to a chained leash.

I nearly balked. Nearly shrieked in defeat.

But the hard glint in his eyes had me pressing my lips together instead. Something about his expression conveyed clearly that if I complained a little too loudly, he would throw me back into my room and leave without me.

So I acquiesced. Because I'm desperate. And it seems like I have no dignity left.

I feel a small tug to the collar and hear a subtle clink of metal against metal. My gaze flicks to Gemini, but I don't grace him with any kind of reaction.

He tilts his head, a mocking grin spreading across his lips as he toys with the leather handle of the leash, the chain long enough to hang limply between the gap of our seats.

Everything about his body language conveys casual power. From the way his knees fall open to the relaxed way he's stretched his free arm over the back of his seat. The silence coils dangerously, but I choose not to shy away from his attention, staring right back.

His hair is yellow today. It's hard for me to ignore how it matches my nails, which he so carefully painted while we sat by the water a few days ago. There's a fresh smear of black eyeliner under his eyes, and the two thin upside-down triangles he drew just under his waterline make him appear like a jester even more than usual. The black mesh button-up under his trench coat is unbuttoned halfway down his chest, tucked into tight black-and-white striped pants.

Yellow, black and white.

My outfit matches his.

I've unwillingly become but a mere extension of Gemini Foley. The leash connecting me to him sure seems to solidify that unnerving feeling.

"We've left your neighborhood," I state for no other reason than to cut this daunting tension between us in half.

"And?" he asks. He haughtily raises an eyebrow, his gaze still steady and piercing, watching me with hooded eyes.

I try to act unperturbed, but my heartbeat unexpectedly doubles, as if everything about Gemini is somehow a trap. I shrug and look back out the window.

There's a beat of silence before he speaks again, and I'm surprised when he actually entertains my observation.

"We're heading to the Vorovsky estate." Then he mutters almost to himself, "Technically, we've agreed to stay within the limits of our neighborhoods due to the threat to our lives." He makes a small, dismissive wave, then pins me with his stare, his grin turning lascivious. "But I've never before missed the first day of a bacchanal, and I certainly will not be missing one anytime soon."

My attention snags on *the threat to our lives* said in such a casual manner. It must have something to do with the bombing we heard when I was trying to escape him on the day of the inauguration. I want to press him further on the subject, but my words die in my throat when he adds what feels like an innocuous statement.

"A return to where it all started," he declares as the car makes its slow turn around a looming fountain with carved statues of naked bodies holding large pitchers spilling over with water.

I realize then that there's a reason this route felt vaguely familiar.

The Feast of Fools.

He's brought me back to the maze. My first instinct is sudden and paralyzing fear. My vision blurs, and I recoil, pushing myself as far away as possible from him. He tightens his grip around the leash, shushing me gently, as if trying to calm down a spooked horse.

"Don't be silly, pet," he purrs, blowing me a kiss. "You're safe with me."

I don't have time to reel over the utter nonsense of his statement before the car door opens and Gemini steps out first.

Turning back to face me, he leans down and offers his hand. "Now then," he says, "enough of this dillydallying." There's a wild glint in his eyes. "Tonight, we feast."

My mouth goes dry, but I straighten my shoulders and warily slide my hand into his, stepping out onto the gravel on shaky legs.

13

VEIL

Inside the Vorovsky estate, I'm left stunned.

I'm not sure what I expected. But certainly not *this*.

Growing up in Corutio, I am no stranger to vice and what it looks like to fall victim to the god of excess. I've witnessed it, yes, but I've never experienced it personally. Too tucked away into the dark folds of the city margins to be affected.

Even the Feast of Fools—which the god clearly influenced —held little power over me. In the past weeks, I've had plenty of time to mull over why I was unaffected when the others appeared almost hypnotized. I wonder if it's partly why I managed to survive the sacrifice.

When Gemini said we were to feast, I was naive to believe we were walking into a *real* feast, similar to the one I had been forced to participate in on these very grounds.

But as the heir of the Foley family leads me by small tugs of the leash through the massive foyer, lofty halls, and countless stately rooms, my throat goes dry from the *magnitude* of excess I'm forced to witness.

Maybe there had been a feast earlier today, but all I can

see now are the spoils. And a level of inebriation that I don't think I've ever encountered before in my twenty-five years on this mortal plane. This seems closer to madness, a festive hysteria blackening the gaze of every person we cross paths with.

And the indulgence—*my gods*—the uninhibited indulgence. From gurgling down alcohol straight from the bottles to naked, writhing bodies in every state of coitus.

Eyes black.

Thoughtless.

This might not be the product of the god of lust; however, excess is kin to such gratification. Eroticism perfumes the air and appears to spur these poor souls into a whirlwind of sexual frenzy.

My gaze flicks to Gemini, who is looking at me with a feral grin from over his shoulder, his coat long ago discarded to a nameless servant. I'm a ball of nerves, awaiting what's to come, but try to keep my expression as smooth and hard as the marble around us.

Because of the see-through material of his shirt, I can now see the tattoo sprawling the span of Gemini's back. A snake coiling around a hand. It's the same symbol as the necklace he fastened around my neck. The one I've been forced to wear ever since he kidnapped me.

I'm unsure why it takes me seeing it on Gemini's back to connect the dots, but it dawns on me that I've seen this symbol before, around the Foley neighborhood.

It must be his family sigil.

The medallion pressing against my chest seems to burn my skin with the realization. I'm not sure what's worse—wearing his family sigil around my neck or the collar and leash. Both are claiming me. Tying me to the mortal extension of the god of trickery.

I feel tricked all right ...

"Here we are," Gemini finally declares with a pleased sigh as we enter a room the size of a small house.

He leads me by the leash through the room, weaving us between countless revelers. The lighting is ambient, cloaking the room in a warm, uniform glow. Most of the walls are painted a dark wine-red with images of still life projected across them—depicting a variety of fruits spilling over plates, meats from raw to fully cooked, bread ripped open and half eaten. It only heightens the powerful pulse of excess found in every small crevice of the estate.

The room is stuffed with black couches, burgundy divans, and large, gold-threaded cushions that can fit dozens.

Even with a prudish sweep of the room as we walk, I count at least seven groups of tangled bodies, dispersed around the lofty space.

No one in the room pays us any attention, but my anxiety spikes nonetheless.

What does Gemini expect of me tonight?

"Don't be so glum, doll." Gemini's voice falls down an octave as he faces me, and goose bumps break out all over my body when he smooths his hand down my arm, his nose trailing up my neck. Sensing my apprehension, he answers the question plaguing my mind. "All I ask of you tonight is to sit down and look pretty," he whispers into my ear before catching my earlobe between his teeth.

I startle at the sensation of the quick swipe of his tongue across my skin, but I don't move an inch.

"Can you do that for me, Veil Vulturine?"

At the sound of my full name out of his mouth, my nape tingles. It's uncontrollable, and I loathe my dysregulated reaction every time he speaks it. Straightening back up, his chest still inches away from mine, Gemini pins me with his animalistic stare, and my mouth waters. I swallow hard and slowly nod.

"Yes," I croak out weakly.

"What a well-behaved doll I own," he drawls, dragging his thumb over my lips before he pushes me backward onto the couch behind me with a soft palm to the shoulder.

Before distancing himself, he lets the chained leash drop over my thighs and leans down to level his gaze with mine.

"If you suddenly crave witnessing me spill blood tonight," he says with an arrogant lift of his full lips, "well, it's simple really — all you need to do is let someone touch you."

The shiver that zips down my spine is just as confusing as the squeeze in my chest at the sound of his threat, but I say nothing. I continue to stare and ignore the couple beside me, who are surprisingly fully clothed, indulging in large glasses of red wine, their lips just as red as the slosh of alcohol in their cups.

Gemini keeps his smoldering gaze glued on mine as he steps into a sunken cushioned area a few steps away from where he has me sitting. His face is painted with a mixture of hunger, arrogance, and pleasure. But there's something in the wild undercurrent of his expression that I can't quite place. It's almost like ... he's trying to show off.

When he snaps his fingers and three heads swivel to attention, I realize that's exactly what it is. He wants me to witness his influence over others.

His power.

His dominance.

A young man approaches him first, black curls framing his face. Then, moments later, a woman with auburn hair, reaching the middle of her back, approaches to his right. Both are naked.

Gemini's eyes never stray from mine, his grin turning into nothing but a taunting slit while the duo unbutton his shirt. Another man, just as naked, kneels in front of Gemini and starts on his belt. I can't see his face, only the back of his shaved head and the wings tattooed on his scalp.

I wish I had something to drink, or smoke, or *anything* to dull the edge of watching Gemini be disrobed. Instead, I'm dreadfully sober while everyone else is blissfully intoxicated.

When his shirt comes off, my eyes drop to the small diamond hanging from his left nipple. Undeniably knowing where my attention has fallen, Gemini gives the diamond a small flick with his finger. My gaze flies back to his face.

He laughs.

But I can barely hear it over the loud moans and thudding bass. The ghost of his laughter still manages to skitter across my skin, and my body unexpectedly heats.

His eyes slide down to my chest, and a flush crawls up to my neck and cheeks. I'm repulsed by such a blatant reaction to seeing him like this. Aside from the obvious reason—having been brought here by force—it feels like I've lost a game I wasn't aware we were playing, until now.

The victory flashes across his irises before he reaches back to grab the man on his left by the neck, pulling him into a passionate kiss, his gaze somehow *still* on me.

I'm caught between two wild urges. The first is to continue watching him devour this man whole, and the second is to cast my gaze down to where the woman has now joined the other man on his knees. The latter urge eventually wins. Feeling like some kind of perverted voyeur, I gape all the same.

He's practically begging me to.

Gemini's pants have been pushed down his legs, his long, thick cock stroked by multiple hands at once. I catch a glint of a gold ring at the tip. A piercing. My breath hitches, and I squeeze my thighs together at the salacious sight.

I shouldn't like this.

I shouldn't crave to see even more of him.

But I'm growing hot with need, and I'm not sure what to do

with myself, but toy with the chain now wound tight around my hands.

My attention bounces back up to Gemini's face, and I've somehow missed him curling his hand around the man's hardened cock. His mouth is open near Gemini's cheek, panting in pleasure while one of the gods' favorites whispers in his ear. I'm suddenly desperate to hear those very same words.

Gemini smiles, his hooded eyes flicking to mine, as if knowing exactly what thoughts are aflame in my mind. My breathing turns shallow, and I barely register when I slip closer to the edge of the couch, as if needing a better look.

I watch in consuming desire as the man with the shaved head settles behind the woman. He starts to fuck her from the back while her mouth wraps around Gemini's cock, her cheeks hollowing around his shaft.

I can't tell if the sensation I feel could even be described as jealousy, but it's certainly possessive in nature. There's even a faint bubbling of anger behind my chest. No one can touch *me*, but he can have as many hands touching him as he wants. I fall deeper and deeper into the confusing depth of being forced to watch Gemini being pleasured—and give it back ravenously.

He's breathtaking.

Undeniably beautiful.

Still a snake.

But I've been ensnared.

Hypnotized.

His sexuality drips over every hard curve of his body—his tightening stomach, the clenching of his jaw. Dropping his chin slightly down toward his chest, he peers at me from under his lashes while he continues to fuck the man with the black curls with his fist. Again, Gemini whispers something to him, but this time, he releases him from his grasp to let him step up to the man with the shaved head still on his knees.

I stare with unbridled attention as the one on the floor

opens his mouth, never losing a beat, his hips thrusting steadily against the woman's ass. Cum spurts onto his stretched-out tongue, his eyes closing, as if he were tasting the most delicious of nectars.

My gaze flies to Gemini just in time. His eyelids flutter closed for only a second as he punches his hips forward, both hands on the woman's head. His darkened eyes slam into mine, and for a fleeting moment, I convince myself that the same peaked pleasure painted so magnificently across Gemini's face ravages inside of me.

My clit throbs painfully, but I stay perfectly still as I stare and stare and stare, my fingers twisting even harder into the chain leash. I've been tricked into some of the most heart-wrenching pleasure I've ever had the *dis*pleasure to witness.

Lazily, Gemini smooths his hair back before dropping both arms to his sides, his chest heaving as he catches his breath.

A crowned prince.

A spoiled aristocrat.

The deranged glimmer in his eyes is so quiet yet so loud. Somehow, I know exactly what it means.

I've been caught craving the one thing that should repulse me.

14

GEMINI

There's nothing like the tickle of a secret slithering into my ear, ready to be devoured and consumed to put me in the most delectable of moods.

It's the final day of Tithe Season, and this time, the last day falls on a Wednesday—*my* day. Tithing began at high noon as my faithful followers lined up next to the carousel inside Pandaemonium.

Secrets hold a weightier importance this winter solstice than any Tithe Season that came before. I've been particularly famished for my followers' secrets, knowing that one of them was bound to let slip who was behind the attack at the inauguration. And earlier today, I pulled the secret right out of a little waif of a thing. I now know who tried to kill us, and I didn't have to lift a single finger. I thanked my follower for their loyalty with a long kiss on the lips before having them forcibly removed—I'll have fun with them with Constantine later—and quickly relayed the information to Wolfgang.

I'm one merry servant of the god of trickery.

Hours later, the single file still disappears through the door leading into the underground tunnel, connecting my casino with the Pravitian harbor. I stopped the carousel for the occasion. Sitting on one of the winged horses, I face my audience while, one by one, they step onto the platform and whisper their secret into my ear.

There is no such thing as an inconsequential secret. I love them all. Each and every one of them is wickedly exciting and wonderfully important, no matter the size.

One never knows when the most anodyne of information will come of use.

Gossip is a powerful thing.

For my special day, I've kept my hair blond and donned a simple white silk shirt, loosely tucked into black leather pants. I dressed my Veil in a leather baby-doll dress to match and set her down next to the carousel in a large chair that resembles a throne more than mundane furniture. This time, I chose not to have her on a leash, instead cuffing her ankle to the chair.

To avoid any unnecessary fuss, I detained her roommates for the day so they wouldn't find Veil here and make a public stink. This is *my* day after all.

It's been nearly two weeks since I first plucked Veil from the crowd.

And yet she remains a mystery. An effervescent piece of her keeps escaping me, always just out of sight. I don't believe she knows she's hiding something from me. But she is.

Bringing her to the bacchanal was a test. I was curious to see how she would respond to such excess. And just like I'd suspected, she wasn't affected like the revelers around her. This only solidified my developing theory.

Well ...

Maybe she wasn't affected by the decadent whims of the god of excess, but there was no denying how *I* made her feel.

And, oh ...

I wish I could have tasted the lie on her tongue. Although there was not a word spoken between us, I could see it. The way her body responded to watching me receive pleasure—she couldn't hide it. The flush. The squeeze of her thighs. The widening of her pupils.

Seeing her struggle ...

Fighting it ...

It made me crave her that much more.

I could have her. Of course I could have her.

Nothing is stopping me from taking what's already mine. But where is the gratification in that? I'd rather bide my time. Like a deadly spider, I patiently wait, weaving a sticky web around her, until she inevitably comes to me of her own accord.

I've taken her.

Yet I haven't *caught* her.

But the day she begs for me to touch her, begs to touch *me* in the dead of night ... oh, that's when I will have caught her. That's when I will have truly won this game of ours.

In between two followers, I sneak a glance at her in the mirror on the opposite wall from where she sits. I laugh under my breath, then snap to a passing employee to bring me a fresh coupe of champagne.

Veil doesn't realize that I can surveil her from this angle. And for the past hour, I've been observing her. Studying exactly *how* she would walk right into my trap.

Although she has been acting rather docile since the first day I took her, I suspect she'd try to escape, if given the chance.

And today, I *have* given her the chance.

Tricked her, like I do best.

When I cuffed her to the leg of the chair, I feigned putting the key in my pocket. Instead, I let it drop to the floor, close enough for her to snatch up, but just far enough that it would take a bit of orchestration for her to reach it. I also instructed my guards not to intercept her if she did try to leave her chair.

I knew my petty little thief would rise to the challenge.

She must be running on blind optimism and naivete to think I wouldn't notice.

Especially with the surprising way she bent her body to even retrieve the damn thing.

In the mirror, I watch her pin her attention on me as she tries to inconspicuously unlock the cuff. She appears nervous and fumbles with the key; still, she's swift. And I pretend to be oblivious, sipping my champagne and signaling to the next person to step up onto the platform.

I wait.

I collect a secret.

Until ...

Shoving whoever last spilled their secret, I step off the horse and fling my coupe to the ground before strutting down the carousel.

Veil is already a ways ahead, slipping through the crowd like a silverfish. I keep an unhurried pace and wait for the satisfying moment when she looks over her shoulder and finally notices me. I smile wide and give her a taunting wave of my fingers. Her eyes widen as panic splashes over her face like a bucket of cold water.

Silly rabbit tries to run, and sizzling arousal licks up my body. Visions of me chasing her through the maze enlivens every nerve ending in my body. Gods, how I would love to re-create that fateful night.

I run after her, slamming the doors open that she tried to shut behind her. Her frightened breaths fill the dark corridor, and my manic laugh floats up in the air with it. It only takes me a few more quick strides to snatch her by the arm.

She shrieks, "Let go of me!"

I chuckle darkly as I try to wrangle her into my arms. "You should come up with something new next time. *Let go of me* is beginning to feel stale — don't you think?"

"I'll kill you!" she screams, and even then, I can tell she doesn't believe the words that just flew out of her mouth.

My laugh grows menacing. Taunting.

"We can workshop it when we get home, love," I say with a soft grunt as I try to pin her to the wall, but she's fighting a lot harder than the two previous times. Must be all the food I've been feeding her.

It's then I feel it.

Like a cold vacuum through my senses.

I'm suddenly weakened.

And everything grows dull.

15

VEIL

There's an unbelievable strum running through my veins, and both Gemini and I grow still, my back pinned to the wall as his fingers dig into my bare arms.

His eyes widen, and I feel mine do the same as his mouth falls open on a sharp inhale. But when I see his expression shutter, his typical non-threatening demeanor evaporating, my urge to run as far away from him as possible surges back like a deadly tsunami.

His glare turns cold, and it coats my skin with frost.

"*What did you just do?*" he asks so chillingly, his teeth gnashing with a bloodthirsty threat.

His fingers dig even deeper into my arms, and I know I'll find bruises in the shape of him tomorrow morning.

What did I just do?

Every atom in me is vibrating with the fear of Gemini's righteous anger, but I can hardly concentrate. My mind is pulled to the crowd beyond the deserted corridor. I have an insatiable craving to hunt down every single lie and dirty secret of anyone with a pulse in the main room.

Gemini shoves me hard against the wall, and I snap my gaze

back to him, realizing I was staring toward the closed doors at the end of the corridor.

"Who are you?" he growls, his tone accusing and enraged. His eyes bounce between mine as he stares, his gaze desperate but menacing.

He stares like he's never seen me before, and I wonder if my time has come. If death has finally arrived to collect my soul for the long journey home.

"I — I have no idea what's happening," I manage to croak out shakily as I fight the urge to screw my eyes shut.

Then I sense it.

Like a balloon popping. And whatever it was that I was feeling, it's now gone like a puff of smoke. I can tell Gemini felt it too. His grip loosens infinitesimally around my arms as curiosity flashes through his features.

The silence slithers itself around us, slowly curling around my throat like a lazy, coiling snake. I can hardly swallow, waiting for Gemini to say something.

"Sneaky, sneaky, sneaky." It's a low, threatening hiss. "Pretending to be a weak, little rabbit, when you are anything but." His face now inches away from mine, he snaps his teeth close to my nose, and I wince. "Aren't you, pet?"

My body rattles under his touch as his fingers dig painfully into my arms. "I don't know what you mean ..." I utter quietly, trying to bite down on the panic still filling my lungs.

He releases me and takes a step back. His face smooths back to the Gemini I've become accustomed to. Lighthearted and mischievous. The one skilled to manipulate me into feeling things I refuse to admit out loud. It sends a shiver down my spine, and I'm unsure what to make of the sensation, other than to ignore it.

"Well, Veil Vulturine," he says with a dark curl of his lip, "I think it's time for us to find out."

"WHERE ARE YOU TAKING ME?" ALTHOUGH I ASK MY QUESTION IN a soft tone, my voice echoes through the arched corridor, and I cringe at having disturbed the silence around us.

Gemini doesn't answer and simply continues to drag me by the wrist—I should be grateful that, at least this time, it's not by a leash tied around my neck. I don't have any more struggle left in me. For today.

All that I've gathered is that we've descended multiple flights of stairs to reach the subterrestrial levels of Mount Pravitia—the most prominent building in the city. It didn't take much for Gemini to charm the guards into letting us past the lobby.

There's a chill in the air, and I break out into goose bumps, the stones around us leaching any warmth away from my body. We haven't passed a single soul since reaching this particular level, and I can't fight the dread warning me of what's to come.

Finally, we stop in front of two large, imposing doors. Gemini lets go of my wrist, and I puff out a small sigh of relief while I watch him push the doors open with a small grunt, the curve of his neck flexing with the exertion.

A great, cavernous hall appears on the other side, and before I even step into the room, I'm hit with a strong wave of familiarity, as if a dormant part of me remembers being here before.

Strange.

"What is this place?" I ask Gemini, hoping, this time, he'll answer me.

But he does nothing of the sort, yanking me inside by the arm instead. I pick up my pace, following him in. His fingers are back around my wrist, his rings' sharp edges digging into my skin. My attention falls on the flex of his toned arm, his sleeve pulled up to his elbow, before I snap my eyes back up to observe the lofty hall.

Sweeping my gaze across the room, I question the nagging feeling of familiarity that still tickles my stomach. In the very middle sits a vast, circular platform. It appears to be made entirely out of black obsidian. And even at a time like this, I wonder how much such a thing would cost to make.

Gemini stops us just a few steps away from the platform and turns us so we face the doors.

"Now"—Gemini smooths his hands over his shirt, brushing out the wrinkles, his attention straight ahead—"let me do all the talking."

My tongue burns with another question, but I swallow it down. The silence settles between us as we wait for what I'm assuming is *someone* while the flambeaus on the walls flicker as if dancing with an undetectable breeze.

A woman appears not long after. My heart batters at the sight of her, an inexplicable pull tugging my chest forward, as if I were seeing a long-lost kin.

She's older, her long white hair delicately fluttering behind her as she steps inside the hall. With every slow step she takes, her bare feet peek out from underneath her long gray tunic. Her pale blue eyes are lined with painted gold, and my mind turns hazy when her gaze slams into mine, the feeling akin to a live wire making contact with water.

"Good," she states dryly when she approaches, stopping a healthy distance away from us. "I see you've found her."

Her words ring in my ears, something about her intonation prickling against my skin.

You've found her?

Gemini splutters—a reaction I've rarely seen him do. "Meaning?" he croaks out, seemingly much more serious than usual.

She must have some power over him to have him standing straight, like a dutiful schoolboy.

Tucking her hands into her opposite sleeves, she flicks her eyes from Gemini to me, then back.

"The seventh heir, of course."

The stone beneath my feet turns into quicksand. My knees buckle, and I feel nauseous.

Gemini rakes his hands through his hair as he begins to pace around in a circle before burning me with his accusing stare. "I knew it."

Blood rushes into my ears, but I somehow will myself to stay standing. I don't understand what's happening, the words hardly sinking in, but I continue listening. The woman and Gemini speak about me like I'm not even in the room.

"But the gods chose her as my sacrifice. How could that be?" Gemini says with a small hiss.

"She's alive, isn't she?" the woman intones, clearly unfazed by Gemini's question.

"Because I let her go."

"As the gods had known you would."

They both fall quiet and stare at each other. I can almost hear the unspoken conversation coursing between them.

"What do you mean, the *seventh heir*?" My voice is weak, barely a whisper, as nausea roils in my stomach.

The woman turns to me. "The gods are ushering in a new epoch. The existing *damnatio memoriae* has been dissolved. You are the sole survivor." She gives me a curt nod. "Welcome home."

I struggle to comprehend what any of this means, but the weight of her declaration is not lost on me. I think I'm going to be sick.

"She serves the god of thievery then?" Gemini muses out loud, seemingly connecting pieces that I know nothing about.

The woman gives another short nod. "Yes." Her attention

back on Gemini. "I can count on you to guide her through this new chapter. She'll have quite a few questions, I gather."

Gemini looks at me from the corner of his eye, his grin feral and cunning. "Of course."

The woman turns to leave, but Gemini calls out to her, "Oh! And, Oracle?" His voice is far too amused, making my hackles rise.

Half turned, she waits for him to speak, her expression cold and stern.

"Is it true about the fornication rule? It no longer applies?"

"Correct," she states before turning around without another glance.

It takes a few seconds after she disappears through the doors for Gemini to react.

But when he does, it sends a chill down the length of my body, rooting me to the spot.

He bursts out laughing, big belly laughs that have him doubling over.

Anger spikes through me like an iron rod, as I'm suddenly overwhelmed with the weight of what just transpired. How dare he find this amusing when my life has been anything but?

Without any rational thought, I shove him with all my strength. He stumbles but quickly regains his footing, which only makes him laugh even harder, the sound bubbling up and up and up, until I finally *snap*.

The sound of my hand striking his left cheek detonates through the now-quiet hall, and the shock splashed across his face mirrors the shock twisting my insides into knots.

Although my small outburst has made him stop laughing, he hasn't lost his mirth. It glimmers wildly behind his mismatched irises as he brings a palm to his reddening cheek.

"Oh," he says much too calmly, a smirk slowly spreading across his face, his eyes shimmering with a wild glint, "this is going to be *so much* fun."

16

GEMINI

*V*eil pestered me all the way back across the harbor. I refused to answer any of her nagging questions until we were in the privacy of our own home, away from loose lips and prying eyes.

I have an insurmountable possessiveness smarting my chest; Veil being the long-lost seventh heir is quite the monumental secret to keep, and the urge to hide it from the other heirs—temporarily—is a primal need I can't control. I can almost feel the influence of my dear god of trickery celebrating inside of me with gleeful pleasure.

Because for now?

Veil is *my* perfect little thieving secret.

"Gemini," Veil groans out exasperatingly when we step into the living room. Her tone tickles my ear like the fizz of champagne up the nose.

Ever since we spoke to the Oracle, she's been acting bolder. She claims not to know what any of it means, but there's no denying that having been told she's the seventh heir of Pravitia has certainly emboldened her.

It's a delectable change I plan on cultivating for months to come.

"Patience, love," I respond with the same exasperation.

With a tired sigh, I tug my shirt out of my leather pants, pulling it over my head. I fling it onto the couch before making my way to the patio doors, sliding one open. "I'm in the mood to stargaze."

Veil stands listlessly in the middle of the room, staring at me. She's still in her baby-doll dress, and I consider changing her into something more relaxed, but decide against it. I enjoy drinking in her tattooed skin far too much to cover it up. Ethereal stars, clouds, and suns paint her skin, as if she'd wished she were part of the cosmos instead of being tethered to earth.

She doesn't move, so I signal her with a tilt of the head to follow me onto the terrace.

"It's cold out," she says weakly.

I stifle an eye roll. "I have heaters. Now come," I bite out impatiently. "You want answers, don't you?"

That does it.

My doll springs into action like a wind-up toy and quickly follows me outside.

Settling onto one of the couches facing the harbor, I reach for a small compartment in the table next to me while Veil perches herself on the edge of the love seat, facing me.

I pull out a metal cigarette case and the accompanying Zippo. Popping the case open, I take out one of the pre-rolled joints and slip it between my lips. With a strike of the Zippo on my thigh, a small flame bursts to life, and I light the joint with a deep inhale.

Veil silently watches me through it all, and I inconspicuously preen under her undivided attention. Pushing out a long billow of smoke into the inky night, I languidly stretch my body slightly sideways on the cushions, my free arm draped over the back of the couch.

My eyes slide to pin Veil with my steady gaze, and her shoulders straighten a fraction.

"I know nothing about your god."

Those same shoulders drop, and I barely conceal the chuckle that escapes my lips.

"You said you had answers," she mutters dejectedly.

"I know everything about being a servant to our gods, pet." I take another long inhale, then reach over, offering her the joint. "Just not yours specifically."

She eyes the joint like I'm handing her poison.

"I won't kill you," I say with a sneaky grin.

Her brown eyes flick up warily.

"Besides, I no longer can." I give my hand a small twirl, still holding the joint between two fingers. "Divine law and all."

Finally, she takes the joint out of my hand at the same speed as a snail running a marathon. She studies me as I lean back into the couch, a gentle buzz softly settling over my senses.

Her mouth wraps around the filter of the joint, her lips touching the same spot mine just did. The thought zips straight down to my cock. I drag my tongue over my teeth while she regards me, and my skin heats.

"Divine law?" she says after exhaling the smoke from her lungs.

I nod my head, taking the joint back. "Lesson number one, doll." My gaze turns dark and conspiratorial, my smile just as clandestine. "You are no longer one of *them*," I say, waving vaguely toward the twinkling skyline of Pravitia. "We are our gods' gift to this city. The only *laws* we abide by are those given to us directly from them."

I expect my delivery to impress Veil, but her expression stays flat.

Tough crowd.

I take another drag of the joint and continue with a lot less flair this time, a tinge of vexation in my voice. "Heirs can't kill one another. It's how your family was exiled in the first place."

She furrows her brows together, a small crease appearing between them. "*Damna ... damnatio mem—*"

"*Damnatio memoriae* — correct. Or damnation of memory." I lazily swipe my hand through the air, smoke curling around my fingers, idly rising skyward. "Wiped out of our history records and banished. It's why I know nothing about your dear god of thievery."

She stands up abruptly, like the chair is suddenly on fire, but quickly sits back down, smoothing out her dress.

I chuckle at her erratic behavior.

She eyes me distrustfully, her mouth pressed into a thin line. "How did you know it was the god of thievery then?"

Cunning little thing.

Before answering, I prop my elbow on the armrest and bring my foot up on the couch, resting my other arm loosely on my knee. "Power of deduction, love. And some very *interesting* context clues."

The small drag of the joint she took seems to finally take effect, her body slowly relaxing as she rests her back against the love seat. But her burning curiosity still flares in her gaze. "Like what?" she asks.

I hum, tapping my finger, making a show of pretending to think. "Your *compulsion*, for one."

"Petty theft?" she says almost mockingly.

"Indeed, love. Petty. Theft," I answer, pointing a finger at her to accentuate my two last words.

She seems to be stumbling over more than one question at once.

I don't bother waiting for her to land on one and continue, "I would *surmise* that although a mortal family is banished from the city, their subconscious need to please their god never ceases. As long as the god collects its tithe"—I stub the joint in the ashtray next to me—"well, the divine law does not displease them."

I lean back into the couch and clasp my hands over my naked stomach while dropping my head backward. I gaze up at the stars, a blanket of cosmic orbs shimmering just for us, as I listen to Veil's nervous breathing.

"It's — it's all too much," she says weakly.

I almost startle when my heart skips with a small jolt of empathy for Veil.

My poor little lost doll.

"Tell me, Veil Vulturine," I muse, my eyes still cast skyward, "why did you come here?"

"Here, as in Pravitia?"

"Here, as in Pravitia," I repeat.

It takes her much longer to answer than expected, and I peek a glance her way. She appears to be deep in thought, almost like she's connecting the dots herself.

"What is it?" I ask.

Her gaze finds mine, rosy lips parting on an answer, but then she closes her mouth, as if changing her mind.

"Lesson number two, pet," I say with a bored lilt. "Our powers do not work on each other. It's how I first suspected you might be one of us. Although ..." I say, suddenly sidetracked. I peer at her with a cant of the head, brows furrowing. "You seem to be the exception to the rule."

"How so?" she squeaks.

I fall silent, recalling the incident earlier at Pandaemonium. The one that led me to finally bring her before the Oracle.

I dismiss her question with a small flick of my fingers. There's so much we haven't discussed yet, but it can wait. "That's for another day. *As I was saying* ..." I declare somewhat theatrically, trying to get back to my initial thought. I pin her with my stare, but keep my body relaxed against the couch. "I might not be able to smell the lies and secrets on you, doll. But *do not* underestimate me. I have a plethora of ways to make you speak. Care to discover one of them?" I ask casually, flashing her an arrogant grin.

Her eyes widen, and she shakes her head.

Good. She still fears me.

"I'm not trying to hide anything from you. I just ... I don't know how to explain any of it." She crosses her arms and sighs. "To answer your question"—I don't miss her petulant tone, and I resist the urge to laugh—"I was ... I was called here. I don't know how else to say it. And then after the Feast of Fools"—her voice gets quieter, and she starts to wring her hands together— "I — I tried to leave." Her eyes turn glassy, as if trying not to cry. "But couldn't — I *physically* couldn't leave."

I stare at her while digesting what she just said, a heavy silence rumbling between us.

Then I burst out laughing.

Veil reacts similarly to my earlier outburst. "Nothing about this is funny," she bites out through clenched teeth and a tense jaw.

I jump up to my feet and offer her my hand. "Oh, but it is, love. But it is. And as soon as you accept that we are mere pawns for the gods to play with, I assure you, Veil Vulturine, you'll find the humor in it too."

17

VEIL

I stare at Gemini's proffered hand, his words humming in my head like some kind of eerie prophecy.

"We are mere pawns for the gods to play with."

The unsettling feeling skitters down my spine and burrows itself deep into the pit of my stomach. So much has been left unsaid, and I fear I will suffocate under the sheer weight of it all.

How can this be happening?

How can I even trust anything coming out of Gemini Foley's treacherous lips?

Lifting my eyes up to his, I rasp, "Who was that woman?"

Gemini's eyes have softened ever since he finished smoking his joint, but his gaze still burns against my skin. I can practically hear it turn to crisp.

His voice is just as soft when he answers, "She's the Oracle. She speaks directly to our gods."

Well then ...

Something inside of me, similar to my usual intuition yet so unfamiliar, tells me it'd be wise to believe the Oracle.

The seventh heir ...

I can barely wrap my head around it, let alone accept it.

"I'd suggest you take my hand, love." He wiggles his fingers. "It's getting late, and I'm losing patience."

A heavy sigh escapes me, followed by a sharp inhale when a small jolt of electricity zaps through my arm and down my body as I place my hand in his.

I know Gemini felt it, too, when I witness his bare chest break out into goose bumps. But he does nothing to let on that he felt it, simply pulling me up onto my feet.

When he turns, I get another good look at his sigil tattooed on his back.

Then something he mentioned in passing when he first brought me into the mannequin room comes back to me. *"So many tattoos, and yet you've left your back unmarked."*

He was piecing his theory together even then. And he's right; why *have* I left my back untouched when the rest of my body is covered with tattoos? I never did think much deeper about the meaning until now, and I always assumed I just hadn't found the right design yet.

And what if, this whole time, I was listening to a subconscious desire to please my ... my god?

"What does my sigil look like?" I blurt out as we step into the house.

Gemini swivels around, but doesn't stop, now walking backward as his eyes narrow, studying me. "Why do you think I knew your god was the god of thievery?"

His question to my own confuses me.

"Petty theft?" I respond with suspicion, having a feeling it is the wrong answer.

Gemini lifts his lips, as if amused, but shakes his head. "Like I said, that was just one of the reasons. But!" he says, pointing his finger in the air and turning back around so as not to walk straight into the couch. "The quest to my answer was much simpler. I just had to look to the city where my pretty, petty thief had come from."

"What does that have to do with anything?"

"You never stopped to wonder why Pravitia has six ruling families and Corutio has seven?"

I stay quiet, mulling over what he just said as we step into the hallway. "Keeping up with the ruling class has never been my top priority, whether it be here or back in Corutio."

Gemini chuckles, and I roll my eyes at his inability to ever be serious.

I wait for him to continue his explanation, but I'm distracted by something a lot more pressing.

I stop dead in my tracks. "We've passed my room," I state with the most authority I can muster while my heart has shot up to my throat.

"Indeed we did, doll. Indeed we did," Gemini says over his shoulder, his darkening voice slowly curling over every word.

I stare in horror as he strolls into his bedroom. My eyes blur with the sheer volume of thoughts clamoring in my head.

"I should no longer be your captive," I say with ire.

I'm still fighting against the fear lingering inside of me, but I can't deny the fire that lit up in my stomach when the Oracle declared me the seventh heir.

A tense silence falls between us while Gemini casually turns to face me. My heart triples in rate. His eyebrow lifts with arrogance as he watches me from inside his bedroom. The black eyeliner seems to only intensify the blue and green hues of his mismatched eyes.

"Is that so?" he finally asks.

Feeling like the rug is being slid right out from under me, I nonetheless try to stand my ground and cross my arms, aiming my hard glare directly at Gemini.

"I'm the seventh heir of Pravitia." My voice cracks when I say *heir*, and I internally cringe. "You should treat me as such."

Gemini's dark chuckle prickles over my skin, and I feel it reverberate low in my stomach. "You might be the long-lost heir, Veil Vulturine. But you are still mine to keep." He says the last sentence so flippantly, so matter-of-factly, practically dismissing me as he swivels on his heel, turning his back to me. I hear his mocking laugh, even from the hallway. "Besides, who would believe you, doll, if you told them you were an heir?"

Indignation rises up my throat like bile, and I see red. My rational thoughts shatter, and before I even realize what I'm doing, I'm charging at Gemini like an enraged bull.

I hardly recognize the snarl I hear emanating from my lips as I grab a handful of his hair. I somehow manage to make him lose his balance, his body pitching backward to the ground. Before he has time to react, I leap on top of him, trying not to lose momentum, my fists raining down on his face.

I land a few blows before my crazed haze is pierced by Gemini laughing. I freeze, one tight fist still pulled backward, hovering in the air, my other hand digging into the side of his neck.

His arms are loosely flung over his head, revealing the intricate spiderweb tattoos on his shaved armpits. He appears far too casual for someone who now has a split lip.

My heated scrutiny of his body only lasts a few heart-pounding moments, but the seconds seem to stretch on forever as I take him in. The way his laughter crinkles the thin skin beside his eyes, making two perfect dimples appear on his cheeks. Or the pull of the thin scar over his left eye with the expressive dip of his eyebrows.

My gaze slides to his mouth. The blood from his lip has seeped between his teeth, turning his smile bloody and hauntingly demented.

I suddenly become painfully aware that I'm straddling him with only my panties separating me from the bare skin of his stomach.

My distraction only lasts a few hurried breaths, but Gemini is so fast that I don't see his counterattack coming. His hands fly to my arms, and he flips us with a smooth hook of his leg over mine. My back slams to the ground, and the wind is nearly knocked out of me as Gemini's hips gracefully undulate over mine before pinning me under him.

"There she is," he rasps while his left hand grips both my wrists over my head. The colors of his eyes are now just a sliver compared to the black of his blown-out pupils.

The silence is decadent as I watch his tongue dip out to trail across his bottom lip. The urge to fight him has evaporated, replaced by a much more *carnal* urge, and I internally recoil at the feeling.

"You can fight me all you want, pet. In fact," he says, giving his hips a quick little thrust forward, "I rather enjoy this side of you."

I'm then made aware of his hard length between my legs, and I can feel the second my panties grow damp with his gentle rocking.

My heart pounds loudly in my ears, and the realization makes me want to avoid his gaze altogether. But I don't. I can't seem to rip my eyes away from him.

Not when his smoldering eyes overwhelm me with a hunger that I would rather not name.

Using his free hand, he walks two fingers up my stomach, his attention now on his hand moving up my torso.

"Do you think it's a coincidence I found you?" His voice is but a whisper, and my nape tingles at the sound. His eyes flit to mine, then back down. His fingers continue their tantalizing trek up my body. "Tell me, Veil Vulturine ..." His gaze is back on mine, his eyes now as black as night. "Why would the gods make you *my* sacrifice if it meant"—his hand reaches my neck, his fingers slowly and deliberately circling my throat before applying the smallest pressure—"nothing?"

"Spoiled brat," I spit, my lips curling into a snarl. "I am not a *thing* for you to keep locked away. You can play house as much as your black heart desires, but I will never *truly* be yours."

My words hang between us. My heart drumming erratically against my chest, I wait for him to react. I swallow hard, his palm still clasped around my neck.

His brows lift in surprise, but he quickly grows serious, studying me while his body heat pulses through me like toxic radio waves. Then he laughs, and the burning urge to spit in his face consumes me.

But before I can fathom doing such a thing, he pushes himself off me and says, "Want to bet, love?"

Hastily getting back onto my feet, I stare him down, my body buzzing with adrenaline. "I'm sleeping on the couch."

I barely turn around before he pulls my back against his hard chest. His hand winds around my hair and tugs hard so that my head falls back onto his shoulder, and I hiss at the sting.

His mouth feathers my ear before he whispers, "Your little ragtag crew has been causing quite the stir in the neighborhood since you disappeared. Shame if something happened to them." His nose trails up and down my extended neck, and I break out into goose bumps. "Get in bed, pet."

My breathing stutters at the thought of me being the cause of my friends' deaths, and the humorless chuckle he lets free tells me he knows he has me backed into a corner.

There's nothing I can do—for now.

I must accept my fate and share a bed with a poisonous snake.

18

VEIL

My bare feet pound against the dewy grass as I run in terror. If I dare pause and look down, I know I would find my feet cracked and bleeding.

Even worse, I'm naked, lost in a hedge maze while a monster with haunting eyes relentlessly chases me.

I look back over my shoulder and scream.

His hands drip with blood and gore, reaching, grasping, clawing.

If I stop, he catches me.

If I stop, he catches me.

If I stop—

I JERK AWAKE IN A COLD SWEAT. DISORIENTED, I SCRAMBLE TO SIT up in bed, swiveling my head side to side. The room is dark, but the slivers of light from the waxing moon filtering through the windows illuminate enough of my surroundings for reality to snap back into place. That, and the scent of blood oranges and cloves clinging to the threads of the T-shirt I've been forced to sleep in.

Laying a shaky hand on my pounding heart, I try my best to

regulate my breathing while my gaze falls to the body slumbering next to me.

Having to share a bed with the same man who hunted me for sport must have triggered my recurring nightmare. Admittedly, waking up from said nightmare now doesn't bring the same relief as it did before.

The monster has already caught me.

When I finally resigned myself to my fate last night and agreed to sleep in Gemini's bed, he promptly gave me a shirt to sleep in before jumping under the covers, completely nude.

I acted unaffected and kept my eyes cast down until I had no choice but to crawl under the duvet next to him. Curling my body into itself, I laid on my side on the very edge of the mattress, deliberately facing away from him.

He didn't protest and simply turned off the lights with a few claps of his hands.

The only silver lining with having to share a bed with Gemini Foley is that his mattress is ridiculously massive. If I stretched my arm out now and tried to reach him, my fingertips would still fall a few inches short of his naked arm.

Idly, I watch him sleep. One arm flung over his head, his lips slightly parted as his chest rises up and down, breathing deeply in and out. He appears harmless like this, with his eyes closed, face smoothed away from any conniving expression. He could nearly pass as a sane member of society like this. Almost.

I stifle a sigh that seems to originate from the very center of my soul. Bone-deep exhaustion soon replaces my pounding heart, and my mind turns to fog. Settling back onto my side, I gently rest my head on a pillow that smells like Gemini and let my drooping eyelids close, eventually falling back asleep till morning.

I've been reading all afternoon on one of the terrace daybeds when Gemini returns. He was gone for most of the day —most likely to do with the large crowd I could see, even from this far away, making its way through the city streets.

He's relaxed his control over me in the past couple of days, but I would be naive to believe I could walk out of his home without anyone stopping me. Although I never see them, I can feel his security team's eyes on me, surveilling me when Gemini can't watch me himself.

I'm like a bird with its wings clipped. I can't escape, even when the yearning for it has become almost unbearable.

I lift my gaze to meet his when he approaches me, and I'm nearly knocked over by the surge of energy emanating from him. His eyes are wild and bright, his black eyeliner even more pronounced today. Whatever *celebration* was happening down there, he certainly dressed for the occasion, looking quite regal in a yellow tailcoat and white lace gloves.

"Come with me," he orders with an enigmatic smile, and even his voice strums with electricity.

I notice his split lip is now almost healed, but his black eye is still purple. I feel no remorse at the sight.

Instead, I wonder what happened today for him to seem so enlivened. But I don't bother asking, my curiosity having dulled with the passing days of my captivity. However, the suffocating boredom of that same captivity has me following him without a single protest.

When I realized he was taking us into the city, I tried to conceal my excitement. But the subtle lift of Gemini's mouth as he watched me from his seat on the boat told me I wasn't hiding it as expertly as I believed.

After crossing the water, we take the town car. A few

minutes later, we arrive in front of a dilapidated building just a few streets away from the harbor. I recognize the facade of Animus immediately.

Antoinette, Madeline, and I would come to watch Zazel perform at the Pravitian circus whenever we could afford it. My heart aches at the memory, and I hope that maybe Zazel is inside.

Something about Gemini's demeanor tells me that he's waiting for some kind of reaction, but I refuse to give him the pleasure of one. I keep my face as smooth as stone and take his hand while stepping out of the car, following him inside.

To my dismay, the circus is deserted.

Cloaked in darkness, it appears to be closed for the day.

"Sit," Gemini says, pointing to the stands facing the stage.

I roll my eyes at the order, but still do as he said. He misses my small protest, too busy jogging away and disappearing to the back.

I wait, my impatience manifesting as a bouncing knee and me biting the skin around my thumb. Finally, a single spotlight turns on, illuminating a large circle at the very center of the stage. I perk up, wondering what will happen next.

Gemini returns, his smile just as mischievous as ever. He's changed into a striped pair of jeans and a cropped leather vest, his chest bare underneath.

Strutting up to me, he offers me what appears to be a pale pink leotard.

He hasn't yet said a word, simply waiting for me to take the outfit out of his grasp. I let the silence hang for a little while longer, staring back at him.

Eventually, I cave. "Why are you handing me this?"

His smile widens, as if he won the game, and I immediately regret asking.

"Oh, this?" he says in an infuriatingly innocent tone. "It's for your audition."

19

GEMINI

*V*eil's eyebrows dip in the most adorable furrow, and I start to salivate at the thought of her slender body poured into the leotard that I'm *still* holding up for her.

"My audition?" she repeats after a few failed attempts at speaking.

"You were a gymnast, weren't you?"

"Yes, but I haven't—" she begins to protest.

I tilt my head, hovering over her. "I didn't miss how you bent your body when you retrieved the dropped key." I shoot her a wink. "When you thought I wasn't looking."

Flinging the leotard onto her lap, I stroll up onstage, stepping into the spotlight. I stretch my arms out on either side of me and circle around to face her.

"I can offer you freedom," I say magnanimously, walking back to where she still sits, her brown eyes as wide as saucers. I drop my voice an octave lower for a better dramatic effect. "Under *specific* conditions."

Her gaze turns hard, and I pause, thinking she's about to cut me off. But she doesn't speak, her lips thinning into a straight line, the pink leotard trapped in her curled fist.

I shrug and continue my little speech, holding up a finger. "All I ask is for one simple audition. And this could all be yours, pet."

"You speak like joining the circus has been a lifelong dream of mine," she snaps.

I drop the smile. "Fine, let's go."

I feign nonchalance as I try to take the leotard out of her hands, but she quickly fights back, pulling it into her chest.

"Wait." Her voice wavers, and I know I have her.

I let out a small sigh, acting bored when I'm anything but.

"What are the conditions?" she says slowly.

And, oh, how I wish I could place my palm over her heart and feel how hard it's beating.

Pinning her with my stare, I allow myself one small drag of my thumb over her bottom lip, and her eyes track my movements.

When I finally speak, my voice is close to a whisper. "What if I asked you to audition before telling you my conditions? Would you still agree?" I let the silence convey the significance of the moment before speaking again. "How much do you crave your freedom, Veil Vulturine?"

I drink up the parade of unspoken words flashing across her irises. It's as if she's trying to calculate all the ways this could possibly go wrong for her.

Eventually, she gives me the smallest of nods and stands up, a hard resolve now written clearly across her delectable face. "I'll go change."

BEFORE VEIL RETURNS, I TURN ON THE SOUND SYSTEM AND deliberate on what music I want to play for my doll's little show.

As if this audition means a godsdamned thing.

I chuckle under my breath, knowing that whatever *conditions* I decide, it will just be another ruse for me to bind her fate to mine. One more way to *ensnare* her so implicitly that she will never find her way out.

I decide on a hauntingly melodic tempo—something to make her body twist and turn, slowly, sensually. As I settle back into the stands, Veil reappears, carefully stepping up onstage. She eyes me warily, and I flash her one of my most beatific smiles, indicating with a small wave of the hand for her to begin.

When the spotlight finally bathes her body with light, I drink her in as desperately as an alcoholic sipping on the finest of champagnes.

What a divine creature she is.

She's pulled her brown hair into a tight bun atop her head, small flyaway curls framing her ears. The sleeves of the leotard hug her arms and torso like a second skin, the slope of her breasts just as mouth-watering as her peaked nipples.

Her tattooed legs are decadently exposed, the leotard cutting into the meat of her ass. I silently preen, knowing I'm the reason why she now has more of her for me to grab and squeeze. My gaze travels down her thighs, and I imagine my tongue laving down the length of them, all the way down to her dainty little toes—which I painted myself.

Vulnerability flashes across her face while I finish up my slow and unabashed perusal of her body. She tries to conceal it, but I catch it before it disappears. And something about it makes my mouth water.

"What do you want to see from me?" she asks, her voice rising just above the music.

I tilt my head at her question, a sick thrill bubbling up my chest. "Your flexibility." I purposefully add a pregnant pause to my answer as she squirms under my calculated attention. "Your grace. Impress me."

She breaks eye contact and looks away. I can feel her nerves, even from here; they strum in the air like a plucked cord. A silent melody, regaling me of tales of Veil Vulturine and my effect on her.

It's addictive.

Closing her eyes, she seems to center herself, her shoulders straightening, body lengthening, her arms moving away from her body while placing her hands into a delicate repose.

Then she begins.

And nothing about her performing is amusing any longer.

I swallow hard. Mesmerized. Her dancing body is a masterpiece, a work of art in a constant flow of movements. My body responds immediately, and I'm engulfed with erotic pleasure so potent that I choke on it.

It's as if, suddenly, *I'm* the one who has been ensnared.

My balls tighten with insatiable greed, and my quickly hardening cock pushes achingly against my jeans. My eyes never leave her. Glued to my seat, I track her intoxicating journey across the stage.

She curves her back, one foot pointed behind her while her arms reach far up into the air. She unfurls her body with such unimaginable grace that I can't hold myself back any longer.

I spring up to my feet.

"Hold that pose," I bark.

Veil's body reacts to my voice but stays poised, her body stretched in the most ravenous curves, her extended arms making her small breasts jut outward, her peaked nipples pressing against the thin material.

I swallow down a groan, trying to keep my expression impassive, slowly circling around her, like a ruthless coach evaluating her technique.

She keeps her chin high, the only movement coming from her eyes, which are tracking me wherever I go.

I skate my palm over the twist of her torso, my hand hovering, but never touching.

My cock throbs. Begging. Pleading.

"Show me another pose." I say it so slowly that I wonder if I'll manage to successfully deliver my next sentence without my voice cracking over the sheer weight of my need to watch her like this. "Something I can use for the circus, pet."

She falls back to a relaxed state, her piercing gaze shining bright with defiance. She stays silent while she hesitates until she lifts her right leg toward her back, her toes pointed. Keeping her eyes on me, she arches her back and brings her arms backward, taking hold of her foot and pulling it over her shoulder.

There's a faint throb of victory at seeing her contort her body like this.

I knew she could do it.

I just couldn't imagine how talented she truly was, her body bending in ways mere mortals only wished they could. My obsession for my thieving doll only tumbles further down into the pits of my black heart.

Humming in approval, I begin to circle her again. When my devouring gaze eventually lands on the small piece of gusset barely covering her pussy, I'm almost brought to my knees.

My mind scorches with visions of impaling her with my cock over and over until her cunt is so full of me that my cum drips down her thighs.

I gnash my teeth like a frenzied animal, completing a full circle around Veil while she strains to keep the pose, arms taut and muscles shaking.

I've been a good boy until now ...

But it's getting rather boring.

"Don't break your pose, or you won't get your freedom — understood?" My voice is tight with lust while my fingers pop my jeans open, quickly pulling the zipper down.

I grip my cock with such force that it hurts, but it's followed by overwhelming relief when I drag my thumb over the tip, toying with my ringed piercing.

Veil's cheeks were already rosy with the exertion, but a renewed flush crawls up her neck as her gaze dips to me fisting my cock. She looks back up, her expression a beautiful symphony of concentration and barely tempered desire. Her eyes smolder, and I wonder how far I can push her until she snaps.

She licks her lips and rasps, "Understood."

Time slips, and we face each other for what feels like an eternity, the same hauntingly melodic tempo welcoming us into this new debauched season we've found ourselves in.

Keeping my eyes pinned to hers, I spit in my hand and bring it back to my cock, slicking it over my throbbing length. I'm a live wire, thrumming with the most intoxicating energy. That, paired with the perverse thrill of parading Dizzy's corpse down the street of Pravitia earlier today, has me ready to explode. The desire to channel this erratic energy into Veil has become unbearable.

My attention falls on the tremor in her arms just before her grip on her foot slips.

"Hold it," I bark.

She straightens back into position, a small bead of sweat sliding over her temple and down her cheek. With my cock still in hand, I stroll to face her back, and I'm met with the most ravishing of visions.

The thin patch of fabric stretched over her cunt has grown damp. My taunting chuckle is anything but amused, and the urge building behind my chest is akin to bloodthirst.

She's wet.

She's *fucking* wet.

"What do we have here?" I muse innocently.

Bending down, I lean closer and softly blow right between

her legs. She jolts at the sensation, and my laugh turns that more provoking.

"Hold the pose a little while longer, pet," I groan darkly, trailing a finger down the damp fabric and pushing it into her pussy so it molds to her even tighter. "I promise you, the reward will be worth it."

20

VEIL

’m a trembling mess. Every nerve in my body is engulfed in the most intoxicating of infernos. My muscles are burning with the effort of keeping the pose for this long, but somehow, I find the strength to stay perfectly still.

Gemini's finger is a slow tease over my covered slit, and the twisted need for him to continue to touch me—deeper, *harder* —just might be the thing that finally kills me. And the melodic tempo languidly wrapping itself around us only heightens the experience.

His finger hooks under my leotard, stretching the fabric and making the other side of the cutout dig into my thigh. A relieved moan escapes my lips at his exploratory touch.

My body trembles, and he hums with delight.

"Is this what you crave, love?" he says so casually, dragging the same finger through my arousal, never quite touching where I need him most. "A needy mess for one of the gods' favorites?"

I still have a small shred of rational thought warning me not to answer his question. It's a trick. It's always a trick.

But the slow push of his finger inside my pussy has me

crying out a choked *Yes* followed by a small sob of relief when he tugs my leotard fully to the side and adds a second finger.

I should be disgusted by how wet I sound when he begins to finger-fuck me with zeal, but somehow, it only fuels the shameful lust building inside of me. He's transformed me into his doll, using and playing with me as he pleases while I stay locked in my pose. I'm so close to the abysmal edge, yet he's hardly touched me.

That same sick and twisted part of me wishes I could watch him stroke his cock while his fingers pump into my pussy with the same cadence. I ache to see his expression. The wildness of complete abandon I know I'd find painted across his face.

I hear Gemini curse under his breath, and the sound has me squeezing hard around his fingers. My body begins to visibly shake, and I don't know how much longer I have it in me to stay in position.

Gemini's hand twists, his two fingers hooking over the most sensitive of spots inside while his thumb finally makes contact with my swollen clit. I hiccup around a pleasured sob, my mouth falling open.

"That's it, pet. Let go," Gemini coos darkly. "Give in to me."

The force by which my orgasm crashes through my body shocks me, and it's anything but gentle. It ravages me, wringing me dry. I buckle under my weight and let go of my raised leg, narrowly missing Gemini behind me. I lose my balance, but my captor quickly catches me.

Somehow, he's managed to keep his fingers inside of me as he pulls my back into his chest. He continues to fuck me through my climax, which seems never-ending—a perverse desire that craves to keep me prisoner, that demands I yearn for Gemini like this.

It's sick.

I'm sick.

Yet the slow glide of Gemini's fingers out of my core leaves me wanting—*no*, aching—for more.

"Remind me, Veil Vulturine," he says near my ear, his hand now digging into the thick of my thigh, wet with my arousal. "How can you claim not to be mine?"

Repulsed, I yank his arms off me and swivel around to shove him in the chest.

"You must be mad to think that this meant anything," I spit with so much bitterness that I feel it cover me, cold against my burning skin. "I had no choice."

Stumbling back, he laughs like a psychopathic jester, unceremoniously shoving himself back into his jeans while glaring at me with hooded eyes. He clearly didn't finish by how hard he still is, and I hate myself for even noticing. I'm half naked and feeling painfully vulnerable, but I try to save face and glare back, crossing my arms.

"Oh, but you *did* have a choice, pet."

"Coercion isn't a *choice*."

He rolls his eyes, as if speaking of morality bores him. I expect him to throw me another retort, but his response surprises me.

"It will be of a boundless delight to watch you turn." He takes a challenging step forward. "This isn't you," he says, his lips curling with disgust. "This — this,"—he waves his hand in the air in a lazy circle, as if looking for the right words—"fragile humanity. It's becoming quite the nuisance."

My stomach drops as a puzzling premonition sinks deep into my psyche, but I ignore it. I swallow hard and try to keep my body language as defiant as possible.

"I will never be like you," I growl back.

My response only makes him smile wider.

"Naive little doll," he drawls with so much condescension that I feel his words spill over the crown of my head like a cracked egg. "Your god would beg to differ."

The urge to throw his point back in his face scalds my throat, but I'm suddenly exhausted. I will never win this demented debate as long as Gemini is alive. Or until he tires of me, which, at this rate, will be never.

"I'm going to change," I say, defeated.

Gemini's beguiled expression cracks just long enough for me to see disappointment behind his jokester mask. It's gone just as quickly.

"Don't you want to know about your conditions now?" he says, his voice slightly raised as I walk away from him.

"Does it matter?" I yell back over my shoulder.

I expect Gemini to bring us back to the pier. Instead, the town car heads northbound, deeper into Pravitia. I don't recognize this part of the city, and the question of where we're heading lies heavy on my tongue. I chew and chew and chew until it becomes nothing but a pulverized pile of words before choking it back down.

I try to appear as uninterested as possible while I watch the sun set beyond the skyline, the shadows lengthening like nocturnal ghosts as the orange orb makes its ritualistic descent into darkness.

When the car finally stops, my gaze slides to meet Gemini. He sits opposite me, his seat facing mine. His reclined posture is as relaxed as a debonair prince casually surveying his dominion. I'm greeted with another one of his unnerving smiles as his head rests between his finger and thumb. I keep my expression detached, which only seems to tickle him further.

"Tell me you don't want to perform at the circus," he states simply.

It sounds like a command.

My reflex is to agree, spurred on by spite and to be as difficult as I can be in a vain effort to gain back a semblance of control.

Unfortunately, whatever fabricated freedom he's currently dangling under my nose is better than rotting inside his house until my sanity slowly withers away. Or worse, I forget who I am and metamorphose into the very doll he claims me to be.

"I do want to perform," I say so quietly that I wonder if he can even hear me.

He nods slowly, as if he unequivocally knew my answer. I stew over the thought while I wait for him to speak.

"Condition number one," he says smoothly with a maddening quirk to his upper lip.

I consider stomping my heel into his crotch just to watch him buckle over in pain, but I resist the tempting image. Although considering how he reacted when I landed a few punches the other night, he'd probably get aroused. The thought is meant to be aggravating. Instead, lust pulses deep in the far reaches of my stomach, a taunting, throbbing presence.

"No one can know you are the seventh heir of Pravitia," Gemini declares.

I puff out my disagreement. "How is that fair?"

"Fair is for the weak, love, and I'm anything but."

There's a bite to his tone, and I break out in goose bumps. It's as if even my body is warning me not to test him further. I reluctantly agree to his condition with a curt nod.

He then rattles a few more conditions, his body language staying as relaxed as a dozing cat: Gemini must accompany me whenever I frequent Animus, and I must practice alone *or* with him. His smile turns roguish, gaze darkening, as if he's recalling what transpired between us earlier today. My breath shallows as I unconsciously cross my legs. I hold his stare, painfully aware that I'll concede to all of it for a taste of string-tied freedom.

"Is that all?" I grit out.

He hums, looking upward, as if thinking about it, but the pit in my stomach alerts me otherwise. This is just another one of his taunts.

"I've saved the best for last, doll." His grin slices across his face. "I want an heir," he says quietly as he gazes out the window before his scintillating stare falls back to mine. "When the time is right," he starts, "you shall give me one."

21

GEMINI

J watch the flush crawl out from under her peacoat and up to her freckled cheeks with selfish gratification.

"An heir?" she says much too delicately. As if catching herself, she quickly furrows her brows with indignation. "You must think me a fool if you think I'll ever agree to ... to *that*"—she can't even say the word, and I don't bother hiding my merriment—"in exchange for your sick and twisted version of freedom."

"Tell me, Veil Vulturine"—I pause, keeping my gaze pinned to hers as I place my forearms over my knees, leaning into them—"as the servant to the god of thievery, do you *think* continuing your bloodline won't be required of you?"

Her eyes bounce from left to right as she studies me.

She knows I'm right. And I'm so close to having her exactly where I want her.

"Not with you," she says oh-so quietly.

"Then who?" I cant my head. "A pathetic rube whose entire purpose is to marry into the ruling families?" I scoff. "Don't be so mundane."

"I won't agree to this," she hisses, her arms tightening across her chest.

"I thought you said there was no chance I would *ever* have you, pet?" I volley back.

Her eyes narrow. "There isn't."

"So why are you so up in arms then? Shouldn't this be an easy condition to agree to?"

"You said 'when the time is right.' "

I shrug. "Maybe the time will never be right, doll. Only the gods know for sure."

I move another chess piece across the imaginary board. Always countless steps ahead. Her expression shutters, and I know I have her. The feeling is as salacious as having her come all over my fingers. I watch her from under my lashes as she deliberates. She chews on her bottom lip, and I give her a dazzling smile in return.

"That's all of it then?" she says peevishly while looking down her nose.

It tickles me how she glosses over the final condition, but wordlessly concedes nonetheless. It's as if she's attempting to ignore it, hoping that it will somehow cause me to forget.

Oh, but she's dreadfully wrong.

Every day, every *second*, I weave my sticky web tighter and tighter around her.

As we stare at one another, my tongue swipes over the healing cut on my lip. The consequence of Veil's little domestic tantrum the other night. She might think that she's fighting back, somehow resisting me. In reality, she's barely struggling. Deep down, in the dark recesses of her mind, she's finding satisfaction in this perverted push and pull. And sinking her perfect cunt on my cock is just as fated as me breeding her full of my heirs.

All she needs is a little bit of convincing, whether she first agrees to it or not.

AFTER SEALING OUR AGREEMENT WITH A TENSE HANDSHAKE, I escort us into Laveta—a cabaret bar nestled in the heart of the Carnalis neighborhood. Now that the threat to our lives is a thing of the past, the rebellion squashed and forgotten, we can finally travel freely around Pravitia once again. And ever since discovering Veil's true identity, I've been itching to visit one very *specific* heir.

Laveta's dark reds, velvet, and black decor gives it an unassuming air of luxury without being too loud and garish. It's a private establishment, only fitting a maximum of fifty people, inaccessible to the general public. The small stage faces circular tables, and is where Belladonna comes to sing.

A little birdie told me she'd be here tonight, and after nodding to the bouncer manning the door, I lead Veil inside with a hard tug of the wrist.

I find Belladonna crooning onstage, dripping with lust and white lace, red hair cascading in loose waves over her freckled shoulder. A single spotlight draws everyone's attention to Belladonna while she cradles the microphone seductively in both her hands, her red lips a stark contrast against her pale white skin. Every patron in this joint is under her spell, panting over her as if she were a siren singing a divine melody. Her dear god of lust must be so proud.

One look at Veil, and I know she recognizes her from our fateful night during the Feast of Fools. And her lack of enamoredness for the woman on stage further confirms that she is indeed one of us.

"Why did you bring me here?" Veil hisses under her breath. "I thought you said to keep my identity a secret?"

"I did not bring *you* anywhere, doll," I reply smoothly, coaxing her backward and toward an empty table. "I have business to attend to." I push her down by the shoulders. "Now sit."

She settles into the chair with a huff, crossing her arms and avoiding eye contact. I chuckle under my breath as I walk away, tickled by her recent bout of defiance. With every passing day, Veil slowly becomes more and more brazen, and it pleases me immensely. It's also a rather mighty aphrodisiac.

I sit at the bar and order a glass of champagne, idly flipping a coin between my fingers while Belladonna finishes her song.

The Foleys and Carnalises have never been close. Always some old family feud causing tension between them. My aunt's demise at the hands of Belladonna's father during the Lottery thirty-eight years ago explains the chill between us. My aunt was only eighteen. It's what spurred our parents' generation to have only one child. That way, it would ensure the continuation of the bloodline and prevent any siblings from possibly being sacrificed during the Lottery.

I've never cared to keep up with silly feuds, but Belladonna has always been the most sensitive of us all. Especially when, nineteen years later, her father was sacrificed by Aleksandr's mother. Killing an heir has always only been allowed during the Lottery. Our generation was the exception since there were no siblings to pass down our gods' given powers if one of us were to be killed. Belladonna was only ten years old when her father passed. Then her mother died of a broken heart not long after.

She's kept to herself ever since.

"Foley," Belladonna says when she approaches the bar. Her green eyes study me with suspicion.

I grin. "Carnalis. Tithe Season treat you well?"

The barkeep slides Belladonna a cosmopolitan without her asking, and she takes a dainty sip before sitting beside me.

Ignoring my question, she says, "Mercy isn't here." Her red-chromed nails tap on the marble bar top as her gaze skates across the room, as if she's already exasperated with our conversation.

"She's not the one I'm here for."

Belladonna's eyes snap back to mine, and she quirks a perfectly sculpted brow, but says nothing.

"This is a business call, love."

"What could you possibly need from me?"

"I need you to lift the fertility barrier."

Her fingers stop tapping on the bar midair, and if she wasn't suspicious before, she certainly is now. She studies me warily, as if trying to solve a puzzle in her mind.

"I expected Mercy and Wolfgang to be the first to ask," she says slowly, her guard still up.

Regarding our powers, the general understanding is that they don't work on each other. But a small facet of Belladonna's powers is an exception to this rule; she controls the fertility of the ruling families. None of us can procreate without the god of lust's consent.

My gaze flicks to Veil, then back to Belladonna, but I'm not as sly as I hoped, as her attention is now on my doll across the room. I don't expect Belladonna to remember her from the night of the Feast of Fools, but her gaze lingers nonetheless.

"Who is she?" she asks with her eyes still on Veil.

"Veil Vulturine, the newly discovered servant of the god of thievery," I answer flippantly before taking a slow sip of champagne. "And I happen to have a sudden and insatiable desire to impregnate her."

Before coming to Belladonna with my request, I knew I'd have to divulge Veil's true identity if I wanted my plan to work. Since Veil is also an heir, I would need Belladonna to make her fertile as well. Of course, Veil knows nothing about the ruling families and the aforementioned fertility barrier, and I plan to keep it that way.

Belladonna's eyes widen while her whole body straightens. "What did you just say?"

I purse my lips, acting like repeating myself is the highest of nuisances. "Her family was banished from the city however long ago. You know," I say with a lazy flick of the hand, "*damnatio memoriae* and all."

My answer seems to flummox Belladonna even further.

"No, I *don't* know," she gripes. "How do you know any of this? Does *Mercy* know?"

I shake my head, and she sputters over her words, seemingly having lost the ability to complete a sentence.

From the corner of my eye, I notice a wayward admirer approach us, but before they can sing any praise, Belladonna hisses, "Not now, you cretin."

When our needless distraction stumbles away, I continue with our conversation. "Don't get your panties in a twist, love. I *will* tell her — when the moment is right. I just need a few more weeks."

"A few more *weeks*?" she repeats incredulously. "We should be having a meeting about this now." She punctuates her last word with a pointed finger on the bar top. "Where did she come from? How do you know she's not a threat to us?"

I sigh. "Don't you think Mercy has enough on her plate already? This can wait; Veil isn't going anywhere. She's harmless."

Downing the contents of my coupe, I stand from my seat and pin her with a hard stare, my usual droll attitude vanished. "Will you do this for me or not?"

Belladonna stares back, red lips pressed into a thin line. "Why should I? I don't even like you."

I chuckle at her flimsy insult. "A debt owed by a Foley is a powerful thing, Carnalis. You don't need to like me to accept my request."

She's quiet, seeming to deliberate, until, finally, her eyes flutter closed while she takes a deep inhale. When her eyes reopen, she nods. "It's done."

"Good," I say, then shoot her a wink. "I owe you one."

She mutters something under her breath, but I don't hear a word she says when I suddenly realize Veil is no longer sitting alone at her table. I recognize the man as a peevish social climber, close enough to the ruling families to frequent the exclusive clubs in Pravitia, but still the equivalent of gum under my shoe.

Scum.

And he dares lay eyes on Veil as if she were a viable option for a fun night.

Dares to *speak* to what is mine.

I cut across the room in seconds. Veil senses my approach far sooner than the living excrement breathing the same air as her. Her eyes widen in surprise, and the small tremor of fear still reverberating under the surface of her skin only makes what I do next that much sweeter.

Our eyes lock, and with a jerk of the head, I signal for her to get out of the way. She must see the violent intent in my eyes because she doesn't balk at my silent command and scrambles up and away from the table.

Her gentleman caller has no time to react before I grab hold of a chair and swing it through the air before crashing it down onto his head. The momentum of my swing has him flying to the ground. Flinging the chair to the side, I spot a spoon on a nearby table and reach for it before jumping on him.

The blunt force to the head must have stunned him because he barely fights back, and I land a few hard punches before I lodge the spoon deep into his right eye. He bellows in pain, and my body sings with ancient bloodlust, as if the gods were here with me, cheering me on. My vision tunnels, and I turn lethal. Quickly pushing myself off of him, I jump to my feet and stomp my foot into his face. The spoon sinks even deeper, effectively killing him.

That certainly staunched his screams.

With a satisfied sigh, I rake my hands through my hair, most likely leaving a red streak of blood in their wake, before glancing around the room. All eyes are on me, but none seem remotely surprised to have witnessed such gratuitous violence. It's a risk they run when rubbing elbows with the elite.

I slide my gaze to Belladonna across the room. "Apologies, love. Didn't mean to steal the show."

She's unimpressed, but she snaps her fingers to two men guarding the door, signaling for them to handle the now-dead body on the floor. I flash Belladonna a smile and blow her a kiss.

Turning to a stupefied Veil, I take her hand and drag her out of the bar.

22

VEIL

"*R*ead to me."

I glance up to find Gemini staring at me with a sly smile on his lips. His lean body is stretched out on his red leather couch, just a few seats away from me, the afternoon sun dancing over his face as his hands cradle the back of his head. His hair is yellow today, and he appears to have some kind of aversion to shirts, always bare-chested, especially when it's just us two at home.

Just us two at home.

That sounds much too domestic when, in reality, it's anything but. It's been nearly three weeks since I've been kidnapped, but somehow, it feels like a lifetime.

I'm struck by the softness in his gaze as he waits for me to answer. His black eye has faded, but is still visible, a pale yellow now coloring the thin skin.

It's been a few days since I witnessed him ruthlessly murder a man. It was shocking, appalling even, but ... somehow, it left me with a deep sense of relief. I'd always known Gemini was capable of such abhorrent things, and finally seeing it with my own eyes somehow satisfied my confusing sense of curiosity.

Seeing the monster behind the jester shifted something inside of me, and most confoundingly, it has left me less guarded around him. I can sense some kind of change brewing within me, but I can't quite place *what*. And sometimes, I wonder if Gemini knows what that change is before I've discovered it for myself.

I crave to know more about my god and, most importantly, my family history. Discovering I'm the sole survivor of the Vulturine line feels monumental. Unfortunately, Gemini has been quite tight-lipped on the subject, claiming he knows nothing more than what he already offered me.

I don't believe him.

Then there's the sensitive matter of what happened during my circus audition. Gemini hasn't mentioned it since. And I certainly won't either. But sharing a bed with him every night is becoming unbearable, and I'm ashamed to admit that I'm disappointed every time he ignores me to simply fall asleep, naked, beside me.

It's as if, to him, I am far from being a temptation.

And if not a temptation, then what am I to him?

Blinking back to reality, I push my troubled thoughts aside and clear my throat. "From the book I'm reading?" I ask.

He grins and nods. "I just want to listen to the sound of your voice."

My heart squeezes in response to his statement. I feel split in half; the first is touched by his words, and the second is outraged by my reaction. I look down at the book on my lap, hoping my eyes don't reveal my warring emotions.

The silence lingers between us before I find where I left off and begin to read out loud.

Gemini's grin widens, and he sighs as he closes his eyes, settling deeper into the cushions.

I have time to read two chapters before Gemini's phone pings beside him on the coffee table. With his eyes still closed, he gropes blindly at the table before landing on his phone, picking it up. When he finally takes a peek with one eye, he swears under his breath, jumping to his feet, now on full alert. His head swivels to the door, then to me, then back to the door, looking frazzled.

"What is it?" I ask slowly, my voice laced with suspicion.

"It's Mercy. She's on her way up to the house."

My heart sinks at the name. Mercy Crèvecoeur, coruler of Pravitia. Even if I hadn't seen her bloodlust firsthand at the Feast of Fools, her reputation precedes her.

"Get up, get up," Gemini says quickly. He doesn't wait for me to move, pulling me up and pushing me into the hallway. "You must hide. She can't see you. Not yet."

"Hide?" I say, bewildered, over my shoulder. "But she doesn't even know who I am."

"I can't risk it." He opens a closet door and tries to shove me into it.

"You *cannot* be serious!"

A faint knock is heard coming from the front door, and Gemini whips his head around, as if Mercy will somehow apparate in front of us, then turns his attention back to me.

"Be a good doll for me, pet," he whispers, coaxing me into the closet.

Infuriatingly, I relent. Meeting Mercy is something I'll gladly avoid for now.

"Don't make a sound, and I promise, I'll make it up to you."

I know it's an empty promise, but I still grit out, "You owe me."

He flashes me an arrogant smile and closes the door, effectively locking me inside the hallway closet.

I CAN'T TELL HOW LONG I'VE BEEN LEFT HERE TO ROT, BUT IT'S long enough for me to have made a complete inventory of the closet out of pure boredom. Even with my ear to the door, I can't hear their conversation, so I rifled through his things instead. I've found countless fur coats, hats of all shapes and sizes, and an alarming number of costumes.

I'm seething when Gemini finally opens the door. Storming out, I clip his shoulder with mine before stomping into the living room.

Gemini, of course, finds the entire thing amusing.

Turning to face him, I cross my arms and glare. "You're insufferable, you know?"

He approaches me on light feet, now sporting wide-legged pants and a yellow knit tank top. He must have changed before answering the door.

"Trust me, Veil Vulturine"—he quirks a smile, eyes bright and shining—"I'm an acquired taste."

I stiffen when he gets close, my arms still crossed over my chest. His hands smooth up my arms, but I don't move. Don't react.

"Says who?"

"Says everyone," he rasps, and his lowered voice sends a shiver down my spine.

His eyes are trained down, watching his hands slowly move up my arms.

"Like all your conquests?" I freeze, shocked to hear a bite of jealousy in my tone. I immediately regret my question and don't particularly want to know the answer either.

His quiet chuckle tickles my skin as he lifts his head just enough to regard me from under his eyelashes. "Don't fret, my beloved; you're the only conquest I crave."

My breath hitches at the new pet name, and it sends liquid heat pulsing through my core. I immediately chastise myself for being so easily manipulated.

"How long was I in there?" I say, changing the subject.

His smile widens, his fingers now curling around my arms and squeezing. If I didn't know better, I'd say he almost looked sheepish. "A little over two hours."

I huff out an exasperated breath and step away from him. Turning on my heel, I take a few steps and then turn back to face him, lifting my arms in the air as a show of protest. "When will you stop treating me like your prisoner?"

Gemini's smile fades, and he turns unusually serious. Which only makes his answer that much more foreboding. "When you start acting like the rightful heir of the Vulturine family."

I drop my arms, the silence pulsing like a heartbeat between us. When I speak, my tone drips with dismay. "I wouldn't even know how to, Gemini."

We stare at each other for what feels like lifetimes, but it's closer to mere seconds until Gemini winds back to life.

"Come," he declares theatrically, followed by two quick claps of his hands. "Let's discuss this further by the pool. I feel like a swim."

Dumbstruck, I mutter, "You have a pool?"

"Yes, it's in the atrium," Gemini says over his shoulder as he walks away.

"You have an atrium?"

23

VEIL

At this time of night, the atrium is veiled in darkness, and only the lights from the pool help to illuminate our surroundings. However, I can still make out the shadows of countless plants and vines hanging from pots or tucked into corners, their large leaves reaching up to the glass ceiling.

I can only imagine how beautiful the atrium must be during the day, when the sun radiates over the pool from every angle.

This might just officially be my favorite room in the entire house.

"Why did you never mention the atrium before?" I ask Gemini as I follow him to a row of lounge chairs, fresh towels already neatly folded and waiting for us.

He made us change into bathing suits before showing me to the pool.

He shrugs, running a hand through his hair, and flashes me a smile. "What's the fun in telling you everything?"

I roll my eyes and look away. His laugh is so carefree. And it caresses my skin much too smoothly.

Strolling up to the diving board, he climbs up and stretches himself into position, arms above his head. His pink swim shorts ride up his thighs with the movement, and my eyes drop to his stretched stomach without even a second thought … then a few inches lower.

I swiftly catch myself, but it's too late. By the time my gaze lifts back to his face, he's staring at me with a crooked grin. He winks and then pushes himself off the diving board. Tucking his knees into his chest, he executes a flawless front flip before disappearing into the water with barely a splash.

I watch him swim a lap before I take off my silk robe, revealing the white one-piece Gemini chose for me. With its plunging neckline and thong bottom, it's just as revealing as a skimpy bikini.

After the first week, Gemini stopped watching me undress. And something tells me even *that* is a calculated move. I just don't know what for … yet.

Instead of diving in like Gemini, I take the steps leading into the shallow end. The water is deliciously warm, and I drop down when I get deep enough, fully immersing my body and head. I pop up, dragging my hand over my wet hair, and let out a small yelp when I realize Gemini is standing right in front of me.

His wet hair is slicked back, and water drips down his face, some droplets catching on his lips. "Boo," he says with a dark sneer.

I physically recoil, blood turning ice cold.

Gemini's expression turns innocent, and even that gives me whiplash. He tilts his head to the side like a curious dog. "What just happened?"

The water trickles around me as I slide my body backward, distancing myself from Gemini until my back hits the side of the pool. He hasn't moved, still eyeing me like I've gone mad.

I certainly feel that way.

"It's what you said in the maze before telling us to run." My voice trails off as I linger on the thought that I'm the only one alive from that small group of sacrifices.

Gemini stays expressionless for a beat, then flashes me a toothy smile. "Such fond memories," he says with a nostalgic sigh.

Rage spikes through me as if I were being skewered from the inside out. "Yet, for me," I spit, my heart slamming into my chest, "the day I met you was the worst day of my life."

"Oh, love," he says with a mocking pout, fixing me with his stare as his body slowly glides to mine. His hands land on either side of me, boxing me in. "Maybe we should rectify that then."

I swallow hard, some needy part of me cracking at the desire for him to pin his body against mine. The odd mixture of lingering fear and adrenaline at being this close to Gemini Foley is as intoxicating as the promise of ever-lasting life.

"What is that supposed to mean?" I rasp.

He tilts his head, his cheek hovering so close to mine, but it somehow feels like an insurmountable distance away.

"Maybe the next time I chase you through a maze, my beloved," he whispers near my ear, "you won't be begging me to let you go." The sound of his voice has my body breaking into goose bumps. His nose trails infinitesimally up my neck. "Next time I catch you, you'll be begging for the hard pumps of my cock inside your greedy little cunt, begging for me to fill you with *heirs*."

He says the last word with a small thrust of his hips, and I'm consumed with the image he just painted. I'm grateful that it's dark enough that Gemini can't see the flush crawling up my chest. Thankfully, I'm still holding on to the last fraying threads of my sanity, and I shove him off of me.

"That's never going to happen." My words are sharp, but the uncertainty in my voice is evident. I consider sinking under the water to drown instead of having to watch Gemini silently gloat a few feet away.

I deliberate getting out of the pool and storming away, but I know how quick Gemini can be. He won't let me go that easily.

He will never let me go.

It's not the first time I've had that thought, but it's the first time that statement holds a different kind of indecipherable weight to its meaning.

"What am I to you?" I blurt out.

"A pretty gift from the gods," Gemini states plainly before turning on his back to float, his arms lazily swaying through the water.

"So that's it?" I'm ashamed of the disappointment threading in between my words, but I continue nonetheless. "All I am to you is a *thing* to possess?"

"You are far from being just a *thing*, Veil Vulturine," he replies impatiently.

"What then?"

"You are the future of this city." He says it so casually, and the fight suddenly tumbles out of me like loose marbles. Turning his body in the water to face me, he pins me with his stare, hard eyes piercing right through me. "Did you ever stop to consider that the reason I'm keeping you a secret is for your own good?"

His words surprise me, the snarl in his tone even more. I open my mouth, hoping to push out an answer, but nothing comes out. In seconds, he has me boxed in again.

"They would eat you alive."

I don't need him to tell me who *they* are. The ruling heirs of Pravitia, Gemini's equals—and mine, if I dare to allow myself to think it. But I balk at the very idea of being in the same room with them again. Untamable fear claws up my throat at the thought.

I stay perfectly still as Gemini's face hovers inches from mine, his chest pressing into me.

"And as long as you hold on to your precious little morals, pet, you will never experience the kind of freedom you're destined for." His parted lips trail over my jaw, and I shudder at the sensation. Gnashing his teeth close to my ear, he adds, "Until then, you are mine to do with as I wish."

I try to shove him away again, but he catches my wrists in his hands, a leering grin slicing across his face.

"I don't believe you," I hiss.

"You don't believe what?" he says, the levity back in his voice.

"That there will ever be a day you'll stop treating me like your prisoner and let me go."

He hums with delight, his eyes shining much too bright for the gravity of the conversation.

"How can I make you understand this, doll? The day you decide to transform yourself into the person you've always been destined to become, you won't *want* to leave. You'll realize then that you've been exactly where you wanted to be all along."

"And where's that?"

This back-and-forth pulses with the echo of our previous conversation weeks ago. I know his answer but still burn to ask the question.

He gives me a knowing smile, as if he, too, is recalling that same conversation. "By my side," he finally says.

I parrot back what I said that day, "Like your trophy?"

Gemini is quick to answer, his gaze darkening. "Like my *wife*."

I study him, water clinging to his eyelashes. "You sound so sure about that."

His response is filled with reverence. "There is no such thing as free will in a city like Pravitia, Veil Vulturine. It would benefit you to remember that."

He's still gripping my wrists while my hands are pressed against his chest, and I can feel the faint rhythm of his heartbeat.

"So it's your gods' will? Not yours?"

"*Our* gods," he says adamantly.

"How can I claim them if I know nothing about them?" I snap.

He watches me carefully, a serious dip to his brow. "Is that what you need?" he asks softly. "To commune with your god?"

His question stumps me. But there's a small, distant voice inside that is screaming, *Yes! Yes! Yes!* and I suddenly feel an unbearable sense of loss. It's as if I've been suppressing this feeling my entire life—born with it in the very molecules of my soul.

I have an overwhelming urge to cry, the tears pricking the back of my eyes as I swallow hard. I nod, knowing my voice will crack if I speak.

Gemini solemnly mirrors my nod. "Give me time, and I will find the answers you seek."

<hr>

My eyes fly open as I jolt out of slumber. Taking a deep, ragged inhale, I push the duvet off my body, feeling like I'm about to suffocate.

I was being chased again.

Except ...

This time, Gemini did catch me, and he—

My clit throbs, and I squeeze my legs in protest. To my dismay, it only seems to intensify the lustful ache. But it doesn't deter me from replaying the dream in a slow, deliberate sequence.

Gemini's harsh push to open my legs wide.

His flat tongue burning a path up my slit.

My throaty moans.

I squeeze my eyes shut, feeling crazed.

Gods.

Letting my head fall to the side, I find Gemini peacefully sleeping beside me. Although, in reality, there's nothing peaceful about an agent of chaos like him. And still, in the cloaked secrecy of his dark room, I yearn to touch a lot more than just the warm skin of his rising chest.

My hand falls between my thighs, a feathered touch over my soaked panties, and I'm now desperate to fall victim to my inappropriate desires.

I chew on my bottom lip, staring at Gemini Foley, my biggest temptation. I'm torn by the familiar feelings warring inside of me. Right and wrong.

Gemini's voice drifts past my ears as I recall what he said earlier in the pool. *"As long as you hold on to your precious little morals ..."*

What if he's right? What if I'm destined for something much greater than this?

Then a thought pops into my head. *What if I can't feel my god because I've been resisting it all this time?*

What if they will continue to stay silent until I finally give in, accept my fate and let go?

My mind empties as I make my fateful decision, my heartbeat drumming in my chest as I crack to the maddening urge. Pushing myself up onto my hands and knees, I quietly crawl to Gemini's side of the bed.

24

GEMINI

*W*arm hands on my stomach. Soft strands of hair over sensitive skin.

Slowly, I drift back from somewhere far away.

The shy rake of nails against my thighs. Pillowy lips trailing down, down, down.

My eyes snap open as my hand flies forward, grabbing Veil harshly under her chin. She gasps, her gaze slamming into mine, and even in the veiled darkness, I find a new flame in her darkening eyes. She stares back at me, her mouth agape as I squeeze my fingers into her cheeks.

Her expression is resolute. I've never seen her like this, never this steadfast in her decision, and it feels almost as divine as her hand defiantly wrapping around my hardening cock.

"Veil Vulturine," I muse tauntingly, her name holding all of the implications of this powerful moment.

"Don't ruin this," she whispers.

I suddenly feel the tightrope under us. One false move, and she'll fall right back to her old self. I clench my jaw, the lust of finally having her like this overwhelming me. She continues to fix me with her stare while her hand begins to stroke my throbbing shaft.

Slowly unfurling my fingers off her face, I let my hand fall to my side while Veil stays completely still, aside from her hand around my cock.

I swallow hard, my face serious. "Spit," I order, my voice still raspy with sleep and rising pleasure.

She looks incredible like this—loose brown strands falling over her face, eyes ablaze with desire. She is sultry brought to life, powerful and lethal.

Gathering the saliva in her mouth, she purses her lips, her eyes still scorching a hole straight into my soul as she lets the spit slowly fall over the head of my cock.

Her palm smooths over my piercing before wrapping tightly around the shaft, spreading her spit all over my cock. My head falls back into the pillow, a small hiss of bliss escaping my lips as my stomach tightens with arousal.

The satisfaction of Veil finally caving to her base urges has my sensations intensifying into molten desire. She's exactly where I want her to be, and when her lips wrap around my cock—*oh*—there's nothing quite like it.

To know I'm the reason behind her acting like this, to know I've led her here—eating out of the palm of my hand, or more accurately, swallowing me whole—it makes the heady drag of her tongue down my shaft that much more enticing.

I have a sudden urge to clap the lights on. To watch with unobstructed vision how her cheeks hollow out as she swallows around me, pushing my cock deeper into her hot, wet mouth. I wish I could see the telltale flush on her cheeks. I settle on listening intently to the sounds she makes instead, worried that by turning on the lights, it would break the spell.

The low, humming moan she lets out while her mouth is still full of my cock shoots straight to my balls, and I lift my hips in response. My hand finds the back of her head, my fingers threading through her hair in a loose grip.

The slurp and small pop that follows when she pulls me out of her mouth makes my eyes roll to the back of my head. But it's her words that finally do me in.

"I couldn't wait to taste you," she mutters under her breath. There's awe in her tone, and I'm almost positive she hasn't realized that she said the words out loud.

A surge of possessiveness flares in my chest, and it leaves me breathless. I don't bother taming it. I flip Veil onto her back in seconds, and she lets out a small squeak. Jumping off the bed, I pull her toward me, just enough for her head to fall over the edge of the mattress.

I'm breathing hard as I look down, our eyes crashing into each other. Fisting the base of my cock, I notch the head against her closed mouth, spreading her spit all over her lips.

"Let me have more of you, pet," I say through gritted teeth, my self-control just about ready to snap. "I need to be deep inside your throat when you swallow my cum."

I've barely finished speaking before her chin lifts, and her lips wrap around my cock, her tongue swirling over the head as a taunting invitation.

I hum with approval, my hand stroking her exposed throat. "Relax for me," I coo as I slowly push myself inside.

When the tip hits the back of her throat, she gags around me, and I continue to caress her throat. Soothing her. Shushing her.

I can hardly recognize the tone of my own voice.

I feel her respond to my praise as my cock slips deeper into her tight throat, until I'm pressed flush against her face.

"That's it," I groan, "my perfect little fuck doll."

Her reaction is immediate, moaning around my cock as her legs fall open on the bed, revealing cotton panties, and I grin in crazed victory. Bending down to grip her T-shirt, I jerk it up her body until her breasts spill out, the moonlight caressing the shadows of her peaked nipples. Pulling out almost to the tip, I start fucking her mouth, slowly picking up the pace as her hand disappears into her panties.

"Take those off," I bark.

She listens far too eagerly, wiggling them off before her slender fingers return to her center. My balls tighten with unadulterated lust as she rubs her clit in mindless circles.

I can feel my climax build, but I'm selfish, and I never want this to end. I might have Veil exactly where I want her—my cock *willingly* in her mouth while her fingers disappear into her soaked cunt. But I know, come morning, she'll crumble under the weight of her useless morality.

I watch her pump her fingers in and out, her muffled moans growing needier by the second, and enjoy every part of it.

"Does that soothe your ache, pet?" I ask darkly, my hips thrusting hard and deep, her gargled noises spurring me on. "Seeking your own relief while I fuck that perfect mouth of yours?"

She can't use her words, but her raised hips are response enough, her free palm pushing against the mattress as her fingers disappear deeper into her cunt.

I groan loudly, mesmerized by the sight of her, and my cock pulses on her hot tongue as her soaked fingers slide out and find her clit. Planting her feet on the bed, her legs fall even wider.

I'm so close to the blissful edge, but I hold off. I need to hear and feel her come while she's stuffed full of my cock first. Luckily, it only takes a few more desperate strokes of her clit for her to moan so loudly that I feel it reverberate up my spine. Her mouth tightens around my shaft, and I grab both sides of her head, keeping myself from fucking her senseless.

Eventually, she relaxes into sated bliss, and her climax quickly morphs into mine.

Bending down, I harshly snatch her hand away from her cunt and take her fingers into my mouth. I bottom out, her lips pushing against my base as her arousal hits my tongue. Groaning loudly, I suck on her fingers as I unload, pumping hot spurts of cum down her throat, my free hand groping her breast mindlessly.

As I settle back into my body, I slip out of Veil's mouth, and my attention catches on her smoldering yet serious gaze. Without breaking eye contact, she turns onto her stomach and pushes herself up, before settling on the edge of the bed. We stare at each other in silence for a lengthy and tense beat as we both catch our breath. Finally, I break the spell.

"Regretting it already, love?"

My question is flippant, and she doesn't answer immediately. Instead, she continues to study me, as though *maybe* if she stares long enough, she'll decipher a puzzling enigma.

"Are you?" she replies softly.

My grin is wistful as my thumb finds her swollen lips. "Why would I regret what is already written?"

Her expression shutters, and I can see the exact moment she closes herself off. I can't help but be amused by her predictability.

"Ah, yes," she says resentfully before standing up. Her gaze levels with mine. "Your beloved gods."

She pushes me out of her way and disappears into the bathroom.

THE SILENCE IS TENSE THE NEXT MORNING AT BREAKFAST. AND according to Veil's body language and the fact that she keeps avoiding my gaze, it's bothering her a lot more than it's bothering me.

The dining room echoes with the delicate clinks of cups

placed back on saucers and the soft crunch of teeth biting into pastries. I stopped hand-feeding her a while back, and my senses tell me she'd bite my finger off if I tried such a thing this morning.

I find the entire affair rather humorous.

Finishing my last bite, I clear my throat and stand up. Fishing out a small vial from my pants pocket, I stroll up to her chair—as far away from mine as possible—and quietly place it in front of her. She stares at it. And I know she recognizes its contents immediately.

It's a contraceptive tonic.

She lifts her gaze to meet mine, eyes narrowing. We have an entire conversation without having to utter a single word.

She wouldn't need the tonic if she stayed true to what she'd declared so vehemently just a few days ago. But after last night ... it's only a matter of time until she's fucking herself on my cock.

She knows it.

I know it.

The tonic is a small peace offering. No threat of an heir, until the time is right—as I so benevolently declared.

Except ...

The tonic does not affect the servants of the gods.

Only Belladonna's powers can control our fate.

But Veil does not need to know that. She can bask in her false sense of security until her belly inevitably swells with our heir. And hopefully, by then, she'll have come to her senses and accepted that we are bound to share this life, she and I. Tricking her is simply the most natural way to lead her to her fate.

I leave Veil to her silly deliberations, knowing that when I eventually return to the dining room, I'll find an emptied vial in front of her vacant seat.

25

VEIL

As promised, Gemini escorts me to Animus almost daily. I soon realize that this small piece of freedom might be worse than being stuck in the house. On the plus side, I'm surrounded by people here, but Gemini's menacing glare makes everyone steer clear of me. All it does is make the abject loneliness more acute.

And where is Zazel?

I've been here for a few days and have not seen them anywhere. I try to remember if they had a fixed schedule, but my mind has a hard time conjuring up *anything* from before my kidnapping. However, the thought of Zazel discovering the truth of my disappearance has my skin crawling with apprehension. Maybe it's better if my friends think I'm dead.

But even that morbid hope is futile when Gemini plans to have me perform onstage in front of a large crowd of Pravitians in less than two weeks.

I've been practicing for a few hours now with Gemini carefully watching me from his spot in the corner of the room. It's a private space, and no one is allowed inside while I'm practicing. A floor-to-ceiling mirror spans an entire wall, and there's even a trapeze hanging from the low ceiling. The apparatus is novel enough that I've started incorporating it into my routine, just for something new and stimulating to master.

When straining to execute a rather difficult sequence of movements atop the trapeze, I slip and almost fall. I curse under my breath as I dismount, pushing the small hairs sticking to my forehead away with irritation.

I'm breathing hard, both hands flat on the back of my hips as I stare into the mirror.

"What's wrong, my beloved?" Gemini casually asks from behind me. His gaze is down, flipping through a tabloid magazine as he sits on the floor. His back rests against the wall, legs sprawled in front of him while he idly flips a coin over and around the fingers of his free hand.

My gaze finds him in the glass. The feeling of unease I've had since I woke up this morning sits heavily on my chest. That, paired with his new pet name, which *feels* like so much more than just a pet name.

"Nothing is wrong," I snap.

Gemini's eyes flick to find mine in the mirror. His eyebrows rise in a hint of surprise, and a subtle grin appears at the corner of his lips.

Then, in the most embarrassing turn of events, I burst out crying. Shocked and mortified, I bury my face in my hands, keeping my back to him. But Gemini is next to me in seconds, grabbing me by the shoulders so I can face him, even though I'm trying my best to keep my face hidden as I hiccup through the tears.

"Veil, look at me," he says with a slight bite to his voice. "Tell me what's wrong."

Knowing he won't let this go, I force myself to calm down before sheepishly lifting my head up to face him. "I don't know," I answer truthfully.

I attempt to shake myself out of his grip, but his fingers dig harder into my shoulders. I roll my eyes in exasperation at his refusal to let this go. Averting my gaze, I try my best to furiously wipe my cheeks dry from the damning tears.

"I've been feeling restless, like — like something is missing." I slide my gaze to his. "There's an urgency to the feeling, and it's only been building as the days pass." I chew on my lip nervously. "I can barely put words to it."

Gemini is quiet. He studies me, as if holding a much larger piece of the puzzle than I ever knew was missing. And something about that fleeting sentiment has the resentment of still not knowing anything about my family's history flaring through my veins, alongside the growing restlessness.

"How long since you last collected tithe?"

His question further irritates me.

"Speak plainly, Foley."

He pushes out a small chuckle before speaking again. "When was the last time you *stole* something?"

Surprise prickles my skin like a fresh set of goose bumps, but it's quickly subdued by how ridiculous I find his question. "How long since you kidnapped me? Then you'll have your answer."

Impatience flashes across his face, but he is fast to erase it away and laughs dryly before finally letting me go. His gaze turns arrogant. "Still hung up on that, I see."

I'm about to fling my retort back in his face, but he beats me to it. He begins to pace in front of me, hands clasped behind his back. He looks especially dapper today, wearing a black velour suit, the top buttons of his dress shirt undone.

"Do you want this feeling to cease or not?" he hisses, clearly growing tired of my crossness.

I snap my mouth shut and let the silence temper the rising tension between us before muttering a small, "Yes."

"Good!" he chirps, his mood shifting instantly. He snaps his fingers and points to the floor. "Sit."

I balk for a split second before Gemini flops down and crosses his legs. I follow suit, settling in front of him as I eye him suspiciously.

He drags both hands through his pink hair in some sort of theatrical pause before giving me his full attention. "You must feed your god, Veil Vulturine."

"But—"

He waves me off like a pesky fruit fly. "You've been doing this all your life. Now you must learn to do it intentionally." His gaze turns serious. "With purpose."

Confused, I make a show of looking around the empty room. "How am I meant to steal anything when it's just us two?"

His smile turns devious. "Steal my power."

I stare at him, dumbfounded. "I — I can't."

"You've done it before."

My mind drifts back to the day at Pandaemonium, when he caught me trying to run away. Something happened between us that day, and I never quite had the words to press Gemini about it. Just one more thing cloaked in maddening mystery. And I always seem to be the last one to know.

"Whatever *that* was, I don't know how that even happened, let alone how to do it again."

"Not everything needs words to be understood, pet," he replies far too dismissively. Placing his hands palm up between us, he adds, "Put your hands in mine."

I resist his command and instinctively curl my hands into fists instead.

Gemini scoffs, followed by a dry laugh. "You are incorrigible."

Admittedly, I'm not sure why I'm being so difficult right now when he seems to genuinely want to help. Or as genuine as Gemini Foley can be.

I conceal a small sigh and delicately place my palms in his.

Electricity zaps through me, and I'm flooded with images of us. Of *him*. His naked body towering over me as he fucks my mouth with abandon. A shiver travels down my spine, and I try to swat the image away as quickly as possible.

This isn't the time to think about *any* of that.

I try to hide where my mind has gone by looking away and fidgeting into a more relaxed position on the floor. But Gemini never misses a thing, and I pretend not to see the twinkle in his eye when my gaze slides back to him.

"Ready?" he says.

I nod.

"Close your eyes."

Again, I unconsciously resist, taking a few unnecessary seconds before I do what he said.

I inhale deeply. The heat of his hands against mine is now heightened with my one missing sense. It takes longer than expected for Gemini to speak again, the pause feeling intentional, as if he's trying to teach me something, even in the quiet spaces in between.

"There is no such thing as a rift between you and your god," he says, his tone sounding quite solemn. "You are an extension, a mortal rendering of their divinity. This means there will always be a connection — inside of you. It's from that source from which you draw your powers."

His fingers curl around my open palms, and I break out into goose bumps.

"It's time, Veil Vulturine, for you to find that loose thread. To *feel* that power pulsing through your veins."

What if I can't?

The reaction is immediate. Still so unsure and questioning, let alone accepting, that I have some kind of divine ability—no matter how amoral the gods are or how frightened I am of them. I swallow down my insecurities and take a large inhale, dutifully keeping my eyes closed.

Gemini falls silent, his presence still imposing, even without my eyesight. But the touch of his skin against mine grounds me, and I don't linger on how uncomfortable that thought makes me. Instead, I use it as my first stepping stone, hoping that maybe it will lead me to this ever-elusive place inside myself.

I don't know how long we sit there for. It's long enough for time to start feeling like an elastic band being stretched and stretched and stretched. I don't know if and when it will eventually snap.

Gemini is right. The words evade me. Like smoke, they become immaterial, and I lose myself in the feelings.

I float.

I drift.

I linger.

Until, suddenly, I snag on something.

I almost miss it. Almost pass right by it.

I curl my hand around it, like a thin gold thread, and *tug*.

26

VEIL

The sensation that follows is akin to a rush of adrenaline. It surges from the tips of my toes up to the crown of my head as every single hair on my body stands on end.

My eyes fly open to find Gemini beaming, his wide smile warm, eyes shimmering.

A shocked laugh tumbles out of my lips. "I did it," I say breathlessly.

Without thinking, I leap toward him, my arms circling his neck in a burst of giggles. The impact of my body on his makes him fall backward onto the floor as his arms wrap effortlessly around my waist.

I push myself up to look him in the eye, and my laugh slowly fades. Our gazes turn serious, and I'm suddenly hyper-aware of my body on top of his.

"How does it feel?" Gemini rasps.

A part of me yearns to break this loaded moment. The rest of me craves the exact opposite. All the pieces of me are at war, and I'm standing directly in the line of fire.

I decide not to move.

I give him a shy grin. "The feeling has many layers to it," I muse. "I feel my god's connection inside of me, but then ..." I pause, lingering on the foreign sensations, "Then I feel the power I stole from you like a second presence. Almost like a separate entity." I smile. "How does it feel to *you*?"

His expression turns boyish, his gaze moving up and around, as if trying to decipher the feeling. "Quiet."

I expect to sense something, maybe a prickling at the nape that lets me know if he's lying or telling the truth, but there's nothing.

"I can't tell if you're lying," I say, perplexed.

His hands dance up my spine and back down again. "Our powers don't work on each other, remember?"

"But I thought maybe since I have your power ..." I trail off, knowing Gemini will decipher what I mean.

"Power or not, beloved," he says with a wink, "I'm still the chosen one."

We fall into another loaded moment as we silently stare at one another until Gemini is the first to move. He gently pushes me to his side so he can jump to his feet, then gives me his hand.

"Now let's go smell some lies," he declares with a wide grin.

Still sitting on the ground, I meet his gaze as my brows furrow. "How do I give your power back?" Suddenly, I feel nervous.

He shrugs, wiggling his fingers to signal that he's still waiting for my hand. "I'm sure *the* servant to the god of thievery will know how."

AT THIS TIME OF DAY, THE CIRCUS ISN'T OPEN TO THE PUBLIC, BUT there's enough of a crowd for me to metaphorically stretch my legs and try to test Gemini's power on those around us. Acrobats practicing high up in the air, a knife-thrower lodging sharp blades inches away from his beautiful assistant, and—

"Zazel!"

They quickly turn around at the sound of my voice, and I leave Gemini's side to run up to where they are standing.

My heart pinches when I watch the overwhelming relief wash over my friend's face.

"Veil, we've been so worried," they say in a rush.

I pull them into a tight embrace as they continue to mutter their relief into my hair. Pushing me back, they keep their hands on my arms while they survey my body.

"Are you okay? Where have you been?" Their voice is tight with emotions, and tears prick my eyes at the thought of what I've unintentionally put them through.

"I'm so sorry, Zazel." The ball in my throat grows bigger and bigger as I try to find the words while a small voice in my head hisses at me not to tell them that I was kidnapped. "I didn't mean to scare you. I, uh ... it's just been a weird few weeks," I say weakly, feeling guilty.

I turn my head to look at Gemini over my shoulder. He's watching us, but to my surprise, he seems to have no care in the world, and I realize then that he wouldn't even be bothered if my friends knew the truth.

He's above it all.

And ...

By the same logic, I am too.

I feel a large, gaping fissure start to form between me and Zazel before I even know how to process it. I turn back to them, their gray eyes narrowed as they bounce between Gemini and me. "Have you been with Gemini this whole time?" they ask slowly, their tone suspicious and somewhat incredulous.

My shoulders fall just as their hands let go of my arms.

"It's complicated," I reply with defeat.

We stare at each other for a few tense seconds until Zazel

breaks the crackling silence. "Well, whatever this is, I hope you're being careful. I'm happy for you."

Gemini's powers flare inside of me. *A lie.* But I wouldn't have needed it anyhow. Their false statement hangs heavy between us like an accusation.

Zazel's hard expression shifts, as if just noticing my leotard and loose jogging shorts. "Are you working here now?"

I rub my hand on the back of my neck, suddenly feeling awkward. The shift in mood is giving me whiplash, squashing the happiness I originally felt at finally seeing Zazel after three long weeks.

Now I'm desperate for this conversation to end.

"I am." I pause. "Contortionist," I add with a shrug of my shoulder.

Zazel's brows dip in confusion. "You never told me—" They stop abruptly, their expression shuttering, as if realizing something I'm not privy to. They study me like it's the first time they've ever set eyes on me.

My throat tightens, but my words stick to the roof of my mouth.

"I guess ... I'll be seeing you around," Zazel mumbles.

They turn their back to me and walk away. I do nothing to fix the chasm between us as I let the confusing relief of this conversation ending settle over me.

I sense Gemini approaching, and a wave of anger crests, engulfing my confusing feelings. Spinning to face him, I shoot him a hard glare. I can't decipher if the anger is misplaced or not, but I direct it at Gemini nonetheless.

"What have you *done* to me?" I hiss under my breath.

Gemini throws his hands in the air in a show of surrender as he laughs darkly.

"This isn't funny," I snap.

"What have I *done* to you?" he repeats, the spark of amusement dancing across his irises. "Why? Because you feel no connection to the people from your past life?"

His words stun me. *Past life?* My mouth opens, then shuts. Why does he always seem to be one step ahead of me? Always the one with the answers?

"You speak as if I died," I snarl.

"Have you not?" he muses, stepping closer as his eyes darken. "Am I not witnessing the most beautiful of rebirths before my very eyes?"

His question strikes me as far too powerful for me to answer. I barely have space for his words to find a place inside my chest.

But they do.

Oh, they do.

Something inside me shifts. I let go of the gold thread connecting me to him, and I feel the very second his powers siphon back off to where they belong.

He closes his eyes and takes a large inhale, as if reveling in the feeling of being whole again. His eyes snap back to mine as his fingers slip under my chin, raising it slightly so that we're eye to eye. My heart triples in rate.

"When will you learn, little rabbit?" he whispers much too softly. "You belong with us."

27

VEIL

"*D*o you feel ready?"

Grabbing my duffel bag with my change of clothes off the floor, I look over to Gemini and answer his question with a nod and a timid smile.

I've been practicing every day for the past week. My body is sore, beat up, and tired, but my physical ailments are overshadowed by the excitement of what comes next. And Gemini has sat in the same corner of the same room, never seeming to grow bored as I fine-tuned my very first contortionist routine.

My debut is tomorrow night on the grand stage, and I need it to be seamless. Maybe performing at the circus was never a dream of mine, but now that it's part of my reality, it's hard not to want it to be perfect. I missed this creative side of myself, tucked away ever since I had been called to Pravitia.

Gemini returns my smile as he heads for the door. Opening it, he waves for me to walk out first. "Wait," he says as he grabs my wrist, pulling me the opposite way from the exit. "Let's unwind first."

His cold rings feel pleasant on my skin, and I don't try to remove my arm from his touch. The reflex has become

155

dormant, and even that small action—or lack thereof—tells me I'm slipping.

The road ahead is a treacherous one. I don't want to trust Gemini, but I can't seem to control the bricks being removed one by one from the wall I've built around me. We've fallen into a routine, and I loathe to admit that it no longer feels like I'm his captive. Instead, it almost feels like we're ... partners.

Then there's the rising tension between us.

It has only gotten thicker as the days pass and nothing more has happened.

It's a game. I know it is. But Gemini appears to be steadfast. Unbothered, he continues to casually sleep naked beside me every night.

Then why am I the one who feels like I'm cracking?

The circus is deserted at this time of night. Something about the emptiness helps me concentrate when I practice. Gemini took notice early on and started taking us to Animus after the crowd packed up and left for the night.

I follow him in silence, passing the grand stage until we stop in front of a large net. Gemini turns on his heels, a playful expression splashed across his face.

I give him a flat stare back, narrowing my eyes before slowly lifting my gaze upward to the tightrope high above us.

"Unwind?" I ask sarcastically when my eyes land back on Gemini.

He scoffs disdainfully, clearly bothered by my lack of excitement, but I can still see his cheeriness bubbling under the surface. "Where's your sense of whimsy, love?"

Before I even have time to respond, he grabs his shirt by the back of the neck and pulls it off. He chucks it to the side, leaving him in only tight leather pants that hang low on his hips. Crouching down, he begins unlacing his boots.

"Shouldn't you wait till I've agreed to this first?" I try to make my voice sound serious, but I can't hide the smile tugging at the corner of my lips as I cross my arms.

As he continues to untie his boots, he lifts his head, a bleached-blond strand falling over his forehead. "Like most things"—he winks—"I know you'll eventually give in."

I act shocked by his answer, taking a step backward as I place my splayed hand on my chest. Our laughs merge in a melodic levity, and I forget myself in the innocence of the moment. It feels much too good, but I don't care.

I toe off my shoes as Gemini finishes taking off his boots. "Have you ever walked the tightrope before?"

"A few times," he says slyly before springing back up to his full height.

I peer at the tightrope, placing my hands on my hips. "I never have."

"Something tells me you'll be a natural, doll," Gemini replies nonchalantly.

When my gaze lands back on him, I'm struck by his change in demeanor. His eyes have turned dark, watching me from under hooded lids. Something about his wide stance and slow breathing reminds me of a predator in wait.

Weeks ago, my initial—and *only*—reaction would have been to flee, but tonight, I find myself taking an unconscious step forward, a steady throb of heat pulsing low in my stomach.

We don't move as we stare at each other with intensity. I could pluck the tension between us like a stringed cord. I bet it would create the most alluring of melodies. Something I'd yearn to record and capture forever so I could listen to it over and over again.

Finally, Gemini breaks eye contact and lifts his head up to the tightrope. My gaze falls on his parted lips. My throat goes dry.

"Ready, beloved?"

My body breaks out into goose bumps.

I nod.

He smirks and then points to the ladder. "Take that side; I'll take the other," he says, gesturing over his shoulder with his thumb.

"What if I fall?" The words rush out as my stomach flutters with nerves.

His smile widens, and his eyes sparkle. "I'll be there to catch you."

I shoot him an incredulous look. "You'll be all the way on the other side."

"Don't you trust me?" Then he adds quickly, "Don't answer that."

Not waiting for my response, he walks to the ladder and begins to climb. I follow suit, heading to my side and grabbing on to the first few rungs.

At the top, I step onto the small platform on shaky legs, audibly gulping when I look down. I've never had a fear of heights, but the thought of falling through the air into a large net isn't really soothing my nerves either.

Gemini stands on the other side, watching me intently. There's an ease to his stance that makes me think he lied to me earlier and that he's done this a lot more than just *a few times*.

His voice floats across the tightrope. "Mirror my movements, pet." He flashes me a smile as he stretches out his toned arms on either side of his body, using them to balance. "You'll be fine."

My words stick to the roof of my mouth, so I nod instead and dutifully mirror his pose. I watch him take a slow step onto the tightrope, then another.

He's mesmerizing. The muscles of his abdomen contracting as he uses his core to maintain his balance. His smile is arrogant as he keeps his gaze pinned to mine, chin straight.

"Your turn, Veil Vulturine."

I push out a long, anxious breath and look down, chewing

on my inner cheek. After tense deliberation, wondering if I should take the cowardly way out, I take my first step. But my left foot is still firmly on the platform, and I squeeze my eyes shut for half a second before taking the final step onto the tightrope. My stomach leaps up into my throat as I try to gain balance, my arms swinging on either side of me.

"Steady," Gemini says.

His command irritates me, but unexpectedly grounds me into focusing on the art of staying balanced on the tightrope. After a few seconds, I gain my composure and straighten back up.

I giggle in shock, beaming at Gemini. There's a proud look in his eyes, which spurs me to take another tentative step and then another. Until finally, we are only within arm's reach of each other. I can't stop smiling, an intoxicating adrenaline thrumming inside of me as I stare into Gemini's darkening eyes.

"Look at you, love. I knew you could do it," he says, his voice low and seductive.

My smile fades, and my mood shifts to something a lot more carnal as Gemini watches me with blatant hunger. He takes another step forward, swallowing the space between us. His skin glistens with proof of his exertion, his chest rising slowly and steadily.

"How did you know?" I ask softly, my tone meaning to convey a lot more than just that one question.

He stays silent for a long, tense beat.

"I see your potential just as clearly as I see your destiny, my beloved. I've never doubted you."

His next movements are so fast that I barely have time to react as he snatches me by the back of the neck, pulling me forward. He pushes his body into mine, his arm around my waist as he keeps me hard against him.

Our lips crash together in a blaze of desire as we fall.

28

VEIL

The fall only lasts a few seconds, but it's long enough to be born anew. Gemini's lips on mine emulsify and transform me. It's as if my soul was anticipating this very moment to finally remember itself.

I am breathless and aching.

I am desire come to life.

Gemini manages to turn our bodies midair, his back hitting the net first while his arms hold me tightly around my waist. I hardly notice the landing, the kiss consuming me, devouring me with every bite of his teeth on my lip and the lashing of his tongue on mine.

The net envelops us, as if understanding our need to stay as close to one another as possible, our embrace intensifying, along with our quickening breaths.

Gemini's hands find the sides of my face, and his forehead presses against mine as he breaks our kiss. "Do you sense it now, beloved?" he whispers harshly against my lips, his voice low and hoarse with need. "Do you see?"

"Yes," I answer. "Yes, yes, yes."

Desperate. Aflame. Obsessed.

I slam our lips back together while bringing my knee over his waist so I can better straddle him. His fingers dig into my hips, making me grind myself on his hardening cock over and over again. The net constrains our movements, but I don't care. I am blinded with need, and nothing else matters now but the feel of him underneath me. Pulling away, I splay my palms against his chest, pushing myself up.

Our eyes clash in a heated dance of darkness and desire. I feel myself getting wet by just the weight of his gaze on me. His eyebrows dipped in famished concentration, Gemini's expression is intense, adoring in ways I've never seen him. The pink in his cheeks humanizes him. His chest rises in the same fast staccato as mine. His razor-sharp attention is solely on me.

And—

Oh gods.

He's a masterpiece.

I can hardly breathe.

A perverse beauty promising me every wretched thing under this burning star. My chest flares like a supernova, recognizing the universe it's been forever bound to.

My nails dig into his chest, promising more, before I pull away and reach for my tank top. I yank it off over my head, along with my sports bra. I don't have time to fall back onto Gemini's chest before he reaches for me, his hot mouth latching around my nipple.

I gasp out a breathy moan as my back arches into him. His hand palms my free breast with such dominance that I find myself growing even wetter. My clit throbs as I push myself harder against his cock, the sensation only heightening the need to feel him entirely.

"Gem," I say breathlessly.

"Yes, doll?" he asks in between sucks and kisses, his tongue circling my nipple, slowly turning me into a blithering mess. I pick up a hint of humor and something about hearing his usual lightheartedness during such a loaded moment has me falling even deeper into maddening arousal.

"I need to fuck you," I rasp. "*Please,* let me fuck you."

Gemini's body tightens around me like a bow ready to snap. His free hand slowly slips down over my ass and *squeezes* as his gaze lifts to find mine. His pupils are so blown that I can only see black, and if I'm not careful, I will tumble into the abyss of his gaze and never find my way back.

He lifts his hips, his cock like a steel brand against my core. "Don't ever dare ask for permission again, pet." His tone is harsh, just like the touch of his hands on my body, and I break out into goose bumps, aching for more.

The net is all around us, making it hard for me to tug down my shorts, but there's something about our precarious position that makes the entire act that more desperate, that more filled with the animalistic need to come together.

Our lips find each other once more as we both do everything in our power to get my shorts off as fast as possible. We do the same with his pants. Push and shove and tug until, finally, his cock is freed.

I nearly sob at the sight.

His glistening, pierced tip beckons me.

Hypnotizes me.

My body shakes with a need so powerful that I become an inconsequential bystander to the sheer force of it. The urge to taste him again is an intoxicating one, but this isn't the moment to satisfy my gluttony, not when my pussy is pulsing with the absence of him.

Nothing about our pressed bodies conveys patience or begs us to savor the newness of what's to come.

No.

It's urgent and filled with the intoxicating promise of *more*. Every atom that makes up who I am sings in chorus.

More, more, more, more.

And somehow, I can hear Gemini's need, too, his skin buzzing under my touch.

Wrapping my hand around the base of his cock, I hover atop him, dragging his head up and down my slit, and relish the groan that rumbles through his chest. I take half a second to enjoy the grip of his fingers on my thighs before sinking onto his cock. I'm soaked, slipping easily around him, but his shaft is so thick that I only make it halfway down.

My hands fall back on his chest at the intrusion, and my mouth opens on a deeply pleased moan now that I finally know what it feels like to have Gemini Foley at my mercy.

He grips my ass, pulling my cheeks open as I rock my hips against him, slowly inching myself further down onto his stiff cock. Our gazes are locked together—the intensity would be terrifying if I had any rationality left in me.

"That's it, pet. Take all of me," he groans through gritted teeth. "I knew you'd be the perfect fit."

I sink down another inch and then another as Gemini's fingers dig harder and harder into my soft flesh until I feel *all* of him, and the fullness is as overwhelming as the first hit of a mind-bending drug.

"*Gods be damned*," Gemini says under his breath as I begin to grind my clit on his pelvis.

I am somewhere beyond words. I can barely even think. All I want is to *feel*.

Our eyes slam into each other, and his burning gaze sends my body into a feverish state. Reaching for his hands, I bring them up to my breasts, making him palm them as I clasp my hands over his.

I'm fucking him mindlessly. Deeply.

It's a passion so deadly that I can see the intoxicating poison seep into his gaze. Gemini's eyes widen, as if he's having the exact same realization.

It makes my orgasm soar through my body, and I chase it with abandon, my clit grinding achingly against him as his cock throbs inside of me.

"Gemini," I whine, feverish for more, even now when my climax builds and builds.

"Use me, beloved," he growls, his hand traveling up to my neck and curling around my throat, as if seeking my racing pulse. "Fuck me until you're sick of me."

His words push me over the edge of reason, and my muscles lock up, as if electrified. My eyes widen in shock, and Gemini's expression only darkens as my pussy squeezes over and over as I come all over his cock.

I only have time to watch his lips lift into an arrogant, taunting grin before he somehow maneuvers me onto my back, his body hot and heavy all around me.

He slides his cock back inside of me in one powerful thrust, his face finding the crook of my neck, nibbling at my feverish skin. His low hum vibrates against me as he takes a deep inhale —it's as if he's craving lungfuls of me—before dragging his nose up to the shell of my ear.

"Did you ever think, Veil Vulturine," he says slowly, his voice dark and tormenting, "that losing could feel this good?"

His words barely snap me out of my haze, barely scuff against the lust of having Gemini's cock pump inside of me again and again.

I knew this was a game.

I fucking knew it.

I lost the second I felt the thick head of his cock stretch me open.

"Is it losing when you're as far gone as I am?" I grit out as he continues to fuck me with senseless abandon.

His laugh is wicked, and it shoots pleasure down my spine.

He lifts his head to meet my gaze, and he's even more breath-taking when his face is only inches away from mine. The details of him are complex and seemingly never-ending. I could watch him like this forever.

"I have never claimed to be anything else," he replies before kissing me with renewed passion.

I feel the net dig into my skin under me, and I savor the sensation, savor the feeling of being held here against my will. Gemini has trapped me in every sense of the word.

And I …

Don't care.

"Now, imagine me fucking you full of my heir," he says with a growl. "How divine it will feel."

My back arches at his depraved words. A second orgasm pushes me to the very edge of sanity, but I still manage to croak a small, "*Never.*"

Gemini laughs before catching my bottom lip with his teeth, then releasing it. "Look at you. Your body craves it, pet." Bending one of my legs upward, he deepens the position and begins to fuck me with even more passion, his cock hitting the perfect spot inside with every thrust. "You'll look so pretty with my cum making a mess of your pussy," he groans, his neck cording with the effort.

My climax crests just as he possessively licks my neck, and my mouth falls open, his name on my tongue. He curses when he hears his name and savagely fucks me through my orgasm until I feel him throb deep inside of me.

"Can you feel it?" he says almost ominously as his voice strains with his own climax. "Even my seed is at home inside your womb."

My pussy flutters around him as if I've lost all control. Gemini's words light me aflame, even when I claim to hate the idea.

His laugh is a lot more sweet-tempered this time, as if his

mask has slipped and it's the real Gemini Foley who's gazing into my eyes while stroking the hair off my face.

No games.

No motives.

Just two burning bodies, entangled in a safety net, ravaged and undone.

29

GEMINI

The circus is abuzz tonight. It pulses under my skin in turn. There's a bouquet of lies floating in the air as I pass the crowded stands, the scent of it just as potent as the perfume of buttered popcorn tickling everyone's nostrils.

There are countless reasons to lie. And the citizens of Pravitia will find any reason not to tell the truth, especially in an establishment like Animus, influenced by the god of trickery.

Lies taste even sweeter here.

It's why crowds enliven me. They are always so full of snakes. Because morality is but an illusion. And nothing tickles me more than people lying, especially to themselves.

Speaking of liars ...

"My beloved," I announce as I stroll into Veil's dressing room.

She jumps when she hears my voice, but resumes what she was doing with a short huff and roll of the eyes. She sits at her large vanity, the mirror lined with bright bulbs, as she finishes applying her lipstick. She's braided her silky hair and twisted it into a tight bun, leaving her neck and shoulders uncovered.

Her gold leotard reflects the light of the chandelier above our heads. I had it installed just for her. It sparkles with countless hanging crystals, catching the light and twinkling across the walls. Nothing too extravagant for my little thieving doll.

My blood heats just at the sight of her sitting there, her attitude at my sudden appearance sparking the flame even hotter.

I have been beside myself since last night. Every depraved thing I have ever done in this life—or will do in the next— holds no candle to watching Veil finally crack and cave to her darkest desires.

And for that desire to be me?

Oh.

What a mouthwatering experience that was.

Her cunt was just as perfect as I'd fantasized.

The gods make no mistake; she was made for me.

Although ...

Our connection might have been a wee bit more powerful than I'd expected. I might have miscalculated how affected I'd be to have her so carnally.

I might have even lost myself a little.

I eventually did find my way back. Just in time to delight at the idea of breeding her full of my heirs. Especially when I knew she was so emboldened by the belief that she was protected against it.

Against *me.*

When will she ever learn?

I squash a maniacal laugh at the thought and stroll up to her chair, standing behind her. "Are you not pleased to see me, love?" I say drolly as I slide my hands from her shoulders to her arms and then back up again.

Her expression shutters as our gaze meets in the mirror. She's been closed off since last night. I'm sure a part of her regrets it, but the subtle flush of her cheeks tells me she's fighting her attraction. I pay it no mind. As if anything will stop me now.

"I'm just nervous," she mutters, breaking eye contact as she caps her tube of lipstick, carefully placing it next to her mascara.

Leaning down, I trail my open lips up the curve of her shoulder, and she cranes her neck as if wanting to grant me more space. Her lust is unmistakable. I smile against her skin before pressing a tender kiss on her racing pulse.

"Your act will be the talk of the town, beloved. No need to fret," I whisper into her ear before swiveling her chair around so she can face me.

Her eyes are wide and innocent as she peers up at me from her seat. I lean down to kiss her, but she turns her head, her chin to her shoulder.

The flare of impatience in my chest is violent.

I let out a tsk. "Are we still playing this game, pet?" I ask harshly.

Her eyes burn with ravishing defiance, and I feel it all the way down to my cock.

"I just applied a fresh coat of lipstick," she says with a bite.

My eyes narrow, and I realize then that this little rabbit might enjoy games more than she's letting on. "You think I would care about wearing your lipstick on my lips?" I drawl. "I'm sure that shade of red would suit me perfectly."

She chews on her inner cheek, as if trying to conceal a smile, and looks away when she answers me, "You know that's not what I meant, Gem."

The small show of familiarity with the shortening of my name on her red lips has the low embers of my arousal transforming into engulfing flames.

"Fine then," I bark.

My next few movements are brusque and guided by blind desire. Falling to my knees in front of her, I grab her thighs and tug her forward so that her ass drags closer to the edge of the chair. I throw her leg over my shoulder and shove her leotard to the side with my other hand.

"What are you do—"

My tongue flattens over her cunt, and I lick up to her clit before sucking it into my mouth. I savor her breathy moan as her hand falls onto the back of my head, and she immediately begins to squirm wantonly under my touch.

Still, she tries pushing back with her words while the grip of her fingers through my hair tightens. "Did you think after last night, you'd be allowed to do anything you please with me?" Her words are waspish, but my cock hardens nonetheless.

I don't even bother looking up; her glistening cunt ensnares me the more I taste it. "Cease your pointless babbling," I spit between two sloppy licks of her slit. "You're boring me."

I successfully shut her up when I thrust two fingers inside her drenched channel, and I feel Veil's body seize under my touch.

"*Oh my gods ...*" she says mindlessly as I begin to fuck her with all the impatience and irritation I have boiling inside of me.

The only thing that will satiate me now is having her come all over my face.

The feel of her swollen clit on my tongue has me acting like a rabid dog. Taking my free hand, I spread her open just to have my fill, and like a long-lost lover, I stare at her pink cunt, shining so beautifully with her arousal and my spit. The sight does nothing to tame my need for her.

My mouth finds her clit once more, tonguing it and devouring it while I continue to pump my fingers in and out of her soaking hole. It doesn't take much longer for her to strangle my fingers with her orgasm and drench my face while she comes.

It's positively the most delectable meal I've ever had the pleasure to consume. And I already hunger for my next serving. As long as I'm alive and breathing, my plate will always be full of Veil Vulturine.

***

Shortly after, I leave Veil to compose herself and make my way back to the grand stage, where she will be performing. Flopping into my seat in the front row, I turn to Constantine and flash her a sated smile.

After a month, her leg is still in a cast, but she's traded her wheelchair for bedazzled pink crutches. She tilts her head to the side, her ponytails swaying with the movement, as she narrows her eyes at me, then bursts out into giggles. Fishing through her purse, she pulls out a pink handkerchief.

"For your face," she deadpans.

I snicker and yank it out of her hand.

"And what if I left it there on purpose?" I say with a laugh as I wipe all evidence of Veil off my chin.

"I know you did, silly boy." She flashes me an exaggerated pout. "But if you're not willing to *share*," she says with emphasis, crossing her arms, "then *I* don't want to see it."

"Still peeved about your cast?" I ask with a dry chuckle, knowing she has been bored out of her mind since her injury.

"I feel *fine*," she laments. "You'd think I was gravely injured by the way Sasha mother-hens me."

She rolls her eyes, and I laugh even harder.

"Tinny, love, you had a beam fall on you."

"That was *weeks* ago," she answers petulantly.

My attention shifts to the dimming lights, and my heart makes an unexpected leap when I know Veil will soon be onstage.

I lean over to Constantine and whisper conspiratorially, "Ready to meet our newest servant?"

Constantine's eyes widen, and her pink-painted lips pop open as she regards me with the same shock Belladonna did two weeks ago. But I don't give her the chance to speak, shooting her a wink as I lift a demure finger to my lips to signal her to be quiet.

There's nothing quite like the thrill of a secret freshly revealed.

30

VEIL

My heart is in my throat as I step up onto the stage, the crowd's presence pushing heavily against me. I'm still shaky from Gemini's *visit* backstage. Although I have to admit, it did help to loosen me up and unwind the knot in my stomach, where all my nerves had been locked up.

I'm still nervous, but the fear is nearly gone, and I loathe to admit that he's the reason for the calming breaths I'm now drinking deep into my lungs.

As if his touch is the remedy to my woes.

Gods.

How could that ever be?

I give my head a small shake. This isn't the time.

Concentrate.

My gaze sweeps over the spectators, and my attention snags on Gemini in the front row. One foot over his knee, his chin resting in his palm, he looks every bit the aristocrat with his black tailcoat suit and cane with a gold snake winding down the shaft. He even matched his gold satin shirt to my leotard. There's a faint ring of dust on his knees, as if he deliberately kept the telltale signs of his debauched escapade for everyone to see.

He's staring right back at me, the smirk on his lips widening as time passes. Before I step into the spotlight, my gaze flicks to his right. A cold shiver zips down my spine when I recognize Constantine Agonis from the maze hunt. Her glare is burning a hole through me with how strongly she's staring, and I know then, beyond a shadow of a doubt, that Gemini has told her who I am.

The dread I'm expecting to hit at the realization never surfaces; instead, I feel recharged.

Have her see me.

Have her take in all of me.

Because I am Veil Vulturine and I *belong* here.

After a few quick, centering breaths, I begin my very first performance at Animus in front of a crowd of hundreds. Gemini has been advertising my new act for the past week, and I can feel the anticipation thrumming in the air. The elite rubbing elbows with the bourgeoisie; some are dressed to the nines while others are dressed in simple, casual clothes. All here to see me.

The trapeze becomes an extension of me, the music fast but moody as I lose myself in my well-rehearsed routine. I ride the high of such a feat, and it reminds me how much I used to love the stage. It reminds me of how free I felt when I performed back in Corutio.

Unknowingly, Gemini has given me exactly what I needed to remember myself.

Halfway into my act, my gaze lands back on Gemini. He's still watching me, but his attention is split, his body leaned to the side as a man I don't recognize whispers into his ear. He's delicately placed his hand on Gemini's thigh, and the jealousy suddenly coursing through my veins is all-consuming.

It burns until I myself am split in two. The one performing

onstage and the one whose sole focus is on the man touching what is *mine*.

The music ends. The audience erupts in a cheer, and I pretend to take in the applause, smiling widely and bowing.

But my eyes are pinned on the man, now laughing at something Gemini said. But Gemini's eyes are still locked on mine, and I feel like I've been dunked into boiling water. The man's body is leaning forward, lanky fingers now trailing up and down Gemini's arm. They appear intimate, like they've shared private laughs before.

I can barely breathe. I smell blood.

Knowing I can't stand here any longer without the crowd starting to question my lingering presence, I exit the stage with a clenched jaw and a pounding heart.

I DON'T BOTHER RETIRING TO MY CHANGING ROOM. INSTEAD, I charge through the backstage corridors and ignore the congratulatory yips from fellow circus performers.

My brain is on fire.

And only one thing will quell the burn.

Turning a corner, I finally spot them. Constantine is walking with her pink crutches in front of the duo. She spots me first and must see something she likes in my expression because her face lights up, her mouth open in excitement.

The corridor is crowded enough that I have to weave through a few bodies before reaching them. Gemini has followed my trajectory the entire time, a quiet grin on his lips, and a minute and rational part of me wonders if this was all on purpose.

But I don't care.

"Beloved," Gemini says when I appear before them like an enraged animal.

His casual tone only manages to pour gasoline on my already-raging fire, and I send him an icy glare before yanking his cane out of his grasp.

I'm half aware of people giving us a wide berth as I swing the stick backward before slamming it down on the man's head with a loud crack. He didn't see it coming, too busy making doe eyes at Gemini, and crumples to the floor.

When he goes down, I jump atop him. The sight of the first bloody split of his forehead is as satisfying as a warm bath. I hit him with the cane again and again as if I'd never tire of this kind of senseless violence. I break his nose and bloody his eye and lips before taking the stick with two hands and jamming the tip into his throat, crushing his windpipe. I feel the faint splatter of blood land on my burning cheeks.

Then I stop.

With the cane raised above my head while I straddle the wheezing, gurgling man.

I take in the spoils of my rage.

And I feel ... nothing for him.

Only a vague satisfaction for exacting my revenge.

I begin to take in the sounds around me, as if slowly returning to my body. I can hear gleeful laughter, and somehow, I don't need to look up to know it's Constantine. I could never forget the sound of her laugh, even in a moment like this.

Then someone begins a slow, deliberate clap, and I lift my head to find it's Gemini.

"There you are, Veil Vulturine," he says, his eyes sparkling with pride as he tongues his cheek in victory.

My gaze flicks behind him, and I find Zazel staring at me with such disgust that I barely recognize them. Their face is devoid of familiarity, as if regarding a stranger. A stranger who just bludgeoned someone for the pettiest of reasons. We hold eye contact for a few loaded seconds before they turn and walk out of the backstage corridor, taking with them my old life and friends.

I should feel shame.

Remorse. Guilt.

Anything.

But the only emotion still wreaking havoc inside of me is the insatiable and undeniable need to publicly claim Gemini as mine.

I fling the cane to the ground with a clang and scramble off the now-unconscious man, throwing myself on Gemini.

He's laughing when he catches me, his laughter bubbling and effervescent as he grabs me under my ass and lifts me with both hands. Turning us around, he pins me to the wall with my legs circling his waist.

I'm vaguely aware that a small crowd has formed, but Gemini addresses it immediately, his eyes never leaving mine.

"Everyone," he says magnanimously, "please welcome the seventh heir of Pravitia." I can feel him undo his pants as he continues, "And if anyone moves before I say so, I'll have Constantine collect your blood in vials until you're bone dry."

I faintly hear Constantine let out a whoop before she giggles and claps, but nothing else matters right now, except for the way Gemini is looking at me. It's devotion, in the most disturbing of forms, maniacal and unhinged. I crave it all.

Nothing else matters but our perverse show of connection.

Gemini harshly pulls my leotard to the side, and when I finally feel his cock thrust into me, I think I might be dying. I think I am reborn again and again.

His grin turns into a carnal snarl as he takes his free hand and grips my face, under my chin. He fucks me brutally, mercilessly, as he drags his thumb over my lips. Then he takes the same thumb, his eyes darkening, and smears my red lipstick over his lips.

His greedy actions have me spiraling into mindless arousal,

and I catch his lips with mine. I need to taste him. I need to consume all of him and devour his life force into mine. Nothing feels like enough.

Empty attempts at trying to match the emotions exploding inside of me.

I need him beyond our two bodies fucking against this wall. I need more than just being witnessed by others like this. I need to become *his* entirely.

My soul is begging for it.

My fate demands it.

And none of it is frightening. It only beckons me closer. Faster.

Gemini breaks the kiss and stares into my eyes, his hips pounding into me, his cock filling me so perfectly. A bead of sweat follows the path of his scar over his eyebrow while strands of blond hair fall out of place. He's a mess of perfection.

The small crowd around us is a blur when Gemini is my entire world. A vision of my exalted future.

"I would have chased fate since I took my first breath if I knew it was *you* I was chasing." His words come out all in one breath, jaw clenched, as if he's holding himself back.

His confession has my head falling backward onto the wall. His name is on my lips as my nails dig into his neck.

"I don't want to run anymore," I say breathlessly. "Keep me, Gemini. Keep me."

Gemini groans into my neck, licking a path up my throat before tugging on my earlobe with his teeth. "I must be our gods' favorite," he says darkly, "to have won such a divine prize."

He kisses me deeply, and my climax soars like a shooting star. I am devoured from the inside out. Metamorphosed into someone entirely new. Someone who recognizes Gemini on a molecular level. I turn into an addict. A greedy fool.

If there's only one thing I can steal for the rest of my life, let it be Gemini Foley.

Gemini slams a fist into the wall next to me as he fucks me through the aftershock of my orgasm until he follows shortly after, pumping his cock hard and deep as his forehead presses into mine. Our mouths are open in ecstasy, quickened breaths mingling together as our fiery gaze burns and burns and burns.

Nothing else matters.

Nothing else exists.

But me.

And fate.

And Gemini.

31

GEMINI

The meeting started five minutes ago, but I don't rush Veil as we walk through the high-arched corridor of Mount Pravitia. There's a raging thunderstorm outside, the rain thrashing against the stained-glass windows, cloaking us in heavy shadows even though it's mid-afternoon.

I can feel Veil's heart pound in her chest as if it were my own. Her energy is wild and unsettled. I relish it. Would bathe in it. I know the reason for her apprehension is partly about meeting the rest of the heirs, but her energy has shifted since her little performance at Animus last night.

And I'm not talking about her contortionist routine. I knew her time had finally come the second I saw her storm through the backstage corridor, thirsty for blood.

Oh, what a sight she was.

Before reaching the boardroom, I turn to Veil and grab her gently by the shoulders. She lifts her chin to meet my gaze. Her brown eyes shimmer as she watches me. She's breathtaking. Especially in the yellow corset I chose for her.

We both know she's not my prisoner anymore, but she still

let me dress her this morning. It makes me want to lock her up all over again and never leave the house.

"Who are you?" I ask her seriously.

Her eyes bounce from side to side, as if studying me, before she answers softly, "Veil Vulturine."

I grin proudly and nod before pulling her into a short but passionate kiss. "It's showtime," I declare with a mischievous wink.

With Veil's hand in mine, we walk in. The boardroom is hushed. It's the kind of silence that means something, the air charged with every single atom of the words not yet spoken. Five sets of eyes stare back at us, and the entire affair makes me want to burst into a wild, senseless laugh.

Mercy sits at the head of the long quartz table, next to Wolfgang, her hands clasped tightly on the table. She's dressed in her usual all black, her plunging neckline revealing a small chained necklace that I've never seen before. A quick look at Wolfgang, and I find a similar necklace tucked under the collar of his suit jacket.

Belladonna sits to their right. She narrows her eyes when she sees me, her loose curls a shock of red against the cream of her pantsuit. I don't linger long on her accusatory glare, smiling at Constantine and Aleksandr, who have chosen seats on the other side of the table.

"You know better than to bring one of your zealots to a meeting, Gemini," Mercy snaps.

"Who, Veil?" I ask innocently as I lift her hand to my lips. My skin is buzzing with anticipation. I flash her a bright smile and tsk teasingly. "That's no way to address the seventh heir of Pravitia, love."

The following silence is as thick and cold as a block of ice. There's not a sound, except for Constantine snickering into her pink lace gloves and Aleksandr quietly shushing her.

"What did you just say?" Wolfgang says with a threatening curl of his lip.

I sigh, as if bored when I'm anything but. "I *said*, Veil Vulturine is not one of my zealots."

I pull out a chair and gesture for my doll to sit. She does as I said, her movements slightly unsure, but nonetheless unshaken.

"She is the servant of the god of thievery."

I take my seat beside Veil just as Wolfgang tries to stand up, but fumbles with his chair and nearly falls down. He tries to ignore his misstep by kicking the leg of the chair and leaning his palms menacingly on the table. I'm barely concealing my chuckle when he glares and points a finger at me.

"God of *what*?"

Mercy places a hand on Wolfgang's arm, and his head immediately tilts downward to look at her. Her face is stony and impassive as they share a quick, wordless conversation, and Wolfgang eventually sits back down, peeved. He drags a palm over his beard before crossing his arms.

Under the table, Veil's leg is bouncing up and down, but her expression is cool and collected. I place my hand over her thigh and squeeze. She stops.

Mercy doesn't speak. She appears to be trying to intimidate me with silence, as if I were bothered by any of this. She should know better; this is what I live for.

I can feel my god snickering alongside me.

She continues to throw metaphorical daggers at me, and by the look of her severe brow, I'm sure she's envisioning lodging her real dagger into my neck. Wolfgang is sporting a similar expression, now wringing his hands together compulsively as he stares.

I smile.

They glare.

Somewhere to my left, Belladonna clears her throat.

I turn impatient and let out a long sigh.

As soon as I open my mouth, Mercy hisses, "Explain your-self." I start to speak, but she lifts a manicured finger. "Not you. *Her*."

I turn to Veil, and by the look on her face, she seems taken aback by the sudden shift of attention; then she blinks, and it's gone. It's replaced by a poised expression that has me grinning from ear to ear.

"I was just as blindsided as you are now," she finally says.

"Do not presume you know how I am *feeling*," Mercy spits.

"Mercy," I interject, my tone now a lot graver.

Her gaze cuts to mine. I know Mercy all too well; she's boiling with rage even if her exterior appears as calm as still waters. Slowly, she leans back into her chair just as a flash of lightning illuminates the room. The thunder soon follows.

I give Veil's knee a pat, signaling her to continue. She breathes in deeply and rests her folded hands on the table. She takes the time to look at all six of us before returning her full attention to the ruling heirs.

"I didn't know I was the servant of the god of thievery until it was revealed to me two weeks ago."

"By whom?" Wolfgang grits out slowly, seemingly trying to appear as calm as Mercy, but the bulging vein in his neck is giving him away.

"The Oracle," I reply.

I hear Aleksandr curse, but I keep my eyes on Mercy, whose eyes have widened in disbelief.

"You spoke with the Oracle?" Mercy asks.

I shrug and nod with nonchalance. "I needed my suspicions confirmed."

"How could you keep something like this from me?" Mercy seems to realize her small slip. Her green eyes slide to Wolfgang and then back to me. "From us."

I tilt my head to the side and give her a droll look as I

casually drum my fingers on the table. "You've been busy, love." I flick my hand dismissively. "I'm telling you now, aren't I?"

"Gemini told me last night," Constantine pipes in, just as comfortable in chaos as I am. "He also told half of his circus before fucking Veil against a wall."

Aleksandr rubs his brow in exasperation beside her, his face almost as red as his tracksuit. Wolfgang, on the other hand, blanches upon hearing this, his eyes practically bulging out of his head.

"Dimwitted twit!" he snaps. "You announced it to a handful of plebeians first before even speaking to us? This is *sensitive* information."

"Apologies," I say with a smirk. "It was in the heat of the moment." Then, just to rouse them further, I add, "Belladonna also knew."

She flashes me an appalled look, the apple of her cheeks turning bright red. "You swore me to secrecy, you two-faced buffoon!"

Constantine falls into another fit of giggles, and Aleksandr groans into his hand.

"Silence." Mercy's voice is like the crack of a whip, and silence returns.

Her eyes meet mine, piercing gaze imploring me to be serious. A lifetime of friendship has me listening to her wordless command.

"What did the Oracle say exactly?" Mercy asks.

"*Damnatio memoriae*," I respond.

"From what I understand, my family was banished centuries ago. I only came back to Pravitia a few months ago," Veil adds.

Wolfgang's eyes narrow, studying Veil. "Why, and from where?"

"I'm not quite sure," she says with a sheepish shrug. "And I was born in Corutio. I never left the city before I was ... called here."

"Called?" Mercy repeats.

Veil sneaks a glance my way before answering, "It's the only way I can explain the feeling."

"The Oracle says it's due to the new epoch." I wave two fingers between Mercy and Wolfgang. "It *seems* this new epoch is full of surprises."

"Like a reset?" Aleksandr muses.

"Maybe," I respond as I lean toward Veil, draping my arm over the back of her chair. "The Oracle was quite vague about it all."

Mercy tracks my movements, staying quiet for a beat before addressing Veil directly, "Why do you look familiar?"

I puff out a small laugh, and Veil flashes me a warning look, which only makes me laugh even harder. She ignores me and turns back to Mercy and Wolfgang.

"I was his sacrifice at the Feast of Fools." Veil quickly clears her throat before adding, "He let me go."

This time, everyone's reaction is stunned silence.

"You never killed your sacrifice?" Constantine says, bewildered, and I think she's more offended by the lack of spilled blood than me keeping this from her.

"Lucky I didn't, is it not?" I respond flippantly.

"How could this be?" Mercy mutters under her breath just as Wolfgang says, "We need to make this official."

I roll my eyes. "How? With another one of your puff pieces?"

"Stop acting like an ingrate little troll and take this seriously," Mercy snaps. "She will need an official public appearance whether you like it or not."

"Whatever it takes," Veil says beside me, and pride blooms in my chest.

"Her family sigil," Wolfgang says.

Mercy finishes his thought. "She'll need it tattooed." Then she looks at Veil up and down, seemingly cataloging her tattoos. "Is your back bare?"

Veil nods. "It is."

"Interesting," Mercy says under her breath, and then she changes the subject entirely. "What is the nature of your relationship?"

I don't allow Veil the time to answer. "She is the future mother of my heirs."

As expected, Veil appears to choke on the weight of my words, but Mercy just scoffs and clenches her jaw.

"It's, uh ... romantic in nature," Veil says, her voice cracking as she tries to be helpful and answer their questions seriously.

"They certainly did look romantic last night," Constantine quips, sending us heart eyes our way.

Wolfgang ignores her and says, "However serious this fling is, you cemented your fate with the stunt you pulled last night. She's not just another rube to discard; she's an *heir*. From now on, you're a couple."

I push out a dry chuckle and raise Veil's hand to my lips while longingly staring at her. "Don't worry your pretty little head, my dear Wolfie." I disregard his insulted hiss at the nickname, my gaze continuing to bore into Veil as her cheeks pinken with my steadfast attention. "My fate was always Veil Vulturine."

There's a beat of silence.

"We're getting married," Mercy blurts out.

This time, I'm the one left in shock—but evidently not surprised. There are happy gasps and muttering of congratulations around the table as my mouth falls open and my attention shifts to an awkward Mercy. Wolfgang, on the other hand, is puffing his chest, looking very pleased with himself.

Mercy waves us off. "All I meant was, our wedding can be your first appearance as an official couple — in two weeks."

"Two weeks?" I repeat, tonguing my cheek. "Someone is in a hurry."

Mercy flashes me an irritated look, and I laugh, clasping my hands on the back of my head.

"If you say so, your magnificence," I say. "And what about the circus?"

"What *about* the circus?" Wolfgang volleys back.

I nod toward Veil with a flick of my chin. "She's my new act at Animus."

Mercy groans. "Of course she is."

Wolfgang studies us both, as if calculating some kind of secret Vainglory Media formula, and nods. "Just keep your tomfoolery contained to your neighborhood until then."

32

VEIL

A day later, I'm back at Mount Pravitia.

Gemini escorted me up to the entrance doors, but Mercy made him turn around and leave. He did, but not before making a show of kissing me goodbye.

Now, I'm deep underground with one of the rulers of Pravitia, trying to convince myself that I belong here when Mercy's presence is so imposing. I focus on the cadence of her black stilettos on the stone floor as I follow her down a damp, low-lit corridor, chewing on my inner lip and wondering if she'll ever say another word to me.

"Here," she finally says, and I hide the small wince upon hearing her voice echo against the walls.

There's no door to open, just a large threshold beckoning me inside. I glance at Mercy, her face blank and impassive as she waits for me to walk in first. I'm still unsure of what we are doing here, and now does not feel like the most opportune time to ask. So I swallow down the rock in my throat and enter on tentative steps.

The room is spacious. Dark but lit with flambeaus lining the side walls. I startle when my gaze lands on the Oracle, sitting at the far end of the room between two large stone columns.

She appears as still as a statue, her hands in repose on her lap, as if waiting to be roused from a deep slumber. She's veiled under a gray shawl, her black dress long enough to pool on the ground and cover her feet. Her hair is loose, falling over her shoulders.

I look over to Mercy behind me in a flimsy attempt for some kind of encouragement, but she just impatiently flicks her hand, signaling me onward.

A narrow walkway, flanked on each side by water, leads up to a wider platform, where the Oracle sits. I idly wonder how the water even got here as I warily take my first few steps with Mercy following me close behind.

As I get closer to the Oracle, I realize her eyes are cloaked in a white film. Her focus is nowhere and everywhere, all at once. When Mercy walks up to where I'm standing, the Oracle's eyes shift, the white film fading, revealing the pale blue underneath.

"Servants," she declares. She pins me with her stare, and a cold shiver travels down my spine. "Ready, I see."

Her last words feel far too similar to what Gemini has been repeating to me over the past few weeks. I fight the odd, petulant urge to stomp my foot and ask why everyone assumes to know me better than I do.

Instead, I simply play along and nod solemnly.

The Oracle pauses, shifting her attention to Mercy. "Why are you here, child?"

It's the first time I've seen Mercy flustered, stumbling over her words as she tries to explain her presence here.

"The gods chose me to rule the city," she manages to say. "Shouldn't I be privy to such a conversation?"

The Oracle seems displeased. "Then where is your counterpart?"

Mercy fumbles over her answer again, and the interaction

gives me a sick sense of satisfaction. It humanizes her, and suddenly, I can breathe easier.

"I thought it best to come alone; he understands."

The Oracle stares at Mercy. The moment feels infinite before she slowly lifts an arm and points to the corner of the small platform. "Stand there and do not utter another word."

This shouldn't be a humorous moment, but a manic wave of laughter bubbles up my throat, and I flatten my lips, trying my best to hold it together.

When the Oracle's steadfast gaze settles on me, I revert back to seriousness, clasping my hands behind my back and straightening my shoulders.

"What do you seek, child?"

The question momentarily confounds me, and I take a few moments to respond. "I know nothing," I finally say. "I lack even the questions to lead me to the right answers."

Somehow, the Oracle seems pleased. She nods and appears to be thinking before speaking again.

"You know more than you think."

A small *Oh?* escapes me before the Oracle continues, "Even banished, you couldn't stay away; your god has always beckoned you close."

I try my hardest to decipher her words but fall short.

"I'm not sure what that means ..."

"Where did you live in Corutio?"

"The neighborhood?"

She nods.

I chew my bottom lip. "I lived in the Larcine District."

She hums as if I've revealed information that should mean something to me.

"And whose district was that?"

It dawns on me where she's trying to lead me to. I feel foolish, not realizing it sooner.

I'm now the one fumbling over my words. "I never—"

"Paid much attention?" she interjects.

I swallow hard. "Correct. But what I meant to say was, I never participated in the city's traditions; one neighborhood didn't matter over another."

"You never participated in the city's traditions because Corutio was not your birthright — Pravitia is," she says solemnly, "but it did not prevent you from ever straying far from the god of thievery. Larcine is another one of its servants."

I blink. A bizarre irritation simmers inside my chest. "Is there a point to this?" My words come out a lot harsher than I expected, and I sense Mercy shifting in place to my right. I pretend my heart isn't racing and hold the Oracle's piercing gaze.

"What is your sigil, child?" she asks.

My first reaction is to blurt out *I don't know*, but realize I must know if the Oracle is asking me that question. I take a long inhale and close my eyes. It feels absurd not to recall such an important detail of my daily life in Corutio, but my memories are so blurry that it makes me wonder if I was even awake or dreaming.

Until I returned to Pravitia.

Now every memory is as vivid as the day I lived them.

Opening my eyes, I find the Oracle staring back.

"A hand holding a key."

I can almost discern a small smile on her lips as she nods, folding up her sleeve to reveal my sigil tattooed on her arm, just above Gemini's and two others I don't immediately recognize. It looks fresh on her skin, as if she was expecting me all along.

"Welcome home."

33

VEIL

The surge of pride coursing through my veins at the Oracle's words is incomparable. It's as if I'm sensing my god's power for the first time in its entirety. Unadulterated and infinite.

I feel invincible.

"Thank you," I reply demurely. My smile drops as countless other questions try to clamber out of me all at once. I start with the one at the forefront of my mind. "Why did my family get banished?"

Again, I'm almost convinced I see a sliver of a smile on the Oracle's lips before she answers, "Long ago, your ancestor killed a servant of the god of trickery, thus resulting in *damnatio memoriae*."

"Trickery?" I repeat as a cold chill travels down my body. "The Foley family?"

She nods.

I try to gather my thoughts quickly, not wanting to waste more of the Oracle's time. "Is this why I found myself as Gemini's sacrifice during the Feast of Fools?"

"Perhaps," she answers. "The gods have their reason." She

192

pauses, tilting her head and peering upward, as if listening. She then pins me with her pale blue eyes. "It isn't the first time your paths have crossed."

"Do you mean—"

She gives me a short, dismissive wave, and I know my time is running out, so I change the subject and ask one final thing.

"I must know more about my god. I still feel so disconnected. How can I learn more?"

"Your god is always speaking, child. Listen. *Feel*. And trust that all that needs to be revealed shall be revealed." Then she looks to my right. "Mercy can teach you how to listen."

Mercy's brows lift in surprise, and we both sputter to politely dismiss the invitation.

"Leave," the Oracle declares.

Her command is final and we snap our mouths shut, whispering thank-yous before walking out on quiet steps.

The silence as we make our way back up to the ground floor of Mount Pravitia is stifling. However, this time, I'm not as affected by it. I'm beginning to wonder if this is simply more a part of Mercy's personality and less to do with *me* than I originally thought.

Before reaching the large doors of the main entrance, someone who appears to be an employee scurries up to Mercy and hands her a blood-red envelope. She opens it in front of me and audibly groans when she reads the letter inside, the parchment matching the color of the envelope.

Her attention reluctantly falls on me. "Tinny is inviting us to high tea."

"Tinny?"

"Constantine," she responds with an impatient puff of air.

"Us?" I ask incredulously.

It seems I can't utter more than a single word at a time, let alone fully process what she's telling me. She nods, her gaze as hard as the stone floor beneath our feet.

"When?" I rasp.

"Now."

"You're here!" Constantine chirps, followed by happy little bounces as she stays seated on one of the chaises, her injured leg elevated on a pouf. Her dress is a cloud of pink ruffles and gauze, paired with equally eccentric platform shoes.

"Did we need to have high tea in *this* particular room?" Mercy huffs as she looks around in disdain.

If I focus only on the rugged area near the fireplace—with its chaises, divans, and short tables containing towers of scones and macarons—the atmosphere is inviting.

That's if I ignore the countless shelves of Victorian dolls, locked behind glass cases, all around us. Then the atmosphere turns from inviting to uncanny. I have the strange feeling of hundreds of eyes on me as I find my way to where Constantine and Belladonna are sitting.

Constantine makes a vexed pout, as if Mercy is hurting the dolls' feelings. "They wanted the company." She turns to the dolls. "Didn't you, darlings?"

Belladonna lets out a dry chuckle, but her gaze is fixed on me, a delicate hand perched atop her crossed knee. She's just as mesmerizingly beautiful as ever in her silver satin shirt, white pencil skirt, and red stilettos. Her green eyes hold the same bottomless depth as the ocean.

I turn awkward, but she casually waves to an empty seat, and I take the invitation, sitting on the chaise beside hers.

A tense silence settles between us four, and my intuition tells me that conversation wouldn't be so strained if I wasn't here.

Constantine takes a sip of tea, her lace-gloved pinkie primly raised, before she asks, "So, you can steal our powers?"

Her question is innocent, but I feel the air shift once again. Three suspicious pairs of eyes fix on me while I deliberate how to answer.

I decide on the blunt truth. "Yes."

Constantine's mouth falls open, as if she's barely containing her excitement, blue eyes sparkling. She bounces in her seat. "Do me! Do me!"

"Tinny," Mercy interjects, her voice stern, as if scolding a child.

I'm surprised by the lethal stare Constantine sends Mercy; it's quick and gone in a flash, but it sends a chill down my spine. It's as if unexpectedly glimpsing her true nature—the one behind all the pink and bubbly personality.

"She's a *servant*," Constantine says slowly. "Let her act like one." Her voice is devoid of warmth, and I can't do anything else except stare at Mercy to gauge her reaction.

Her upper lip curls into a subtle grimace as she looks away and crosses her legs. When she brings her attention back to Constantine, she says, "I'm not *doing* anything."

I'm hyper-aware that they are discussing me as if I weren't in the room with them, but I don't dare interrupt. After a lengthy pause, Belladonna starts to laugh softly, breaking the tension. But Mercy doesn't seem to approve of the shift in tone and pinches her lips at her.

"And you," she says hotly, "why did Gemini tell you before me?"

Mercy doesn't spell it out, but I can still sense the wordless implication that the two aren't as close as her and Gemini.

Belladonna's smile drops. Her gaze slices to me, then back to Mercy. The silence has time to curl and slither around us before she says, "It's not for me to say," then quickly adds, "and frankly, it has nothing to do with you."

Premonition prickles at my nape. She's holding on to one of Gemini's secrets, and it must have something to do with me. I have the ridiculous thought of falling to my knees and begging her to tell me, but thankfully, Constantine interrupts my train of thought.

"Macaron?"

I stare at the offered plate of pastries for a few seconds too long. Finally, I choose a lavender macaron and take a bite while the stuffy silence returns.

"So tell me about your first kill."

It's Constantine again. And for a split second, I think she's joking, but the innocent expectation on her face indicates otherwise.

I swallow my bite, suddenly wishing I were anywhere but here. "I've never killed anyone."

"Never?" Mercy repeats, wrinkling her nose at my response.

I sneak a glance at Belladonna, and she's sporting a similar expression.

"I would have thought after last night ..." she starts.

I shake my head, confirming that the man I attacked is still alive—if barely.

"Well then," Constantine says with a honeyed laugh, "we must rectify this immediately."

"That's not necessary," I respond awkwardly.

"Nonsense. Killing is the best part of living," she says flippantly. "You poor thing — you've missed out on so much!" She sucks in a sharp gasp while her gaze skates around the room. "Why don't we come with you? Wouldn't that be so fun?"

Feeling whiplash by this odd turn in the conversation, I fail to find the right words to politely decline her invitation.

"I'm sure Gemini would want to share such a moment with Veil — don't you think?" Belladonna says before taking a slow sip of tea.

"Right," Constantine says with an annoyed pout. "Her *lover*."

I smile, appearing to agree with Belladonna's comment, but inside, I'm reeling from the entire exchange. Shockingly, it has a lot less to do with the idea of taking someone's life and more about the realization that Belladonna is right.

If it *is* bound to happen ... then I would want Gemini by my side, witnessing it all.

34

GEMINI

I sense her before I even open my eyes. And for a few seconds, I keep them closed, letting the soothing jet of water wash over me as I finish my shower.

I haven't seen Veil all day, and my skin has started to itch. I should stitch us together so she would have no choice but to drag me along wherever she went. Grinning at the thought, I open my eyes, finding Veil's vague form through the foggy shower glass. I turn off the water and step out, reaching for a towel and wrapping it around my waist, my eyes never leaving hers.

"Beloved," I say softly as a way of greeting her.

The rain drums loudly on the stained-glass windows, muffling the sounds around us, even my voice. But although she doesn't respond, I know she heard me. She regards me with intensity, arms crossed as she leans against the large double sink.

I slowly pad toward her, my skin buzzing with electricity the closer I get.

"Have fun today?" I ask.

198

Her eyebrow lifts in quiet amusement as she purses her lips before saying, "It was ... something."

"Which part?" I ask, my voice full of levity.

Finally reaching her—as if those handful of steps were the same as crossing a desert to find an oasis—I slide my palms up her arms and crowd her with my body.

Her chuckle is dry, but I can still feel the warmth in her tone as she lifts her chin ever so slightly to keep eye contact. "All of it."

She uncrosses her arms, allowing me even closer into her space, and I take it, pushing my hips into hers. I keep one hand on her shoulder as the other slowly curves up her neck, my thumb trailing across her jaw.

"Oh?" I rasp, my cheek pressing against her.

When she speaks again, her voice is thicker than before. "I saw the Oracle."

"Did you?" I say before catching her earlobe between my teeth.

My hands glide back down her arms, and I feel her goose bumps under the pad of my fingers.

"Yes," she says breathlessly as her hand caresses my waist. She stays silent for a loaded second. "It was the servant of the god of trickery."

My lips trail over her jaw, my palm finding her breast over her silk shirt, and she curves her back to press harder into me.

"What was, pet?"

"The reason my family was banished."

I lift my head to look her in the eyes. There's a wary expectancy in her soft gaze as she waits for me to speak.

"Thievery killed trickery?"

Her nod is slow, almost apprehensive.

My laugh rumbles deep in my chest as I grab her firmly under her ass and perch her atop the sink. She widens her legs, and I slip in between, my hands smoothing over her waist and then down to her thighs.

"No comments?" she says, her arms linking around my neck.

Pulling her thigh higher up my waist, I drag a hard thumb into the meat of her thigh—pleasantly fuller now that *I'm* feeding her. I lift my eyes to hers. "Why would I care what our ancestors were up to?"

Her thighs fall wider with my careful ministrations, and she swallows hard, her blinks slow and pensive. "Strange coincidence that our paths have crossed like this, is it not?"

"Strange?" I say coarsely before finding her lips with mine. The kiss is a slow reawakening. A smoldering flame deep within the glowing embers of our souls. "When will you learn, Veil Vulturine?" I whisper against her plump lips. "Our two paths were always meant to become one."

Veil's hands turn hungrier, pulling me into her while still chasing our kiss. "How do you know, Gemini Foley?"

I pull away, and the sight of her rosy cheeks has me grinning from ear to ear. I take her hand in mine, lifting it to my lips. Slowly, I trail kisses up the length of her arm, my eyes never leaving hers. She squirms against me, pushing against my hardening cock, but says nothing, her eyes wide and seeking. When I get to her elbow, I stop and let the silence percolate between us before speaking.

"My beloved," I say against her warm skin, "all I need is to look into your eyes to know." I press another kiss up her arm. "The gods speak through you, and I listen."

I bring both her arms above her head, and she keeps them in the air as I pull her top off, revealing her black lace bra underneath.

"And you listen ..." she says, as if needing to repeat what I just said.

She brings her arms back down as I tilt my head to bury my

face in her cleavage. Cupping her perfect tits in my palms, I deeply inhale the fruity mango scent clinging to her skin and lick the slope of her breast, eager to taste her.

Our movements are still slow and steady. But I can feel the tension tightening between us. Our breaths quickening, heartbeats racing.

I unhook her bra with deft fingers and flick it somewhere beside us. My hands find her thighs again as I slowly push her pleated skirt up, inch by slow inch. Both our gazes are cast downward as the silence now promises sweet release. My finger hooks around her thong, and Veil leans back into her palms to lift her ass so I can pull it off.

Her cunt is a perfect, glistening little thing, and I salivate at the sight.

I look up to find her eyes hooded and dreamy; still, I see a cloud of turmoil behind her gaze.

"What is it, doll?" I ask as I drag a slow thumb up her wet slit.

She tilts her head backward at the sensation, her mouth falling open with a gasp, and my balls tighten wantonly at the sound.

I have time to start circling her clit before she rasps, "What is it like to take a life?"

The carnal lust that flares inside me almost brings me to my knees. My grin is wicked as I flick her swollen clit with a finger. "What makes you ask that?"

Her eyes flash in irritation as she snaps her mouth shut, but still, she widens her legs for me. Something in her shady look tells me she won't be begging me for an answer.

But I yearn to tell her.

Anything for my pretty doll.

Reaching for her nape, I pull her into my chest just as I slip two fingers into her tight pussy. I taste her moan in the charged air between us before saying, "Come on my fingers first, pet, and I'll tell you anything you want."

I ravage her lips with mine, tugging, biting, sucking, as her eager hands pull against the towel around my hips. By the time it falls to my feet, her hand is wrapped tightly around my hard shaft, and I suck in a sharp hiss. But I plunge back into our kiss just as my fingers plunge into her cunt.

Her moans are poetry, written in a tongue only I understand, hungry, cryptic words only my soul can decipher. And I starve for more. Her free hand tugs on my shoulder, nails digging into my skin, as if she's wordlessly demanding for more of me.

In between countless feverish kisses, I circle her clit with my thumb and curl two fingers into her until I feel her release a soft whine. Her legs lock up around my hips, and her fist tightens around my cock.

"Tell me," she says, on the crest of her orgasm, eyes still closed, and I am untethered.

Dragging her even closer to the edge of the sink, I cradle her face into my palm and slap her hand away. Fisting the base of my cock, I drag my shaft through her soaking slit, never entering her.

"Look at me," I command through clenched teeth.

Her eyes snap open, and an inexplicable thrill shivers down my spine. I flick my gaze down to where we connect, tapping the head of my cock on her clit.

"It's hard to describe in words, pet," I say heatedly.

"Try," she replies, a small plea to her tone.

I tsk, dragging the tip down to her entrance, circling it tauntingly. "Impatient little thief, let me speak."

Her giggle is drowsy, as if drunk on the same torrid lust coursing through my veins.

"Killing is your birthright, Veil Vulturine," I say harshly, my thumb tugging on her bottom lip, her mouth falling even wider open.

Her eyes burn, and I consider teasing her longer, but I'm desperate for her hungry cunt to devour my cock. Slowly, I sheathe myself inside of her while pushing my thumb into her mouth. She wraps her lips around it and sucks. The feeling of her warm, wet tongue has me thrusting deeper into her pussy, until I sink to the hilt.

"We are gods to them, my beloved," I say, my voice tight with need as she moans around my thumb, her fingers clawing, digging into my hips. I start to fuck her slowly, trying to keep my composure. "Spilling blood is like breathing."

I slide out to the tip, then push back in with one hard thrust. She moans long and deep, her mouth still full of me.

"Necessary. Life-giving." I start fucking her harder, faster, while my free hand carves divots into her thigh. "Your soul — it craves it. The extinguishing of a life. It's the most carnal of acts." My hips slap into hers, the wet sounds of our union spurring me on. "We live." Sliding my thumb out of her mouth, I smooth her spit on her lips like the most luxurious of lipsticks. "They die."

"Show me," she says desperately. "Teach me."

I grip her cheeks with one hand, my gaze searing into hers. "I'll spill as much blood as you desire, beloved."

Her moan spikes, her cunt squeezing around my shaft, and I groan mindlessly.

"Bathe in it if you so wish."

I can sense her mounting climax as if it were my own—and maybe it is. I slide my hand from her thigh to her clit, needing her to come again. "What else do you want, Veil Vulturine?" I ask between punishing thrusts. "Tell me, and I shall give it to you."

Instead of answering me, she tugs me into a kiss, her lips hot and ravenous. Her tongue swipes inside my mouth, finding my own, and my mind bursts aflame. Pulling away quickly, I tilt her head back toward the mirror and spit in her open mouth. I chuckle arrogantly at her surprised expression while her walls flutter around me.

I dive back into our kiss, my hand curling around her throat as I fuck her with endless desire. With every deep thrust, I push her closer to where I need her until she finally comes undone. Her hands dig into my arms, my waist, my hips.

"Your secrets," she says with such erotism that I almost spill every secret I know to exist right then.

Her eyes snap to mine, and I fight the urge to look away. It's as if her gaze threatens to capture me and never let me go. I curse under my breath, my balls tightening with the promise of rapt pleasure.

"Give me an heir," I grit, "and I will give you my secrets."

A sick thrill zips through me, knowing I could potentially impregnate her here and now. It's my most treasured secret and possibly my most insidious. A toxic and intoxicating cocktail, and the very thought has my orgasm detonating inside of me.

I coat her walls, thick with my cum; long, hard thrusts push it deeper and deeper until she is bursting full of me. I pull her into me, needing one last kiss while I breed her with purpose—with every desire to have her bear my offspring. I continue to fuck her through my orgasm, spreading my cum up and down her tight walls.

I wish I could carry her into bed and place her legs above her head without it being suspicious. Instead, I keep my cock sealed inside her cunt, my last request hanging above our heads as we both try to catch our breaths.

I don't expect an answer.

Because I don't need her permission.

Not when I have the gods' inescapable blessing.

35

VEIL

$\mathcal{I}$'m awakened by soft, distant music. I stretch my whole body before opening my eyes, finding myself alone in bed. The sun is out today after days of endless clouds and rainfall, and I smile as I peer out the window, content and at ease.

The realization of such peaceful feelings sends a warning to my rational brain just as I hear Gemini's melodic hum approach the bedroom. I don't have time to dwell on my shift in mood before he appears in the doorway, wearing nothing but a checkered kitchen apron.

His smile turns beaming when he finds me awake in bed, holding a tray out in front of him. A single flower—the color matching the lavender of his hair today—stands in a small vase among the array of breakfast foods.

"What a wonderful day to be the gods' favorites," he singsongs, strutting into the bedroom and delicately placing the tray over my lap. "For my beloved," he says before kissing my cheek.

My heart squeezes with affection, and the same flash of warning flares inside of me. My smile drops as I stare at the steaming cup of tea on the tray, the vial with the contraception tonic that I've been taking daily sitting next to it.

"What just happened?" Gemini questions, standing by the bed, his eyes narrowing in suspicion.

My first reflex is to lie. He couldn't tell if I did, but I decide to be truthful instead.

I lift my gaze to meet his. "I keep forgetting how this all started."

It's been half a week since I last visited the Oracle, and we've been attached at the hip ever since. I've performed a few times at Animus, but aside from those handful of trips to the city, we've been here, in this bizarre domestic bubble, and I suddenly itch to kill the illusion.

Gemini's expression is serious. It's only this stern when the topic of *us* comes up, as if speaking about the oddities of our ... relationship is a direct offense to him.

"This?" he hisses.

Regret pulses as if alive inside of me. Maybe I should have said nothing instead, enjoyed this lovely breakfast and his devoted attention. But I can't stop talking.

"Us," I reply.

He sucks on his teeth before turning his back to me, as if needing to peer out the window. He's completely naked under the apron, which makes this tense moment feel especially ridiculous. After a few loaded beats, he turns back to face me and sits down on the bed. I can't help but think it's an unconscious urge for us to appear more equal, and my heart pitches out of my chest at the small gesture.

"Why does it matter?" He scratches his head with irritation, the impatience unmistakable in his tone.

"You *kidnapped* me," I reply, stunned. "Paraded me around on a leash."

He rolls his eyes, as if I'm being difficult, and the pang of rage I feel leaves me breathless. Huffing a laugh, he asks, "This again?"

"This *again*?" I repeat, my voice now an octave higher. "You speak as if this were lifetimes ago when, in fact, it's been"—I make a rough calculation in my head—"a month!"

Saying it out loud consumes me with dread, considering how fast I myself have forgotten what those first two weeks felt like for me. The fear I experienced. It makes sitting here in bed —a breakfast tray over my lap, prepared by the same man who stole my autonomy—that much more dystopian.

He drags a palm over his face before pinning me with his glare. "Why are you so obsessed with time, doll?"

"Stop calling me that," I spit, suddenly feeling sick.

His laugh is icy against my skin. "How feisty you are becoming."

I cross my arms, my heart now beating wildly inside my chest as we stare at each other, and I can almost feel the strum of his corded muscles. The rising tension beating through him like a deadly melody.

"You were a monster to me not a few weeks ago," I say, my voice now lowered and even.

His expression shutters, the muscles in his jaw feathering. The moment stretches into anxious anticipation as he stares at me, but says nothing.

Until ...

"Still am," he says coldly before flipping the tray off my lap. It flies through the air and crashes against the wall.

The sound of glass breaking shocks me, but I barely flinch as we continue to face each other down. Then he blinks and his expression changes. The aggression is gone. His gaze turns casual, and somehow, that is the thing that frightens me most.

"I haven't changed, Veil Vulturine," he says. Standing up, he makes a small show of dusting off his apron before pinning me with his mismatched eyes one last time. "It might be time for you to take accountability for your actions, little rabbit." He drags his tongue over his bottom lip before adding, "You haven't been my doll for weeks."

He doesn't give me the chance to reply before storming out of the bedroom, leaving me to stew in my own confusing thoughts.

A FEW HOURS LATER, GEMINI HASN'T SAID A WORD TO ME UNLESS absolutely necessary. He failed to accompany me into the mannequin room to pick my outfit, and I hated the sting just as much as his absence.

I chose a black dress with an open back and hoped my outfit would stir a few emotions, enough for his gaze to linger, but he's kept his eyes averted all the way into Pravitia, and I'm beginning to feel off-kilter by his lack of attention.

The town car slowly comes to a stop in front of a high-rise near Mount Pravitia, and my heart flips when Gemini's hard gaze finally lands on mine. With black eyeliner smudged under his waterline, he's dressed casually in a mesh top and red jeans, but he'd look regal in any outfit.

"Ready?" he asks, his voice flat.

I hate everything about his tone, but I act unperturbed and nod. "Not my first tattoo," I say dismissively.

He looks as though he wants to say something, but changes his mind at the last second and opens the car door instead. He offers his hand, and although I want to ignore it out of spite, I take it. Still, I wonder if he's only escorting me out of the car because we are now in public.

Inside, the building is industrial. The corridor is big and drafty as we pass a number of locales that seem to be all kinds of different workshops. Eventually, Gemini stops and opens a door, waving me inside.

This space is like nothing I expected; it's like stepping into another one of their VIP clubs—or I guess, mine now too. Art from a wide range of styles fills the walls, along with neon signs hanging here and there, most of them directly over tall mirrors. A tattoo station sits in the far corner, near the large windows.

But the decor is quickly forgotten when my gaze lands on the couches set up in the corner of the room.

"Vee-Vee!" Constantine chirps, sitting among the rest of the heirs, her leg still in a pink cast, looking like the happiest of the bunch.

Beside her, Aleksandr drags a hand over his mustache, as if already tired of her antics—but I don't miss the way his leg presses into hers.

"Tinny," I say, slightly stunned.

My eyes rove around the seating area, taking everyone in. Wolfgang is settled on the opposite couch, and Mercy is perched on the arm next to him, as if the couch were literally beneath her, while Belladonna sits on the opposite end.

"What are you doing here?"

I directed my question to Constantine, but it's Wolfgang who answers me. "We know this is typically a private affair," he says casually while adjusting his gold cufflinks, "but we thought this was a ... unique situation."

I sense Gemini move past me. He flops onto the couch beside Aleksandr, giving him a loud kiss on the cheek. I know it means nothing, but my face burst into flames nonetheless, and I see Constantine cock her head. Her gaze shifts from me to Gemini and then back again, and I want to strangle the words I see about to come out of her mouth.

"Oh! A lovers' quarrel, I see?" she says.

I'm about to deny everything when someone appears seemingly out of nowhere. They're dressed in a black shirt and jeans, and most of their visible skin is covered in tattoos, including their face.

"Veil?" they say, and relief washes over me, knowing the charged moment has passed.

I nod and smile, muttering a breathy yes, trying to shut out the rest of the group—especially Gemini.

"My name is Axil. I'm the tattoo artist," they say with a toothy white smile, and I'm immediately put at ease.

Shaking hands, we exchange pleasantries, and I let out a relieved sigh as they wave me closer to their station so we can begin prepping for the session.

I'M AN HOUR INTO MY BACK TATTOO. LYING FLAT ON MY STOMACH, I've brought my arms up to my head, cradling my face. Luckily, the hard scratch of the lining is a pain I've grown accustomed to. I focus on the sting, letting my mind wander to anywhere but here.

I was facing away from the seating area for the first half hour, but my neck grew sore, and I had no choice but to turn my head. Now I have two options—close my eyes and ignore what's right in front of me, or avoid Gemini's gaze.

I choose the latter for now, feeling unexpectedly grateful for the rest of the heirs so I watch them instead. By everyone's body language, I can tell there's an invisible current of boredom buzzing through the six. And it's the first time I can take in their dynamics without the fear of being *literally* killed overriding my careful perusal.

They've gradually shifted seats. Wolfgang is now beside Aleksandr and Constantine. Belladonna hasn't moved from her spot, and Mercy and Gemini are now keeping her company.

As I observe them, it has become clear that some don't get along—the most glaring being Aleksandr and Belladonna. They haven't exchanged a word. And judging by the way

Belladonna eyes Gemini and Constantine, I don't think there is any love lost there either.

When my gaze eventually lands back on Gemini, I find his eyes fixed on me. I have to force my body not to jolt and keep my face impassive, but my heart rate doubles, as if it were the very first time he'd ever looked at me with this level of intensity.

It's not.

But something feels wholly different this time.

I swallow hard, but don't look away. The pain from my back tattoo and the gravity of his stare slowly morph into one overwhelming sensation, and still, I don't avert my gaze.

Gemini's anger today is new. A different breed and pointedly directed at me. It's as if he's trying to convey something with his silence. I don't know how long we stay like this, spending infinity conversing without speaking a single word.

I loathe to admit how much I've missed his attention, and it's barely been a day.

What has he done to me?

To make me crave him in this manner?

My gaze is still fixed, but my mind begins to wander to our earlier spat.

"I haven't changed, Veil Vulturine."

I understood immediately what he meant, but even now, I have trouble accepting it.

That I'm the one who has changed.

Especially when I still feel like an outsider, looking in.

The question is, how much *have* I changed? Even thinking of it now, I find it hard to come up with a tangible answer when the change feels ever-lasting, always morphing, alive, sentient.

Then I feel it.

Like a soft caress against my skin. A slow, drifting wind. A summer breeze.

My expression must have shifted into something akin to

alarm because Gemini is suddenly on his feet, eating the distance between us with quick strides until he's kneeling near my head.

"What is it?" he whispers, as if today never happened, as if he didn't just spend most of the day ignoring me.

But I sense the shift, too. This moment is much bigger than our petty squabble. We can revisit it later because having him by my side right now is far more important.

His gaze is seeking. Imploring.

"I think ... I think I can feel my god's presence," I whisper slowly, not wanting anyone else to hear. "It's almost tangible now like — like I could reach out and touch it."

I glance at the couches, but no one is paying us any attention. It feels almost deliberate, as if they know this specific moment should be private, one shared between us and no one else. Of course, there's Axil still tattooing my back, but they seem to know better than to interrupt or try to engage.

Gemini's eyes glimmer with pride as he slides his hand over my arm and squeezes. "Just another tattoo," he says with a wink.

36

GEMINI

After Veil's back tattoo was completed and carefully protected by an adhesive barrier, I saw the faint exhaustion in her eyes and brought her right back to the house so she could rest.

She resisted going back to our bed, saying she'd rather nap on the couch. She didn't ask, but I could tell she wanted me to stay close. And although the anger was still simmering beneath the surface, I acquiesced with no hesitation, but made us change into comfortable clothes first and foremost.

She's been napping for a few hours now, lying flat on her stomach as I read beside her. Her head is close enough that I can reach over and caress her hair. This time, when I do, she rouses and lets out a moan that sends a warm shiver down my spine. Pushing herself up onto her elbows, she looks at me with owlish eyes, and I smile at her sleepy, slightly off-focus expression.

"How long have I been sleeping?" she asks, her voice low and raspy.

Gods be damned. She's divine.

"It's almost evening," I quietly answer. "How are you feeling?"

She sits up fully, her eyes lifting to the ceiling, as if thinking. "Sore," she says. Her smile is soft but roguish. "Nothing I haven't experienced before."

Her smile falls, and before I can decipher what she's doing, she's crawled up into my lap and circled her arms around my neck. Her actions inexplicably leave me speechless as her head falls onto my shoulder, her warm breath tickling my naked chest. I wrap my arms around her waist, making sure not to touch the sensitive skin of her back.

"I don't think ..." she says, her words stuttering, as if she's figuring out what she actually wants to say. "I don't think I want to apologize for what I said this morning."

I have no choice but to laugh; it rumbles deep in my chest, but I don't speak, wanting to hear what she'll say next. She gives my arm a small slap, as if finding the situation somewhat amusing too.

"But ... how can I fix this?" she asks quietly.

"This?" I say, slightly teasing and intentionally echoing our earlier spat.

"Us," she presses as she burrows the cold tip of her nose into my neck. "You ignoring me. I hated it. I hated knowing you were angry with me."

"I wasn't ..." I trail off, not finishing my sentence because when she called me a monster, I *was* angry. Confusingly upset. And ignoring her was the easiest way for me to evade these uncomfortable feelings.

I've never cared what people thought of me before. And to be described as a monster? In any other context, I would have been pleased by the descriptor and beamed at the implications.

But Veil is not *people*.

And suddenly, the word *monster* tasted as foul as a handful of excrement.

"I wouldn't want your apology in the first place," I reply softly.

She's still hiding in the crook of my neck, so I carefully pull her away, my hand slipping into the sleep-mussed hair near her nape while my thumb rests on her cheek.

As she watches me, her eyes are so wide that I'm almost convinced I can glimpse the entire universe between two blinks. Her throat works around a hard swallow, and I forget the very meaning of anger.

"Then what?" she whispers, her fingers slowly curling around my waist as she waits for an answer, her nails lightly digging into my warm skin.

I let the silence spill into all the cracks between us until the air is so thick with it that I have no choice but to speak. "I want your devotion, my beloved."

Her cheeks flush, and my heart grows thrice the size.

"I want you to bare yourself so entirely to me that I can see every single atom that has the honor of creating the person I'm holding on to right now."

I emphasize my words by tightening an arm around her waist and stroking her cheek with my thumb. Her mouth falls open, just enough for me to have to fight the urge to reach over and suck on her parted lips.

Her brown eyes turn misty, as if she's barely containing the magnitude of her emotions.

Her voice is a near whisper when she speaks. "Give me time."

I grit my teeth at her answer. "Again with that nonsense?" I retort. "Slave to something as trivial as the tick of a hand on the clock." The grip I have on her face tightens. "Don't you understand? We are beyond such a boorish construct. We exist outside the linear ... do you not *feel* it?"

Even though I yearn for her to agree, it still surprises me when she does.

"I do," she says, her piercing gaze steadfast. Her pause is loaded, carrying as much weight as the next words out of her beautiful lips. "But if you can see our future so clearly, then why balk at allowing this simple ask? *Please*, Gem, for once, give me something without the price of a compromise."

Her voice is strife with desire. It's all-consuming, but nowhere close to being carnal. Instead, it's bursting with aching melancholy, the tang of angst as tart as a large sip of wine down my throat.

I pull her into a kiss, a fleeting urge to know how such an emotion tastes on her lips. She melts into me, and I drag my thumb down under her chin to find her racing pulse. My tongue slips inside her mouth, finding hers, and our kiss deepens. Still, I can feel Veil holding back, and I know she's waiting for my answer.

Reluctantly, I break our embrace, seeking her gaze once again. I idly lick my lips as we silently stare at one another, hoping I can still find the essence of her lingering there.

I smile softly and delicately trail my fingers down her bare arm before speaking.

"Time," I rasp with a nod.

37

VEIL

I'm crawling out of my skin, pacing back and forth in front of the tall living room windows. Gemini left over an hour ago, needing to attend to some business in the city.

That's not what's bothering me.

It's this growing tightness in my chest and the itch that seems to evade me anytime I try to find the source, crackling just under the surface of my skin.

At first, I thought the rising tension was because I was left alone and missing Gemini. The mere thought that could potentially be the reason had me rolling my eyes and repressing the feeling. But it's been a few hours, and I am now certain that the two are unrelated.

I stop in my tracks and stare out the window, the large quarter moon hanging heavy above the harbor as I wring my hands incessantly and deliberate my next move.

It's as if an invisible hand were reaching out from the shadows of Pravitia, beckoning me closer. Demanding I come ease the smarting ache.

I might not yet be fluent in my god's tongue, but this is undeniable.

I am being called. And if I don't respond soon, I will go out of my mind.

I promised Gemini that I would stay here while he was gone, but my god is more important than staying put for his sake.

Finally, I make my decision and storm out the door.

***

THE NIGHT AIR IS MISTY, THE DAMP CLINGING TO MY SKIN AS I walk aimlessly through the busy streets of Pravitia. I could have stolen a few watches by now, maybe even a couple of wallets to get my blood going, but I have yet to lift a single finger.

My hands are stuffed in the pockets of my bomber jacket, shoulders raised up to my ears in a vain effort to shield myself from the chill. This is the first time I'll be stealing something while being this connected to my god.

It feels different, like entering a brand-new era of my life. I wander with purpose, if there is such a thing. Flowing on an invisible current, I have faith that my god will lead me straight to my next fateful mark. I haven't left Gemini's neighborhood, my intuition tingling with the knowledge that I will find what I'm looking for here.

As I turn a corner, adrenaline shoots down my spine, and I know my mark must be close. I look around, but can't find the source of this electricity in my veins. Then I look over my shoulder, and a knowing thrill charges through me as my eyes land on the man a few steps behind me.

I quickly turn back around and inconspicuously slow down, hoping he'll pass me so I can start trailing him. But after a few failed attempts, the suspicion that this man might be following me slowly dawns on me.

A month ago, before being thrust into the cutthroat world of Pravitia's favorites, my initial reaction would have been fear. The anxiety of the unsafe and dangerous. But tonight, all I feel is vexed outrage that this man does not know who I am and what I am capable of.

The crown of my head tingles, the feeling slowly moving down to my nape and traveling down my body. And suddenly, I realize maybe my god isn't craving petty theft tonight.

But something a lot more violent.

I make a sharp left down a less crowded street just to confirm my suspicion, and a subtle glance over my shoulder confirms that he's still following me. I walk down two blocks before I hear a short whistle behind me, and I whirl around at the sound.

I should be shocked to find Gemini standing behind me, holding the man by the collar and a butterfly knife to his throat.

I'm not.

I don't question how he got here or found me this easily.

Instead, my stomach flips at the sight of his roguish smile. My mouth goes dry as I stare at his twinkling blue and green eyes. Signaling me with a jerk of his head to follow him into the closest alleyway, he drags the struggling man along with him and disappears into the shadows.

I quickly stalk after them, my heart now slamming in my chest with giddy anticipation. What's coming is inevitable, the final missing piece to slide into place for me to claim my rightful place at the top of the Pravitian food chain.

I follow the sound of Gemini's crazed chuckle, as if still leashed by the neck. When he deems us far enough into the alley, he breezily maneuvers the man so that he has his elbows pulled backward, facing me and unable to move.

It's clear the man knows who Gemini is by the lack of resistance, and despite the wild terror written across his face, not a single cry for help leaves his lips. With one hand still hooked around the man's elbows, Gemini hands me the butterfly knife before pulling him closer in his hold. I take it with a smile, and he blows me a kiss.

I take a moment to observe my very first kill. Graying hair at his temples. Wide-set eyes splashes in terror. A round nose. My assessing gaze lingers on a stain on his beige cashmere sweater. Then on the small chain with a locket hanging around his neck.

Petty jealousy pulses through me, and I wish I could have the same effect on people that I'm sure all six have on the citizens of this city.

I vow to become just as notorious as Gemini Foley and the rest.

To never be mistaken for prey ever again.

"You don't know who I am, do you?" I say mockingly.

The man blubbers and shakes his head, tears now streaming down his face. "If I had known," he whimpers, "that you were one of Gemini's—"

"I am not *one of* anything," I spit.

I lunge forward, and the blade slices across his neck like shears on silk. The cut isn't deep enough to be fatal, but the man gurgles a cry nonetheless as blood immediately trickles out of the wound, adding to his stained beige sweater.

Gemini grows ecstatic behind him, his laugh turning that more sinister. "Again, again." He snickers.

Butterflies tickle my stomach as the pride spreads across his face, and I flash him a dopey smile. It urges me on, and I step closer. Tugging on his sweater to create tension, I slice down the middle, cutting it in half. I rip the rest of the fabric with my hands, revealing the man's heaving chest beneath, the shredded sweater falling to the sides.

The knife thrums in the palm of my hand, as if sentient. It's as bloodthirsty as I am, and I bring the sharp blade up to the man's stomach for it to have a small sip. I nick the skin, and he whimpers, the blood from his neck wound slowly trickling down his chest.

"P-please," he croaks.

Gemini tsks loudly behind him. "Say another word, love, and I'll rip out your vocal cords before she's done with you."

The man cowers in his hold, and Gemini winks, sending me another quick kiss.

My gaze lands back on the man's bloody stomach, and adrenaline slowly morphs into morbid curiosity. I sink the blade deep into his gut just to know how it feels, and Gemini turns even giddier, his laughter drowning the man's cries of pain.

"Try the heart next," he says breathlessly, his eyes as bright as the stars above. "Right here." He lets go of one of the man's arms to press his index finger onto the bloodied skin, indicating a specific spot above the ribs.

The man barely stirs, his head now drooping forward.

I don't think, letting my hand guide me instead, and the blade disappears into the man's chest. I pull out the knife with a jerk, instinctively wanting to see the blood flow out of the wound.

I am hypnotized by the blood, beckoning me forward like a siren song. Dropping my hand to my side, still holding the knife loosely in my palm, I reach for the flow of blood with the other hand. I drag my fingers over the wound, the blood surprisingly warm under my touch.

My gaze lifts to Gemini, who's still holding on to the near-unconscious man. He's beaming, and a shocked laugh leaves my lips, my smile widening. As my attention falls back on the dying man, my brows furrow, as if wanting to concentrate.

Idly, I smear the blood across the pale skin until an impulsive urge overtakes me. With my index finger, I slowly begin to draw the letter *V* with the blood on his stomach, followed by a heart and the letter *G*.

I burst into manic giggles as Gemini sucks in a sharp breath at the sight. With an unceremonious shove, he lets the man crumple to the ground at our feet.

"Come here," he growls before grabbing me by my jacket and tugging me forward.

His lips burn against mine, and I scramble over the heap of limbs on the ground to get my body closer to Gemini. I return the kiss with as much desperation as I can feel in his touch, feeling the rush of life coursing through my veins while the man takes his final breaths at our feet.

"How did it feel?" Gemini hums against my neck, leaving a trail of kisses in his wake.

"Natural," I say between quickening breaths. "Effortless."

His laughter vibrates against my skin before he straightens to gaze longingly into my eyes.

"To watch you emerge from the binding shackles of humanity has been an absolute honor, my beloved. Divine perfection."

He presses a kiss on my forehead, and I circle my arms around his waist. The warmth of his words trickles through my limbs like I'm sitting beside a crackling fire.

"Let's go home," I murmur near the crook of his neck.

Silence lingers before Gemini says, "Home?"

I unfurl myself from his embrace and give him a sheepish look, shrugging my shoulders nervously.

Gemini is serious for only a second before his expression turns into a triumphant smile. "Home it is then."

He starts to lead us out of the alley, but I stop him.

"Wait." I crouch down over the body and rifle through his pockets for his wallet before slipping his watch off his wrist and his gold ring off his finger. I stuff the items into my jacket and bounce back up with a wide grin.

Gemini huffs amusingly, putting my arm overtop his while we begin to walk. "You know," he says, patting my hand, "stealing a measly wallet feels beneath you now."

"Stealing is beneath me?" I say incredulously.

Gemini laughs, flashing me a conspiratorial smile. "I never said anything about stealing."

38

GEMINI

Veil sits in the town car, facing me, and I study her for any signs of nerves as the vehicle slows to a stop in front of Aleksandr's estate. Today was Mercy and Wolfgang's wedding. The ceremony was near Mount Pravitia, but Aleksandr generously offered his property for the reception.

Is it generosity when his god feeds off the excess of a day such as this?

Veil's pale blue gown appears iridescent in this light, the golden rays of the setting sun dancing across her tattooed skin as she peers out from the car window.

Her ravishing face is devoid of nerves. Quite the contrary. And how proud I was of her when we first arrived at the ceremony. She commanded attention and knew her place among us, demanding the space.

"A return to where it all started," I say softly, my attention still steadfastly locked on Veil.

She startles ever so slightly, as if pulled out of a daydream, before turning her gaze to me. Her small, knowing smile tells me she remembers me saying those exact words the last time we came to Aleksandr's estate over a month ago.

"I'll have you on a leash next bacchanal," she answers teasingly.

I purse my lips in tickled amusement. "Promise?" I purr.

Veil's laugh floats up between us, and I wish I could reach out and pluck it out of thin air so as to keep it forever.

The driver opens the car door, and I climb out before offering my hand to Veil.

"Ready?" I ask into her hair after she gracefully steps out, giving her a quick kiss above her ear.

"The daunting part has already passed — don't you think?" she says assuredly.

I know she's referring to the swarm of paparazzi outside the ceremony hall, marking today as her official induction into the ruling families. By tomorrow, the city of Pravitia will be abuzz with the news. Of course, Wolfgang will be carefully pulling the strings of the narrative from behind the scenes.

Veil grins as she pulls me onto the path leading up to the entrance, brown eyes twinkling. "Now let's have some fun."

"Where's your husband?"

I plop down beside Mercy on the long bench outside, facing the backyard, the maze looming majestically beyond it.

For the reception, she changed out of her extravagant wedding dress into something more classic. She's the picture of elegance in her slinky black dress, the slit up her left thigh framing the dagger and harness she can't live without.

There's no one out here but us, and I can tell her guard is down by the shy smile she gives me and her idle toying with the pendant around her neck. I even catch the subtle flush across her cheeks at the word *husband*.

"I'm not his keeper," Mercy answers haughtily, taking a long drag of her clove cigarette as she peers up at the stars.

I stretch my legs out in front of me, crossing one ankle over the other, and clasp my hands behind my head, leaning on the back of the bench. "Could have fooled me," I mutter, my gaze now on the night sky.

There's a long silence until we both burst out laughing. And the sound of her laughter is both a shock and an absolute delight.

"You've changed, love," I say with a pleased sigh.

She turns to look at me, her green eyes piercing. "Don't remind me."

I study her some more as she takes another drag of her cigarette, her wine-red lipstick staining the filter.

"Are you happy?" I ask.

She scoffs, as if dismissing the very notion of my question. "Happiness, such a banal emotion." She pauses. The sounds of the festivities inside are muted but still boisterous. Then, reluctantly, she adds, "Yes."

I choke on a laugh at her admission. She's softened since falling in love. There would be hell to pay if I dared to say it out loud, so I sit with the feeling on my own, beaming up at the starry night.

"And what about you?"

"I'm always happy, love," I respond with a grin.

She slaps my arm, and a chuckle rumbles in my chest. "Don't be facetious; you know I'm talking about the girl."

"The *girl*," I say as I straighten up on the bench, "is a servant just like us, Mercy, and she deserves your respect."

She purses her lips, but doesn't argue. Her eyes narrow, as if studying me, before she turns to stub her clove cigarette in the ashtray beside the bench.

"You love her," she states. It's not a question.

I drag my hand over my face as I look up at the night sky, then back down at Mercy. "Love is so banal," I tease, echoing her earlier statement.

"Then what?" she responds, her expression impassive.

I smile ruefully, letting the silence linger before speaking. "Veil and I, we are fate's favorite ballad."

Mercy shakes her head softly, a hint of a smile lifting her upper lip. "Careful — you're starting to sound as vain as Wolfgang."

I laugh playfully. "Maybe your husband is onto something."

She smiles wistfully, crossing her arms against the night's chill. "I ..." Her smile drops. "I wish I hadn't been the last to know about this," she says tentatively. "About Veil."

I'm surprised to find so much vulnerability in her voice. "As a friend?" I ask. "Or as the ruler of our dear city?"

She avoids my questioning gaze when she answers, her voice close to a whisper, "As a friend."

I have the urge to laugh, to dissipate the rising tension between us. Instead, I slide closer to her on the bench and press a kiss on the top of her hand.

"You were too busy falling in love," I say.

She lets out an offended tsk and rips her hand out of my grasp. I chuckle but quickly grab her arm before she moves to stand up, most likely to storm off in a huff.

"Would a secret appease you?" I ask conspiratorially.

She regards me with suspicion, her arm still in my grip, and I can tell she's debating saying no just to spite me. But I know Mercy, and there's nothing she loves more than a secret.

"Yes." She elongates the word for extra emphasis.

I grin and release her. Pinning her with my stare, I tongue my cheek before speaking, just to make her squirm. "I had Belladonna lift the fertility barrier. Soon, Veil will be carrying my heir."

Her eyebrows lift in surprise, but her eyes immediately narrow, as if she's trying to decipher what part exactly is the secret. "Veil doesn't know," she finally says.

I push out a pleased chuckle and nod.

But Mercy doesn't smile back.

"Silly boy," she says, and her reprimanding tone startles me. "Veil is not just another one of your paramours. She is a servant, just like you, remember?"

"And?" I say petulantly.

She stands up, smoothing out her dress before answering. Her dark green eyes are steadfast. "She will make you pay for this, Gemini."

My smile is arrogant. "I'm planning on it."

39

VEIL

I'm giddy from the three glasses of champagne I've had as I follow Gemini outside. The night air cools my heated cheeks, the earthy smell tickling my nose. Gemini is just as inhibited as me, his eyes twinkling with mirth whenever he finds my gaze to share a laugh.

My merriment ends when I realize he's leading us to the maze. My laughter disappears like smoke into the night. I balk, my feet cementing themselves to the ground, even when Gemini tries to tug me forward by the arm. Turning to face me, he furrows his brow, his hand still circling my wrist, but his grin turns wicked.

"Come now, doll. Don't you trust me?"

My rational mind knows this is not like before. I'm safe. This is just a maze, and so much has changed since that fateful night over two months ago.

But my body does not care; it's still living in the past, reacting negatively at just the sight of the maze's looming hedges. Especially when I connect it to the man currently holding my wrist.

"I don't trust you." My tone is resolute as I shake my head.

His laugh is surprisingly warm as his head falls backward before he locks eyes with mine again. "Smart," he says with a quirk of his lips. "I wouldn't trust the god of trickery either."

A sense of dread trickles down my spine, and I swallow hard at the sensation.

"I promise I have nothing nefarious planned," he adds, tugging on my wrist. "However, it *can* be." He winks. "If that's what you so wish."

I stare back with the most unimpressed look I can muster, and his smile widens. The last of our conversation is exchanged in silence. He urges me on with a quick jerk of the head. I still don't trust him, but after a few seconds and a handful of rapid heartbeats, I acquiesce with a slow nod.

Not long after, we arrive at the center of the maze, the looming statue of an archer with his arrow pointing to the sky welcoming us. A cold chill traverses my body, as if I am walking straight into a haunted memory. If I strain hard enough, I can almost hear the wild thump of my heartbeat before Wolfgang told us to run that night.

We're both quiet as we walk deeper into the maze's center. A crow caws above our heads, and I lift my gaze to catch its flight, its dark shadow crossing the night sky. The waning moon is barely a sliver tonight, and the moonlight struggles to illuminate our path.

"Why did you bring me here?" My question feels accusatory, and I make no effort to rectify it.

"Why do you think, Veil Vulturine?" Gemini smirks as he unbuttons his cuffs before doing the same with the collar of his black silk shirt.

I eye him warily, but I say nothing as my nape prickles with apprehension. When his collar is loose enough, he reaches up to the back of his neck, pulls the shirt over his head, and discards it with a flick of his wrist.

His raw beauty takes me aback, as if it were my first time

laying my eyes on him. His tattooed chest heaves with anticipation, muscles tight and corded, as if he's already holding himself back.

"Another one of your games?" I ask condescendingly. All the while, my heart pounds in my chest.

He laughs, toeing off his dress shoes. "Nonsense," he says, chock-full of arrogance. "I'm simply helping you rewrite history."

I'm fairly certain where this is going, but something in me needs him to say it out loud. Still, I carefully take off my stilettos while I ask, "Whose history?"

His smirk transforms into a leering grin, and I'm eerily reminded of the stranger who was destined to kill me in this very maze.

"Ours."

I gulp loudly, a healthy dose of fear and excitement now coursing through my veins.

His bright eyes darken as his chin dips down. As he stares at me through his lashes, his smile turns threatening and calculated. "*Run.*"

The word is barely out of his mouth before I bolt away, my subconscious leading me directly to the same hedge path I took the first time I was here.

Gemini's laughter rises up in the air like a bleak warning, and my body breaks into goose bumps. My mind knows this is all pretend, but I can't seem to convince my body that it isn't real.

And what if it isn't?

And this past month was just one elaborate hoax?

The taunting fear has adrenaline coursing through my limbs, urging me on. Blood rushes through my ears as I weave through the maze, blindly turning left and then right.

This time, I can tell Gemini hasn't given me a head start. I hear his heavy footfalls behind me like a stalking shadow, and the sound sends me into a frenzy. My heart pounds and pounds and pounds as I continue to run, cold sweat beading across my forehead.

I take a left turn and immediately realize my mistake when I find myself facing a dead end, where the hedge maze seems to reach much higher into the night sky in my frantic state.

"Dead end, little rabbit?"

I squeak out a small cry, as if I didn't expect Gemini to appear behind me.

I whirl around, my eyes wild.

"You haven't caught me yet," I spit, walking backward to keep my distance.

Gemini closes his eyes and takes a large inhale. He hums in delight before his deadly gaze slams back into mine. "Your fear smells just as sweet as I remember."

"I'm not scared of you," I hurry to say, hating how much my body reacts to his threats.

"That's a lie, pet."

"And how would you know?" I growl.

"Haven't you learned by now?" he says slowly in a predatory tone. "I know everything about you."

He lunges forward before I have time to react and manages to grab my waist, but I immediately fight back with a renewed sense of outrage.

"Let go of me!" I screech, pushing against Gemini's arm, my nails digging into his skin.

Gemini snickers coldly. "Back to that same song, I see."

My rage only builds, and I lose myself in the feeling and all the repressed fury I once felt for my captor. I swing my arm backward, aiming for his face, then propel it forward. My fist connects hard against bone as I manage to land a hard blow near Gemini's temple.

His head snaps back, and my first instinct is to fall still and see if I hurt him, but my survival instinct kicks in instead, and I take the opportunity to fight him off.

When his arms fall away, I laugh in disbelief, but don't take the time to look back before sprinting away, making my way even deeper into the maze. The hard, grassy soil hurts my soles, but it only spurs me onward, making me determined to evade Gemini for as long as I can manage.

His cackling laughter reaches me through the depths of the gnarled branches of the tall hedges, and I can't tell if he's behind me or somewhere on another path parallel to me. I let out a small, breathless whimper, my lungs tightening as they burn with the exertion.

I keep running, turning this way and that, letting my feet choose for me, my mind now devoid of rational thoughts, except for the throbbing need to escape.

Suddenly, I hear pounding footsteps behind me and make the mistake of looking over my shoulder, slowing me down.

Gemini is right behind me, a mad look on his face. I yelp and try to speed up, but he grabs a fistful of my dress and yanks me backward to him.

Swiveling my torso around so I can slam my palms into his chest, I lose my footing and fall hard on my ass. Gemini doesn't stop laughing, his tone turning even more manic as he follows me down to the ground.

Panic rises, boiling through my veins as I continue to try to escape his hold, struggling to scramble away. My foot flies out, the heel connecting hard with his nose. His head snaps backward, and he curses loudly, his hands flying to cradle his bruised nose. I take the opportunity to turn my body away from him in a feeble attempt to break free. I've only managed a few measly inches before I'm dragged back across the grass.

"The hunt is over, little rabbit," Gemini rasps, the blood from his nose now running down his mouth and chin. "Quit resisting. It's now time to savor the spoils."

I ignore his command and continue to struggle in his harsh grasp, but my body flares in heat, knowing exactly what will happen next.

And I want nothing more than to be devoured whole by Gemini Foley.

Still, I bare my teeth and spit in his face as he pins me to the ground with a large palm against my neck and collarbone. My actions only embolden Gemini further as he tugs his pants down.

"You'll never have me," I hiss, and part of me is surprised by the harsh intent in my tone.

Gemini roughly pushes my dress up, ripping my thong off in a rush of movements. My core throbs in wanton need, my arousal hungry and aching.

"Your words mean nothing, Veil Vulturine," he growls, his eyes crazed and aflame as he positions himself at my entrance. "Not when I've owned you since I took my very first breath."

He impales me with his cock in one vicious thrust, and my mouth falls open on a ragged moan, my head pressing into the earth under me.

His hand keeps me pinned to the ground, his fingers curling around my throat. He fucks me with abandon, and my breath is nearly snatched out of my lungs when the pleasure explodes inside of me.

Gemini snickers mockingly, and the sound of it makes me squeeze around his throbbing length.

"I knew you'd be soaking wet." He leans close to my cheek, his tongue laving a path up my face, certainly staining me with his blood as he does so. "Listen to how sloppy you sound as I fuck you, my pet. Why would you ever deny us when I can hear it in the panting moans you sing for me?"

It's my turn to laugh. It's delirious and mocking. Gemini appears surprised by my reaction with the way his head pops up to gaze into my eyes, the bottom half of his face smeared with blood.

"Foolish Gemini," I singsong, bringing one of my legs up and over his waist.

He moans with the change in angle, his head dropping for a split second as he renews his punishing rhythm, then snaps back to stare me in the eyes.

"Obsession has made you lose control," I continue. "How could you ever claim to own me when I own every single thought in that pretty little head of yours?"

We share a loaded beat of silence. Gemini's expression shutters, his smile dropping, and I can tell I struck a nerve.

Good.

He pulls out, and for a split second, I think I might have ruined the moment. Instead, he sits on the ground and tugs me onto his lap. My dress flutters around us as I grab the base of his shaft and use my weight to sink down on his cock in one mind-pulverizing movement.

We both moan in unison. Gemini's mouth drops open in what looks like raptured awe. I'm struck by the softness in his expression, as if he's lost all sense of his nefarious and taunting motives.

"Have my heir, beloved," he rasps as his hand slips between us, his thumb stroking my swollen clit. "Give me the pleasure of pumping you full of my seed and watching your belly swell with my child."

His tone is full of grit and determination, his gaze serious and steadfast as his free hand finds the base of my nape, his thumb resting close to my parted lips.

I can feel the shift in his intent—this isn't a game anymore.

I slow my movements down, sliding up and down his cock in a teasing cadence. "Why are you in such a rush, Gem?" I ask sincerely, placing my hands atop his shoulders to help me hover over the tip of his cock.

He audibly groans, catching my lips with his as I sink back down, my pussy fluttering around his hard shaft. He kisses me with abandon, his thumb still circling my clit, sending shivers of pleasure throughout my body. My orgasm rushes over me, and I fight it for a little while longer, eager for this moment to last.

"This is not me rushing," he says after breaking our kiss. His hands find my ass under my dress, squeezing hard while making me grind against him. "This is divine timing."

The numbing tendrils of my climax slither into every small crevasse of my mind, and I lose all sense of self. I can't hold it any longer. My body seizes, and my nails dig into Gemini's shoulders.

He moans loudly, and my breath catches when I feel his teeth sink into the thin skin of my throat, his tongue immediately licking over the bite mark now smarting my neck.

I've barely come down from my orgasm before he rolls us forward, grabbing me behind the knees as my back hits the ground behind me. He pushes my legs up, practically folding me in half, the angle so deep that I can feel every inch of him pulsing inside of me.

"Do you trust me?" he grits, his voice strained by his own climax. He curses under his breath as he stills inside of me, then returns to fucking me.

The fleeting thought of having Gemini's child has my core unexpectedly squeezing around his pulsing shaft while he continues to mindlessly fuck me through his orgasm.

Falling motionless, he finds the bite mark on my neck, peppering it with kisses. I caress his back, and something about his heated skin makes my heart flutter with affection. It's followed by a bizarre pulse of apprehension, as if I sense something before my conscious mind ever can.

I never answer his question.

40

BELLADONNA

The ballroom is abuzz for Mercy and Wolfgang's wedding reception. Half of the dance floor has been filled with round tables, covered in black velvet cloth. The intricate gold, black, and red flower arrangements at the center of each table are reminiscent of the very couple we are celebrating.

Dinner ended hours ago, and the guests have moved on to a more decadent and intoxicated way of celebrating. The wine and champagne flow freely, like blood from a severed artery, and if I squint my eyes just right, I'm sure I'll find plenty of drugs being passed around too.

As a servant of our gods, I'm not affected by the manic need for excess that overcomes most mortals when in the vicinity of one of Vorovsky's celebrations. And normally, I would never set foot on any of that degenerate's properties ... except I have twice now ... in the span of a month.

I can't deny the winds of change. Certainly, there is a new epoch knocking at our door. I must learn to be more adaptable, just like my peers, who seem a lot less bothered by change than me. That aside, I promised Mercy I would enjoy myself tonight, and my glass of Barolo, always topped off by attentive servers, has helped considerably.

Even Constantine doesn't come off as shrill as I usually find her.

After spending some time dancing, I sit beside her at our table. A handful of dessert plates with half-eaten wedding cake still lingers, and I idly look for someone to take them away.

Constantine appears morose—an emotion I can't say I've ever seen on her.

"Something the bother?" I ask over the music.

She huffs theatrically, the puff of air dancing in the pink feathers of her bustier. "I'm about to cut this cast off myself," she whines. "I'm so *bored* ... actually"—she straightens as if something just dawned on her and reaches for a knife still littering the table— "I'll do it right now."

I lunge for the knife. "No, you will not, Tinny."

"Let me do this!" she exclaims. "This is the closest I've ever felt to real pain. Even death would be a more palatable fate!"

I scoff, still trying to wrench the knife out of her hands. "You're so dramatic."

After a short game of tug and pull, I manage to wrestle the knife out of her grip and place it out of her reach. She crosses her arms and pouts, but something over my shoulder catches her attention, and her face immediately lifts into a wide, amused smile.

I turn to find a beaming Gemini strolling into the ballroom, Veil in tow. My nape prickles at the sight of her. The same faint *knowing* throbs inside of me, right at the edge of my subconscious. I quickly push it away.

Now is not the time.

They're both disheveled, caked in what looks like blood and dirt. Veil's pale blue dress is ripped near the shoulder while Gemini's shirt has disappeared altogether.

Their current state isn't shocking—we've all seen and *done* much worse. Still, I know I'll find displeasure on Mercy's and Wolfgang's faces, even before I locate them standing just off the dance floor with Vorovsky.

Gemini whispers something in Veil's ear, and her attention shifts to Constantine and me. She starts for our table while Gemini heads for the disapproving couple, a wide grin on his bloodied face.

"Vee-Vee, my darling," Constantine chirps as Veil approaches.

She gives us a sheepish smile, uselessly dusting off her tattered dress before sitting by Constantine.

"Please tell me what kind of high jinks you and Gemini got into. I'm quite literally *dying* for some entertainment."

As Veil fumbles over explaining whatever Gemini roped her into doing, I reach for a cloth napkin. Pouring a fresh glass of water from the carafe, I dip a corner of the cloth into the water and hand it to Veil. She blinks at me owlishly, as if wondering why I'm handing her a napkin, but takes it from my grasp nonetheless.

"For the blood," I say, tapping the corner of my mouth before flashing her a sardonic smile.

Realization dawns over her face, and her laugh hints of a timidity she's obviously trying to conceal around us.

As she cleans herself up, Constantine presses her for more details, and I pretend to listen as I observe Gemini from the corner of my eye. He seems to be trying to pull Mercy away from Wolfgang.

I can only imagine what insults are flying out of her mouth as she appears to protest his efforts, but Gemini doesn't balk, until finally, Mercy gives up the fight.

Veil has barely started her half-baked explanation about her current physical state when Gemini drags Mercy up to our table.

"Time for the bouquet toss!" Gemini gleefully announces, and Mercy's entire body recoils.

She rolls her eyes with exasperation, but says nothing.

A quiet shock of surprise leaves my lips. "How did Gemini *ever* convince you to do a bouquet toss?"

Mercy's cheeks pinken, and she fumbles over her words, staring at the all-black bouquet. "I — it's —"

"Never the mind *how*," Gemini says with sparkles in his eyes. Now that he's closer, I notice the beginning of a purple bruise under his left eye. "Everyone, up! Let's move to the center of the dance floor."

"But—" Constantine begins to whine in protest, but Gemini cuts her off by yelling across the ballroom, "Sasha!"

Vorovsky looks over, and Gemini signals him to come over with overly enthusiastic hand waves.

"Carry Tinny in your arms, will you?" he asks, still yelling across the room, then turns to Constantine and winks.

I sigh. Gemini's personality always grates on my nerves, but I stand to join Mercy, who wordlessly thanks me for my begrudging participation.

Seconds later, Vorovsky trots over, lifting Constantine into his arms. She laughs gleefully, one arm raised in the air while the other circles Vorovsky's neck, her pink cast sticking straight out in front of her.

After pulling Veil up from her chair, followed by an unnecessary show of affection, Gemini leaves us to flutter around the ballroom and round up as many willing participants as possible. Eventually, a small crowd gathers. I stay on the outskirts, having no intention of catching the bouquet. Mercy stands awkwardly in front of us, and I don't miss her subtle glances to Wolfgang, who is wordlessly cheering her on.

Shoulders start pushing against shoulders when Mercy turns her back to us, and little shrieks of excitement rise from the participants as the anticipation of the bouquet toss rises.

Meanwhile, Vorovsky parades Constantine in front of the whole group, as if winding up for a race.

There's a short lull of silence when Mercy tosses the bouquet in the air until everyone winds back to life and lunges for the flowers. There's a flurry of hands as the heap of people moves forward like a sentient mass, and I step backward, trying to avoid getting an elbow to the face.

A blonde I don't recognize snatches it from midair, but her victory is short-lived when Gemini appears out of nowhere and rips the bouquet out of her grasp. Her mouth falls open in protest, but she doesn't dare say a word as Gemini yelps in victory.

"Where's my future wife?!" he says with the widest smile, his face still stained and bloodied, as he whips his head left and right, looking for Veil.

He finds her beaming, standing in the dispersing crowd, and pulls her into his arms for a kiss before dramatically bending her backward, lips still sealed.

My gaze slips to Mercy, standing a few steps away. There's a ghost of a smile on her lips as she watches the new couple. Her obvious affection for Gemini will forever evade me.

It's late into the night, and the festivities have retired to a far less formal room. It appears to have been designed just for this kind of night with its low, moody lighting and countless couches and chaises filling the space. It's my first time *inside* the Vorovsky estate, having only frequented the gardens and maze during the Feast of Fools.

Aside from us six—now seven—servants, everyone celebrating alongside us has been overtaken by the throes of excess, and I'm struck by how similar some of the facets of our powers are. I've never before stayed long enough in Vorovsky's presence to witness it myself. I'm suddenly realizing that the lack of inhibitions among the celebrants looks a lot like being overtaken by lust. The same wide pupils. The same insatiable hunger.

Except my power is a lot more controlled, dignified. I prefer to keep that facet of my powers for my designated day during Tithe Season.

Still, it makes my throat go dry and my skin itch, as if my god were becoming restless at the sight. To distract myself, I grab a wandering soul by the collar and pull them into a kiss. They're too drunk to protest—although I've never had anyone protest my affections before.

I can feel the effect instantly. The feeling is close to an orgasm, followed by a tingle of electricity from my toes all the way up to the crown of my head. I feel immediately recharged, my heart thumping with renewed energy. After having my fill, I break the kiss and shove them out of the way, now feeling a lot more social.

I scan the dark room for some familiar faces and spot Gemini, Veil, and Constantine sitting in one of the far corners. Not my first choice, but they will do for now. Reaching into my clutch purse for my pocket mirror, I retouch my red lipstick before making my way to them.

They're in a fit of giggles when I approach, Constantine especially.

"What's so funny?" I ask with genuine interest, still strumming with adrenaline from the kiss.

"Veil was showing me her powers," Constantine says, breathy with excitement.

"Oh?" I respond, sitting beside her.

"Veil, now do her, do her," Constantine presses, and I can hear the faintest of slurring in her speech.

My heart sinks when Veil turns to me, a sparkle of determination in her brown eyes.

I begin to protest. "Veil, no, don't—" But it's too late.

I feel my powers siphon out of me like a cold chill traversing through my bones.

I can tell the instant it dawns on her.

Veil's smile drops, her eyes widening in horror.

There's a beat of loaded silence.

Then, she speaks far too calmly. "I'm pregnant."

41

VEIL

Belladonna's alarmed expression only solidifies the pit in my stomach at the realization. I hold on to her powers for a few more seconds as my heart beats out of my chest, desperate for this confusing sense of knowledge to prove to be false.

But I've never been so sure in my godsdamned life.

I'm *pregnant*.

I let the gold thread slip, the god of lust's powers returning to their rightful heir.

I turn to Gemini. Anger floods my veins like a raging volcano.

"You *tricked* me." The accusation comes out as an outraged hiss, and I ignore Constantine's small squeak of surprise beside him.

He stays silent, his emotions locked away somewhere underneath his unperturbed mask until, finally, he smirks. It's cold and calculated, and I feel the ground slip from under my feet.

Leaning back, he places his hands behind his head. "It comes with the namesake, love."

The betrayal hurts more than I expected, and I feel tears prick behind my eyes. Mortification at the thought of showing any type of vulnerability in front of him has me taking a deep breath and blinking furiously to keep the tears at bay.

"Veil ..." Belladonna mutters beside me, and I flash her a searing look before returning back to Gemini.

"That's it? That's all you have to say? Your *god* made you do it?" I spit.

Gemini's smile widens, and it makes my fingers curl into my palms, my short nails digging into the skin.

He tilts his head with nonchalance. "You promised me an heir, remember?"

"We agreed I would decide when!"

My heart pounds in my chest, my breathing shallow and ragged.

He flicks his wrist, as if dismissing what I just said. "Semantics, my beloved. Why delay fate?"

His pompous reaction and laissez-faire attitude have me seeing red.

"How could you?!" I bark with rage before launching myself off my seat and straight onto Gemini, blindly trying to land a punch.

"The baby!" Constantine shrieks beside us.

I can tell Gemini is only half-heartedly defending himself, which further enrages me, but it doesn't take long before I'm ripped off of him by multiple strong hands. I don't bother protesting, satisfied to see that I've managed to split his lip and pull out a chunk of his hair before I'm standing again.

"You disgust me," I snarl, spitting on the ground near Gemini's feet.

It's only then do I find something other than arrogance written on his face. I don't bother looking closer to decipher what it is.

I can't stand the look of him.

"Let's go," Belladonna says, tugging on my arm.

I slowly turn my head to look at her, her green eyes pleading. I swallow hard, trying to calm myself, but my anger simmers for her as well.

She knew.

But ...

Not having many desirable options, I choose to follow her, ignoring Gemini's quiet protest as we leave.

SINCE I HAVE NO PLACE OF MY OWN TO GO BUT GEMINI'S, Belladonna brings me to her condo. The Carnalis neighborhood is not far from the Vorovsky estate. Her residence sprawls multiple levels at the top of a modern skyrise near the Pravitian waterfront.

She hints at me needing a shower and hands me a cashmere set to change into after showing me the way to the bathroom. Even in her bathroom, painted ivory with soft coral accents, the quiet elegance of Belladonna's personality can be felt.

Under the shower's hot stream of water, I realize how tense I am and make a feeble attempt to relax my muscles. I sigh loudly, my head falling forward, and let the water wash over me as I stare at the blood and dirt circling the drain. The last remnants of Gemini cleansed off my body.

My head pounds with racing thoughts, the most intrusive of them all being that I'm pregnant.

And Gemini Foley is the father.

My shoulders tense, my teeth grinding together, the longer I linger on the offending thought.

"Do you trust me?" His taunting voice echoes loudly in my head.

Why ask me that question in the first place? And how on earth did he do it? Was the tonic ineffective?

I suddenly feel like the biggest fool. I trusted him enough to believe he was giving me the correct tonic all along.

I need answers.

Luckily, Gemini isn't the only one with them.

I find Belladonna in the living room, sitting on her green velvet couch, gazing out of the window. They sprawl so high that they make up a small portion of the ceiling, too, making the panoramic view that much more astounding. She changed out of her wedding clothes, lounging in a gold satin set with a matching robe, her red hair up in a loose bun.

Her eyebrows furrow when she hears me walk in, as if already apprehensive about what's to come. I sit opposite her on the couch, and slowly, reluctantly, she turns her body to face me. The silence coils around us like a snake, fangs full of poison. But Belladonna does not cower, keeping her gaze steadfast, and waits for me to speak.

"You knew." My voice comes out a lot weaker than I would have wanted, but I keep my expression hard as I wait for her to answer.

"Yes," she says, followed by a slow nod. I think I'll have to prod for more information, but after a tense beat, she adds, "In fact, I helped facilitate it."

I blink in disbelief. My head feels full of cotton. Exhaustion washes over me, but I power through.

"The tonic?" I ask, having no other avenue to choose from.

She shakes her head. "The tonic does not work on us."

"Us?" I grit.

She tilts her head and narrows her eyes, as if I were being purposefully obtuse. "Those who carry our gods' powers, of course."

I push out a wry laugh. "Of course." I drop my smile. "Then *what*?" I seethe.

Belladonna's lips thin at my tone, but she answers anyway. "I control the fertility of the chosen families—most specifically, the servants"—she shifts in her seat, showing discomfort—"to avoid unplanned pregnancies."

"How ironic," I hiss between clenched teeth.

She shrugs her shoulders and crosses her arms, avoiding my accusatory glare.

I'm reminded of the day Gemini brought me to Belladonna's cabaret, the same day I idiotically agreed to give him an heir. I was so sure of my intentions that day, convinced I would never fall for Gemini.

Look where it got me.

Just a doll for him to play with however he chooses.

"Was that the purpose of his visit that day?" I finally ask, not caring to elaborate.

Just as I thought, she knows exactly what I'm referring to.

She nods, her gaze slowly sliding to meet mine. "For what it's worth, I regret agreeing to it."

"For what it's worth," I repeat, chuckling coldly. I narrow my eyes, feeling sick to my stomach at the loss of agency and control I've had to endure just this past month. "How long has Gemini known about the pregnancy?"

The thought that he's been keeping such a monumental secret from me but still parading under the guise of consent has anxiety clawing up my throat.

She shakes her head. "He didn't know. I only learned about your pregnancy today." She pauses, seemingly thinking. "You weren't pregnant when you came for high tea at Tinny's." She shrugs. "So, sometime between then and now, you conceived."

That was almost two weeks ago.

I fight the urge to storm out, my emotions expanding dangerously in my chest, threatening to explode.

I reach for a damp strand of hair, toying with it as I try to regulate my current mental state. The edges of me are fraying, and it's getting harder to stay whole.

"I would think there was a law written somewhere about both servants needing to consent if the fertility barrier was lifted. Or are all of you so lacking in morals that you disregard those laws entirely?"

Her brows dip, and by the way she shifts in her seat, she's feeling defensive. Her lip lifts in something close to a smile, but it never reaches her green eyes.

"Self-righteousness doesn't suit you, darling," she snaps, but when she speaks again, her tone evens out. "Were you aware that there was a divine law, one which was only recently dissolved, preventing the servants from fornicating with one another?"

I narrow my eyes. "Vaguely, yes."

"Then why on *earth* would there be a law about having two servants consenting to the barrier being lifted?"

I fall silent, feeling slightly foolish, but her answer doesn't manage to quell my indignation.

She huffs out a sigh, gazing out of the window. "But," she says, still looking away, "you are right."

Butterflies flutter in my stomach at her admission, and I suppress my surprised reaction, waiting for her to continue.

"You had just as much right as Gemini. He used my unfamiliarity toward you to his advantage. I should have never agreed, and for that, I apologize."

Tears spring to my eyes, and I fight the tremble in my lips. I didn't realize how much I needed an apology—from *anyone*.

"Thank you," I croak.

She flashes me a weak smile, then quickly breaks eye contact. "It's getting late," she says before standing up. "I'll show you to the guest room."

Ignoring her attempt to end the conversation, I ask, "What if I choose not to keep it?"

Belladonna's brows lift in surprise, and she takes a few seconds to study me before answering, "You can if that is what you desire."

She cocks her head to the side, as if deliberating on her next choice of words. And suddenly, I know I'll hate whatever comes out of her mouth.

"But sooner or later, the gods' will demand an heir from you, Veil ... so why delay fate?"

42

GEMINI

"**W**here is she?" I growl as soon as I open my front door, Mercy and Belladonna standing on the other side.

It's been three long days since I learned that Veil is with child—*my* child—and I'm about ready to raze the entire city just to find her.

"Lovely to see you too," Mercy says, clipping my shoulder as she walks in.

Belladonna glares at me, still standing outside the door, until she relents and says, "She's been staying with me." Pushing her way through the threshold, she adds over her shoulder, "And, no, she doesn't want to see you."

Indignation flares inside my chest.

She doesn't want to *see* me?

Impossible.

Both Belladonna and Mercy stand in the middle of the living room, arms crossed. They are visual opposites—one dressed in all black, the other in all white.

"This is ridiculous," I mutter under my breath but loud enough for them to hear.

Walking to the wet bar, I pour myself a scotch, neat. Champagne feels too festive for the occasion. I don't bother offering a drink to the others.

"What's *ridiculous*, Gemini, is how you thought you'd walk away from this unscathed," Mercy says, finally settling on the couch, Belladonna following suit.

I swallow down the scotch in one large gulp and pour myself another glass before turning to face my jury of two.

"Since when do we care about the consequences of our actions?" I ask dryly as I sit down, forcing a bored lilt to my tone.

Belladonna clicks her tongue, but doesn't answer before looking away.

I puff out a cold laugh. "Don't tell me ... Belladonna's made a friend?"

Her gaze snaps back to mine, and she sneers.

Mercy clears her throat, most likely to try to break the tension. She stares me down, her face as blank as an untouched canvas. "You can't be this clueless," she says.

Guilt pangs against my ribs, twisting my stomach, but I pretend not to be affected. "Whatever do you mean, my dear Cee-Cee?"

She tilts her head, dark hair tumbling off her shoulders, narrowing her eyes. "Tell me, why jeopardize the one thing you claim is your destiny?"

"Jeopardize?" I scoff in disbelief. Finishing off the scotch, I settle my drink on the glass coffee table in front of me. "Who said anything about jeopardizing my destiny?"

"Veil," Belladonna answers.

My heart drops, and I suddenly wonder what kind of conversations they've been having behind my back.

"She's mine," I hiss.

"Please," Mercy volleys back, crossing her arms. "You, of all people, should know that you cannot *own* a servant of the gods. You're living in a selfish fantasy."

I spring up, my chest rising quickly with anger.

"Let me see her," I demand, "before you pollute her head further with more of your silly notions."

"No need to pollute her head when your actions have already done exactly that," Belladonna says.

A sudden and overwhelming fear grips my lungs, and I forget how to breathe.

Did I push her too far?

The room falls silent, ripe with simmering hostility.

Slowly walking up to the windows, I peer out into the inky harbor, the stars twinkling on the surface of the water. I find my reflection staring back at me, and I yearn to see Veil's reflection beside mine.

I turn back to face Mercy and Belladonna.

"And what about the others? Do they think the same?"

There's a flash of pity in Mercy's green eyes as she slowly nods, and my anger flips on its axis, now directed at me.

***

Two days later, I find myself standing at the entrance of Belladonna's condo building, trying to smooth-talk the two guards manning the door. Luckily, since my name is *still* Gemini Foley, it doesn't take much effort for them to agree to let me pass.

I run the risk of running into Belladonna, but I'm much too impatient to wait for Veil to come to her senses. The silent treatment has gone on for long enough. I need to see her. I need to talk to her.

I've never visited Belladonna's condo before, but it doesn't take long for me to figure out the layout, and after a few wrong turns, I find Veil curled up in a reading chair in what looks like the library. It's mid-afternoon, but the pouring rain has darkened the skies, cloaking Pravitia and this room under a moody gray light.

"My beloved," I sigh with relief when I finally see her.

I step into the library without any invitation, but my heart cracks when a look of alarm splashes across Veil's face.

"Gemini," she says, her book dropping to her lap.

This time, the tone of fear in her voice isn't welcome, and I yearn to pluck the sound directly off of her vocal cords.

I fall to my knees in front of her chair, reaching for her hands, but she evades me, crossing her arms, so I rest them on her bare knee instead.

"Forgive me," I say breathlessly, my gaze imploring her to hear me, hear the ache.

She doesn't appear moved, and my throat tightens as I wait for her to speak. My heartbeat fills the silence for far too long before her lips begin to move again.

"For *what* exactly?" she says slowly, her brows furrowing.

"What? I—"

"What exactly are you apologizing for, Gemini?" She pushes my hands off her knee, and my arms fall to the sides. "The pregnancy? For tricking me? For *everything* else?"

"For whatever you want," I rush out to say. "Just as long as I can bring you home."

She lets out a groan of frustration, shoving my shoulder so that I slump backward on my ass while she stands up, distancing herself from me.

"I don't think you are physically capable of showing remorse." She crosses her arms and curls in on herself as her lips quiver. "I was right; you are a monster."

Frustration spikes, but it's mixed with a deep ache at seeing her like this.

"What do you expect from me, Veil? I worship the god of

trickery. How can I apologize for something that I was born to chase?"

"I am your *equal*, Gemini." She seethes. "I am not one of your lowly followers." Her nostrils flare, breathing hard. "Are you so conceited that you cannot see the difference between the two?"

Her words prickle uncomfortably across my skin as the silence falls between us, the rain growing louder outside the library windows. I turn, desperate for her forgiveness, ready to give up anything—everything—for her. Whatever she wants, I'll accept.

"Terminate the pregnancy then. Erase my mistakes. We can start over."

She narrows her eyes as she sneers at me. Whatever I say only seems to enrage her further.

"You can attempt to erase your wrongs, Gemini, but it will never erase the betrayal." I try to speak, but she cuts me off. "And if I *do* decide to get rid of it, it won't be for any reason but my own." Her arms tighten around her chest. "Now, leave."

My chest feels cavernous, a gaping hole where my heart should be.

"You can't stay at Belladonna's forever," I mutter as some sort of weak protest, eloquence escaping me.

"I'm not," she answers primly, raising her chin and straightening her shoulders.

"Then come home," I implore.

"I have my own house now."

I take a step back, my mind reeling, having never expected for this to go this far. "A *house*?" I repeat in shock. "In what neighborhood?"

"Mine."

I'm momentarily stunned, uttering half-finished responses before croaking out a simple, "How?"

She sighs, as if fatigued by our conversation. "Mercy and

Wolfgang thought it fair to donate me some land." She pauses. "They gave me half of your neighborhood."

"Half of my neighbor — and no one bothered telling me?" I sputter out loudly, a mixture of shock and anger lacing my voice.

She shrugs and looks away. "Not my problem."

I gnash my teeth together, my heart beating wildly with indignation.

I need to find Mercy.

I raise a finger toward Veil. "This is not over."

It's a threat. A promise. A vow.

I don't let her protest before I storm out.

43

VEIL

I've been staring at the bedroom ceiling for what feels like an eternity. *My* bedroom ceiling, in *my* house. I never imagined that, one day, I'd be able to say that.

Since I had nothing of my own, Mercy and Wolfgang set up an account for me with all the money I could ever dream of—and then added an even bigger lump sum on top.

"You are part of the ruling families now," Wolfgang declared with a roguish grin. "You will never want for anything again."

I smiled, nodded solemnly, and thanked them both, unable to admit that I *did* still want for something.

And that something is the reason I find myself staring at the ceiling in the early morning hours.

It all happened with such lightning speed. Mercy reminded me that I no longer needed to lift a finger for things to be done, and not even a week after my little spat with Gemini in Belladonna's library, I was moved in.

I huff loudly, shoving the blankets off me. I step out of bed and reach for the fluffy robe I chose for myself, even with Belladonna's and Mercy's loud protests. They insisted that the blue fleece was an eyesore. I ignored them. I loved it.

Buying a brand-new wardrobe made me realize that maybe, at twenty-five years old, I still didn't know who I was. It felt silly to have such a realization over something as insignificant as clothes, but ... my whole life, I could never afford anything but whatever I could get my sticky hands on. Then Gemini came along and treated me like his doll. I'd never had the option to choose before.

Padding across my spacious bedroom, I make my way into the en suite. A claw-foot tub faces the large arched window, dawn barely waxing over the horizon. If I'm going to spend my time thinking, might as well do it in a bath, watching the sunrise.

When I first saw the bathroom's layout, the bathtub facing the windows, I burst out crying. It reminded me so much of Gemini's house. Luckily, no one witnessed my bizarre outburst as I cursed the pregnancy hormones and pretended it'd never happened in the first place.

As I wait for the tub to fill, I undress, letting the clothes fall to the floor at my feet. Catching the reflection of my naked body in the mirror, I stop in my tracks. Turning slowly to face it head-on, I begin to carefully note how my body has changed since I was last on my own.

I've gained some much-needed weight. My hips and thighs are fuller now—healthier. My arms and legs have grown toned due to the weeks I spent practicing my routine at Animus. My heart pinches at the thought of the circus; I'm unsure when I will ever return ... or if I ever will.

I lift my hands up to my stomach, delicately placing my palms just under my belly button. I tilt my head to the side, lost in thought. I claim to be still deliberating my choice—keep it or terminate the pregnancy. But with every passing day, it's becoming harder and harder not to feel fate's damning influence.

But if I choose to keep it, does it also mean that I choose to keep Gemini?

"Veil?" Mercy says as she walks into the ruler's drawing room. "Had we planned to meet? Jeremial didn't notify me of—"

"Can we talk?" I urge, wringing my hands as I chew on my bottom lip.

Mercy's brows lift as she points a manicured finger at herself.

I nod, answering the unspoken question.

"Of course," she says with a softness I'm not accustomed to from her.

She gestures for me to sit on the settee across from her. Smoothing the back of her shift dress, she sits down, crossing her ankles together and carefully clasping her hands over her knee.

The silence lingers, coaxing me to speak.

I clear my throat, shifting nervously in my seat. "Was there ever a time you didn't trust Wolfgang?"

Mercy huffs out a wry puff of air, but I'm unsure why exactly until she says, "I never trusted Wolfgang." Then, almost to herself, she says, "I forget how little you know about our shared history."

"You grew up together, didn't you?" I ask.

She nods. "But we hated each other." Then she cocks her head, brows dipping. "Did Gemini tell you about the Lottery?"

"The Lottery?" I repeat slowly, perplexed.

Mercy sighs. "Unacceptable," she mutters under her breath as she pinches her nose. Her green eyes lift back to mine. "I'll make sure to have some books sent to your house. There's so much for you to learn."

My heart squeezes, and a vague embarrassment washes over me. I know Mercy didn't intend it that way, but I can't help chastising myself that I should know these things already. As if my lack of knowledge were somehow my fault. I wade through the misplaced shame before returning to why I came here in the first place.

"Then when? When did you begin to trust Wolfgang?"

I find no need to elaborate on why I'm asking such a probing question; I'm sure Mercy can easily surmise the deeper meaning.

She idly plays with her pearl necklace as she thinks. "I don't think it was a conscious choice. It never is when dealing with matters of the heart — wouldn't you agree?"

"I'm not sure I *do* know. I've never been in love before."

The word *before* slips past my lips, and I cringe at the implications.

"Before?" she repeats, and I break out into a cold sweat. "Do you love Gemini, Veil Vulturine?" she asks with the faintest of smiles, and she reminds me so much of him in that moment.

My cheeks burn up. "I — I prefer not to say," I croak. "It's irrelevant. If I don't — if I ..." Flustered, I stumble over my words.

Mercy finishes my sentence for me. "If you do not trust him."

Tears blur my vision, and I curse under my breath, quickly trying to catch them with a curled finger under the eye. Mortified, I evade Mercy's gaze. "I'm sorry," I mumble in frustration. "I think this pregnancy is making me more teary than usual."

She sits in silence, waiting for me to compose myself, one hand still clasped over her knee, back straight.

"I might not remember the very moment I began trusting my husband," she says, and I sheepishly slide my eyes back to hers. "But I do know this." She inches closer to the edge of her seat, leaning toward me, as if sharing a secret. "It takes vulnerability to trust. And believe me, Veil, I know firsthand how hard that is. Gemini could promise you the world; he could profess to never betray you ever again for as long as he lives, but if you don't believe him, then ..."

Mercy pauses, her gaze lifting to the ceiling before flitting back to me. My throat tightens, and I swallow hard.

"Trust and betrayal are two sides of the same coin, I fear. You must be willing to live with that harsh truth if you ever want to trust Gemini."

44

GEMINI

It's been nine days, thirteen hours, forty-eight minutes, six seconds since I last saw Veil.

Seven seconds.

Eight seconds.

Nine sec—

Her front door opens, and she appears.

"Your hair," I blurt out.

Her cheeks flush as she reaches up and slightly tugs on the ends of her brown strands, now cut into a shaggy bob, hitting just below her jaw. She shrugs, but doesn't say anything, and I realize that she might think I find her visually unappealing.

"You look divine, beloved." I clear my throat. "May I?" I ask with a wave of the hand, questioning if I can come in.

"Yes, of course," she says softly, widening the door and stepping to the side.

I loathe this awkwardness that now exists between us and vow to fix it as soon as possible. When I walk into the spacious but homey foyer of her new house, I try to conceal the sneer at the material manifestation of our separation. A visual assault against our shared destiny.

This was not part of the plan.

The only thing calming my nerves is the fact that I can see her house from my balcony across the harbor. I would have moved houses in a heartbeat and become her neighbor if I hadn't lost ownership of that piece of land.

"Let's sit in the backyard," Veil declares, snapping me out of my stewing thoughts. "The sun is out."

"Whatever you please, my beloved." My tone is far too polite, and even Veil balks at the sound, but says nothing, leading us outside instead.

Her property is quainter than I expected, with a small garden in the far back and a cozy sitting area closer to the sliding doors, string lights crisscrossing above our heads. Tall hedges surround her property, and I wonder if they remind her of the maze.

Remind her of us.

She settles into a cushioned chair, her gray cotton shirt riding up her stomach, a sliver of tattooed skin appearing, and I feel cracked open at the sight.

Oh, how I wish I could reach over and press my lips against her warm skin.

Sitting opposite her, I stay perched on the edge of the seat, my forearms resting on my thighs. I'm uncertain who should speak first, so I break the silence. "Remember when I locked you in that closet when Mercy came to visit?"

I realize my fumble when Veil's expression shutters and her body tenses.

"What I meant to say is," I add quickly, raking both hands in my hair while I attempt to defuse the situation, "Mercy came to me for advice that day. On how to apologize to Wolfgang."

Veil's brows lift in surprise, and I chuckle dryly.

"The irony is glaring, I know, but I do think it was sound advice — advice I seem to have been unable to listen to myself."

Silence settles between us as she studies me suspiciously.

"What did you tell her?" she asks.

I smile. "That her apology needs to come from the heart."

She laughs coldly at my admission and looks away. "Such a way with words," she says bitterly.

"Veil, please," I beseech, sliding even closer to the edge of my seat, needing to be as close to her as possible. "I am sorry. Deeply, *deeply* sorry. I've mistreated you — I see it now — and I am begging for you to trust that I've finally seen the error of my ways."

She eyes me warily as her bottom lip quivers, and she bites down on it to make it stop.

"How can I believe you? How can I know that what you say is true?" she whispers bitterly. "You'll never see me as your equal."

"I will — I *do*," I press. "I love you, Veil Vulturine."

Her brows rise high up her forehead, her mouth falling open at my soulful confession, and I hurry to finish the words that have been taking up so much space inside of me.

"I love you with every breath I take. My heart beats to the cadence of your very existence. *Believe me*, beloved, I am no man without you. Let alone worthy of our gods' benevolence if I have spit on the most beautiful gift they've ever given me. I was a fool to trick you — a *fool*."

My loaded words hang above our heads like a haunted apparition, and part of me expects her to swat them away and not believe any of it.

"You have hurt me deeply, Gemini," she says softly, her voice cracking around the pain I've caused.

I spring up from my seat, my skin feeling one size too small. "Then punish me!" I say desperately. "Make me pay for what I did to you!" I pace back and forth, waving my hands in the air in agitation. "As long as you keep me, beloved. As long as I am bound to you, *stitched* to you so nothing can separate us ever again."

I stop in my tracks and turn my gaze back to Veil. Her cheeks are wet with near-imperceptible tears, and I want to dig my own grave at the sight. Then I notice her lips twitching, as if fighting a smile, and my chest swells with cautious hope.

"And what about your actions?" she asks. "Those have been the most insidious of all."

I stay silent for a beat.

"Then marry me. Let's start there. Marry me, and I shall take your name as mine. Marry me so the whole of Pravitia knows that I am Veil Vulturine's husband above anything else."

She laughs; it's soft and warm, and the sound tugs on the threads of my dark, devious soul.

"You're being ridiculous," she says with a subtle smile.

"My words are not said in jest," I say as I sit back down. "In fact, I have never been this serious in my life."

My eyes never leave her as I fight every urge, every muscle in my body, to erase the space between us and take her into my arms. I don't move, hoping she erases the distance instead.

She appears to be deliberating, chewing on the mouthful of words I served her on a silver platter. The subtle lightheartedness that was twinkling in her eyes fades, and her breathtaking features shift into something far too serious. Her eyes turn watery, and my breath catches in my throat.

"I'm keeping the baby."

My mouth drops open into the widest smile, but she raises her hand in the air so as to prevent me from speaking.

"Because this is as much *my* heir as it is yours. And, well"— she lifts her eyes to the sky, as if recalling a certain memory, a hint of a grin back on her lips—"why delay fate?"

"My beloved, my divine fated perfection," I utter in awe.

I place my hands over my heart as I drop to my knees. The joy at her words makes me feel light and buoyant, like I could take flight. Instead, I crawl on my knees up to her chair and bring her hand to my lips.

I peer expectantly into her eyes. "Does this mean—"

"I have not yet forgiven you, Gemini," she says very seriously. "But ..." Her shy grin reappears, clearer this time. "Yes ... we can try to fix what you've broken."

Her words sting, but I nod profusely, willing to agree to anything as long as it means she's giving me a second chance.

"I'm moving in," I blurt out.

"What?" she says with surprise. "No, Gemini—"

"Do you think I'll have the mother of my child live *alone*?" I say a little too harshly, her hand still in my firm grip. "I might be a fool, but I am not *that* kind of fool."

She narrows her eyes in suspicion. "This is *my* house," she says, and I can't tell if this is her way of agreeing.

"I am but a humble guest in the Vulturine neighborhood," I respond as a way to further soothe her apprehensions.

Silence settles between us, and I focus on the faint bird chirping somewhere in the tree above us as Veil stares at our clasped hands, appearing to think.

"You can take the guest room," she finally says.

Frustration shoots up my body, but I nod solemnly, vowing to find my way back into her bed as quickly as I can.

45

VEIL

Gemini took no time to move in, reappearing a few hours after our talk with half a dozen suitcases and a satin pillow under his arm. That very night, he slept in the guest room, only a few doors down from my room.

Regrettably, it took me having him so close yet so far to realize that maybe the reason for my recent bout of insomnia had something to do with not sharing a bed with Gemini every night. It only made the entire situation *that* much more irritating.

I refuse to crack so easily, even keeping our physical touches at a minimum, which has proven much more difficult when he is determined to walk around naked most of the time.

Aside from his obvious provocation, Gemini has been surprisingly docile in the week since he moved in, respecting my physical *and* emotional distance.

But that was never the problem, was it?

It's the things he did behind my back that did the most damage. Like broken pieces of glass, I can still see the cracks after carefully placing them back together. The glass might still fit, a memory of once was, but they are still two separate pieces now.

My foot wobbles, and I break out of my pose, cursing under my breath. I bring my hands to my hips and walk in a small circle, head slightly falling forward as I try to catch my breath. I've been practicing a new routine for my next act at Animus, but my focus isn't as steadfast as I want it to be.

"Sore?" Gemini asks from the same corner he always sits in when he accompanies me to the circus.

His attention is trained on a book in his lap, but I can tell he's been carefully watching me this whole time.

I purposely started coming to my practices without him. A small defiance I craved, and admittedly, a part of me wanted to hurt his feelings. After a week of pitiful eyes and morose silence, I finally let him come.

"I'm just ... distracted," I answer, puffing a sweaty strand of hair out of my eyes.

"You shouldn't push yourself, my beloved; it's not good for the baby," he says.

I shoot him a searing glare, but say nothing. He chuckles, undeterred.

Chucking his book to the side, he jumps up. "I need to stretch," he mumbles under his breath. "Maybe a few handstands."

Grabbing his T-shirt with his hands on opposite sides of the bottom hem, he pulls it over his head and bunches it into a ball before throwing it next to his book.

"What is *that*?" I say incredulously, now gawking at his bare chest.

"Oh, this?" he says casually, looking down.

I can barely believe what I'm seeing—*Property of Veil Vulturine*, freshly tattooed on his ribs, just under his chest.

When he glances back up, his eyes are sparkling, and an arrogant smirk pulls on his lips. "You haven't accepted my marriage proposal yet, so ..." He shrugs as his grin widens, never finishing his sentence.

The room is hushed, save for my breath, still straining from my routine. We stare at each other, and I'm not sure what I'm supposed to feel, but after a long beat, I burst out laughing.

My hand flies to my mouth as I continue to laugh, and soon, I'm folded in half, and I can't stop. The absurdity of my life has finally caught up to me, and my fit of laughter feels cathartic somehow—as if I'm releasing something that was lodged deep inside my chest.

"You are a fool," I say as my laughter begins to wane, dabbing at tears that sprang in my eyes with how hard I just laughed.

He struts over to me, his smile full of an emotion I'm still having a hard time processing. Something a lot more terrifying than lust. Tentatively, he reaches for me, and I let him. He presses a soft kiss to the top of my head, then pulls back and winks.

"A fool for you, my beloved."

***

HOURS LATER, I CHEW ON MY NAILS IN THE PITCH-BLACK OF MY room, the blinds shutting out the moonlight, and deliberate. My heart still has many, *many* reservations, but my body yearns to be close to Gemini. After a long sigh and a few anxious heartbeats, I push my duvet to the side, my decision finally made.

Not bothering to turn on the light, I grope my way out of the bedroom and tiptoe down the hallway to the guest room. When I gently push the door open, it creaks faintly on its hinges. Despite the sound, Gemini doesn't stir under the covers.

My heart pounds in my chest. It's as if I were approaching a slumbering hyena while I quietly round the bed. I carefully pull down the bedding, watching Gemini closely for any sign of life.

His brows are slightly creased, but the rest of his body seems relaxed as he sleeps on his side, one hand slipped under his pillow.

I crawl in next to him and push the pillow right next to his, snuggling my back against his warm, hard chest. I hear Gemini inhale deeply and then let out a long, groggy hum, the sound rumbling deep in his chest. His arm curls around my waist, and he tugs me closer, his leg hooking around mine so that we're fully entwined.

"My beloved Veil," he whispers into my hair, his nose burrowing into the crook of my nape.

The raspy sound of his voice sends delicious shivers skittering down my arms and legs. My smile is dopey and wide, but I stay quiet as I feel his hand slip under my tank top. His palm flattens on my stomach, and he groans softly near my ear.

"I can't wait to see your belly swell with my child," he whispers, half asleep, pressing his hips into my ass, and my whole body bursts into flames. "How ravishing you will look, carrying our future in your womb."

I remain silent, simply wanting to soak in the moment as peacefully as possible, my walls crumbling down at a terrifying speed. His palm is searing hot on my skin, and I slip my hand over his, our fingers effortlessly interlocking with one another.

After another lazy kiss on my neck, I feel him settle behind me, his breathing slow and steady. And for the first time since I found out I was pregnant, I fall into a deep sleep until morning.

46

VEIL

Two days later, the town car slows to a stop in front of Vore—a supper club in the Vorovsky neighborhood. It's my first time being anywhere near Aleksandr's territory since Mercy and Wolfgang's wedding night, and I can't ignore the dull sting at the very core of my beating heart.

I glance over at Gemini, facing me. His attention is already trained on me, his mismatched eyes dark and hungry. There's a fresh stroke of eyeliner under his waterline, and his bruises have almost all faded from his stunning face.

His red tank top, tucked into black-and-white striped pants, hides his newly acquired tattoo, but I stare at the spot nonetheless. It shouldn't please me so much, but it does. And the greedy part of me wishes it were visible, even when fully dressed.

I haven't forgiven him yet, but with every passing day, I can feel the ice melting between us. The thaw is especially effective now that we are back sleeping in the same bed. Having his warm body curled around me as we sleep is soothing some of the burn still smarting inside of me. But *sleeping* is the only thing going on between us.

For now.

He offers me his hand.

"Come here." His tone holds a similar hunger as to how I feel.

My lips curl into a grin, and I take his hand. He pulls me onto his lap, and I giggle, the sound surprisingly carefree, wrapping my arms around his neck. He peers into my eyes, his grin turning deviant as his hand smooths up my naked thigh, his fingers toying with the hem of my silver sequined skirt.

I lean down and kiss him. A soft press of our lips, gently parting for our tongues. It's our first kiss since our rift, and the wait has made it taste ten times sweeter. When I slide my hand up to cradle his face, he groans as we deepen the kiss, his hand now grabbing a handful of my ass.

Our embrace doesn't last long, but it's enough to make me feel flipped on my axis. I keep my hand on his face, my thumb stroking his clean-shaven cheek as he gazes deeply into my eyes.

"I love you," he says softly.

The pregnancy hormones and my already raw emotions for Gemini threaten a deluge of tears. Thankfully, we are interrupted by the driver opening the door.

With me still in his lap, Gemini lunges forward and barks, "Give us a minute!" Before slamming the car door closed.

His outburst triggers a fit of giggles as I wrap my arms back around his neck. He flashes me a boyish grin, circling an arm around my waist to keep me close.

"I have something for you," he says, his voice low and conspiratorial.

My brows rise, and my curiosity is piqued, but I say nothing as his free hand opens the middle compartment beside us.

My stomach drops when I hear the sound of a chain before he lifts the leash for me to see. My reaction is instinctual; my mood sours as I push myself off of Gemini's lap, but he quickly holds me in place.

"Wait!" he says, his fingers digging into my hips.

"I'm not wearing that thing ever again," I hiss.

"What makes you think it's for you, pet?" Gemini replies, his smile coy but arrogant, with that telltale shimmer in his eyes.

My breath dies somewhere in my throat, and I grow still in his grasp, my mouth falling slightly open. My gaze flicks to the leash, back to Gemini, then back again.

There's no denying the spike of heat low in my stomach at the thought of parading one of Pravitia's most powerful on a leash. *Especially* after everything he's put me through.

"You're serious," I say, a little stunned.

"Deadly," he answers with such burning heat that I can't help but squirm on his lap.

Slowly, I open my palm between us, and his smile widens as he pushes the collar into my hand. I swallow hard as a surge of power zips through my body.

"I haven't forgiven you," I say somewhat petulantly as I curl my fingers around the soft leather.

"I know." The tone of his voice has me glancing up, finding an aching truth in his eyes. "I am not a patient man, Veil Vulturine, but for you, I will happily wait an eternity for your forgiveness. As long as I am by your side as I wait for it."

I am left breathless. His words, deeply moving, cause another wall to crumble down between us. Dropping the leash beside us, I kiss him with all the words stuck in my throat, curling my fingers into his tank top, dragging him even closer. His hands are in my hair, on my face, my neck, shoulders, breasts. *Everywhere.*

I'm so close to giving in.

So close to letting him ravage me from the inside out.

Instead, I slowly break off our kiss and reach for the collared leash.

The silent tension pulses around us as I slowly wrap the collar around his neck. My fingers delicately graze his skin, and I watch his Adam's apple bob around a hard swallow, his gaze searing and locked on me. I notice he's put his hands on the seat on either side of him, as if trying to hold himself back.

When I successfully fasten the collar to his neck, I trail my hand down the chain, slowly wrapping it around my hand, and *tug*.

Gemini lets out a low, carnal hiss at the sensation. His lips curl, showing his clenched teeth as he strains his neck, his eyes devouring me on the spot.

Another pulse of power, and this one goes directly to my core. I'm left stunned by the amount of lust wreaking havoc inside of me at the sight of Gemini like this. But most importantly, at the sight of *me* like this.

This kind of control is intoxicating.

Pushing myself off of him, I unfurl the leash out of my grip and sit across from him, still keeping the tail end firmly in my palm.

While my gaze is still fixed on Gemini's, I slowly hike my skirt up my thighs, letting my knees fall slightly open, but stop just before revealing anything interesting.

Gemini's body language turns taut, the toned muscles of his arms and shoulders cording with restraint. With a subtle snarl dragging his lip up, he looks like the very image of a feral dog on a leash.

I tug on the chain, and Gemini's laugh is so deliciously succulent and dripping with lust that I can feel myself grow wet at the sound *and* sight.

"Take your cock out," I order. "Show me how good of a whore you can be for me."

His eyes flare, but never stray from mine as he quickly but

steadily pulls out his already-hardened cock. My starving gaze dips to his thumb, rolling over his thick head and toying with his pierced tip.

Needing to feed the power growing restless inside of me, I pull the leash hard enough for Gemini to have to double over on himself.

"Spit," I bark, and his dark laugh continues to stoke my flame.

He does as I said, his saliva slowly dripping over the head of his cock, and I loosen the chain for him to settle back into his seat.

When his gaze lands back on me, his blown pupils have swallowed his eyes whole. There lies a darkness I no longer fear, but yearn to match in its intensity.

Slowly, Gemini twists his fist down his shaft before tugging on it harder, his jaw clenching over and over with the rhythm of his fist. "Am I being a good enough whore for you?" he rasps, his mouth falling open in strained pleasure.

My clit throbs, and I resist the need to open my legs even further. *Not yet.*

I don't answer immediately. My lips curve into a mischievous grin as I slowly extend my leg, placing the tip of my stiletto between his legs. "Not nearly enough," I taunt as I lick my lips with such hunger that I half expect Gemini to lunge forward and pin me to the seat.

Instead, he stays perfectly still as I press the toe of my stiletto on his balls with slow, deliberate pressure. Gemini's head falls backward, closing his eyes as he groans in pleasure. His fist pumps up and down his shaft, and the harder I press down on his balls, the harder he seems to fuck himself.

"Fuck," he whimpers before his gaze snaps back to mine, a roaring inferno raging behind his blackened eyes. "I won't last long if you keep going like that," he pants, his voice low and gravelly. "Please," he begs, "let me come inside of you." He swallows hard, his hips pitching upward as I keep my foot between his legs. "Let me feel you squeeze around my cock before I die from this agony."

We both fall silent, our eyes devouring one another as our rapid breathing fills the space between us.

I planned to toy with him some more.

To savor this moment until the very last drop.

But suddenly, I'm scrambling out of my seat, and Gemini practically catches me midair as our lips crash together in a rabid confession of shared desire and devotion. Our movements are reckless and frantic, a flurry of greed and lust so potent that I can taste it on his tongue.

Shoving my panties to the side, I take no time to sink onto Gemini's cock, and we both groan in relief as he stretches me full of him. Our kiss turns sloppy and mindless. There's no gentleness to our union. I fuck myself on him with absolute abandon as I keep the leash taut between us.

"You were made for me," Gemini says against my kiss-swollen lips, his thumb slipping between us and finding my clit already soaking with arousal.

I'm breathing hard, grinding against his hips, his cock reaching places I ached to have touched.

"You were made for me," I repeat, our foreheads pressed together.

He groans into my mouth before pulling out and flipping us over, my back hitting the seat. He leans down and drags his flattened tongue up my slit, sucking on my clit, and the sensation has me exploding into a million little pieces, my orgasm ravaging my senses.

Gemini ruts back into me with the force of a rabid animal, never letting me come down from the soul-wrenching place he just sent me to. My climax crests once more with double the force, and I curl my fingers between the leather collar and his neck as his dark eyes lock on mine. I witness the very moment his climax overcomes him. His hard, throbbing cock pulses deep inside me, fucking me full of his seed, and my body breaks into pleasured goose bumps.

This is mindless rapture.

Stripped bare and painfully human.

It's breathtaking.

Powerful.

And just for me.

47

ALEKSANDR

Taking a slow sip of my drink, I invite the familiar burn of cold vodka down my throat and swallow deeply. The harsh feeling is the closest thing I will ever get to true inebriation. A human experience that is always dangling at the very tip of my finger, but I can never quite grasp it.

It's a bore.

The frenetic energy inside of Vore tonight makes the bar feel damn near sentient. An invisible force surging with life and gorging on everybody's hunger.

At least something in here is.

The scantily clad burlesque dancers shimmer like living, breathing disco balls, dripping with diamonds and Swarovski crystals as they writhe on large swings near the ceiling. I hire them directly from Animus, one of the many business deals I've made with Gemini throughout the years for my clubs and restaurants.

Tonight, all seven of us are expected at Vore to celebrate Constantine finally getting her cast removed. Before this year's Lottery, having all of us in one room—by our own free will—

would have never occurred. But the wheel of change is turning —and turning fast.

With a sigh, I rest my chin on my palm while my gaze flicks to Constantine. She's been glued to the stripper's pole she had me install in the middle of the VIP section. To my dismay, she hasn't stopped moving since the cast came off two days ago. She promised me swift dismemberment if I even *tried* to attempt to have her rest.

My stomach twists into knots as I watch her hook her recently injured knee around the pole. As she bends herself backward, sliding her leg up the pole, her ruffled pink shorts ride up her ass, and my stomach does a lot more than just twist into knots.

How can I hunger for someone with such conviction when I've never experienced *physical* hunger in the first place? A conundrum.

My own little paradox.

Wolfgang drops down beside me. My gaze slides to him and then to Belladonna and Mercy talking a few seats over, but my attention eventually returns to Constantine.

"Have you said anything to her yet?" He utters the question close to my ear, but my body jolts, as if he yelled it into the club's speakers for everyone to hear.

I shush him loudly as I straighten up. He says nothing more, smirking into his drink, his gold signet ring catching the light as he takes a slow sip of bourbon.

I answer him anyway. "It hasn't been the right time, and besides—"

Constantine's squeal of delight rises above the loud music, causing both Wolfgang and me to turn our heads at the sound. She bounces up and down on her chunky platforms, her pink-tipped pigtails bouncing right along with her.

It takes me a second to find what has made her so giddy,

and I hear Wolfgang loudly groan beside me the moment I finally spot it myself.

It's Veil. She's cutting through the crowd with Gemini following right behind her.

And she's leading him by a leash.

"Children," Wolfgang mutters with exasperation, suddenly acting like our father.

Something about his reaction, the dejected pinch of his nose, and the absurdity of our newest couple making such a show in public has me barking out a laugh.

No wonder Constantine is so pleased to see them.

Whatever makes existing more tantalizing, more vibrant with life. Because I am the only one who will ever understand the all-consuming emptiness that accompanies the lack of such a primal sensation like pain ... or hunger.

She will reach dizzying heights just to feel.

I'm usually right beside her when she does.

When Veil reaches our section, Constantine leaps into her arms, her foot snapping up behind her. She then promptly drags Veil by the hand to where we are sitting. Gemini eagerly follows Veil like a lovestruck puppy.

The leash is long enough that Gemini sits beside Mercy, joining her conversation with Belladonna while Veil and Constantine join ours.

"Can you believe it?" Constantine snickers into her hands before sighing wistfully and looking up at the ceiling. "True love."

Veil, who usually reeks of anxious energy, appears quite calm today, chin high and shoulders straight. She toys with the leash resting on her lap before saying, "It's the least he can do."

The accompanying smirk and arrogant lift of one eyebrow further solidify her newly centered energy. No one at the table needs any elaboration on the *why* behind her statement.

"Make sure he suffers," Constantine says with the deadliest smile.

By the way Veil laughs and brushes it off, I can tell she thinks Constantine is simply joking.

But the servant of torture never jokes about such things.

Pain and suffering are her magnum opus.

"And the pregnancy?" Wolfgang asks.

I roll my eyes and stare into my glass. Wolfgang just can't help but be in everyone's business.

Veil's cheeks turn bright red, but she smiles and nods. "I'm keeping it." She says it so quietly that her voice is nearly drowned out by the loud music.

Wolfgang nods solemnly, still uncomfortably masquerading as a father figure.

Setting down my drink, I twist the cap off a glass water bottle and lean over the table to hand it to Veil before giving her a quick wink. She appears surprised by the gesture, but takes it out of my hand nonetheless, followed by a small nod as a thank-you. I realize then that we haven't spoken much since she crash-landed in the middle of all our lives.

I should make more of an effort, especially since Constantine seems so smitten by her.

Anything shiny and new.

Raising my glass, I turn my attention to Constantine. "To Tinny and her well-deserved freedom," I declare.

Constantine's face smooths into the brightest of smiles as she picks up her watered-down mojito. "And to the next generation of Pravitia!" she says, clinking her highball against Veil's water bottle.

As if summoned, Gemini pops from behind Veil, a demented smile on his face. "Did someone say *the next generation of Pravitia?*"

He kisses Veil's neck before sliding beside Wolfgang. "Don't worry, Wolfie; your day will come," he says so condescendingly that I know the only reason Wolfgang doesn't tackle Gemini to the ground is for Mercy's sake.

Wolfgang's jaw feathers. "Unlike you imbeciles, we are in no rush."

Gemini's eyes flick to where I'm sitting for only a split second before turning to Constantine. "Maybe Tinny will be next then."

My heart drops into my stomach at his implication, but Constantine, as always, doesn't pick up on it. She simply falls into a giggling fit at the mere thought.

I promise Gemini a swift death through my silent glare, but he's unperturbed, and he sends me a kiss from across the table.

I should make my infatuation less obvious if Gemini picked up on it.

Then again, what's stopping me now?

48

GEMINI

I pretend to read the words on the page, the book propped up on my knees as I wait for Veil to join me in bed. Instead, I'm listening to every sound my beloved is making in the en suite, envisioning what the sounds are attached to.

The brush raking through her hair. The running water as she washes her face. The small clink of the lid from her face cream touching the counter.

Whoever first paired the word *domesticated* with the word *bliss* sure understood the meaning of life. I can't get enough. I haven't been back to my house since I muscled my way into hers three weeks ago. I haven't left her bed in the two weeks since we've made up.

I don't miss my house, not when I find great pleasure in watching Veil slowly decorate hers to her liking. With each new decoration or furnishing, she learns about herself—her likes and dislikes. And to witness her come into her own is a divine gift I will not be so brash to spoil.

Things might be going a lot more smoothly now, but there's

still some resistance from Veil. I pretend not to feel it. She pretends not to know I can feel it.

Veil is teaching me patience ... not everything needs to be an instant gratification, especially when my reward is a life spent with the servant of thievery.

And the heir currently growing in her belly.

From the corner of my eye, I see her step back into the bedroom, the en suite door facing the king-size bed. She takes a few steps forward, then stops. I feign to be riveted by my book as she makes a sharp right and takes another few steps, but never distances herself from the foot of the bed.

She's acting like a malfunctioning wind-up doll. Not that I would ever call her my doll again. I like my place next to her throne far too much.

My queen.

Finally, I lift my gaze and find her rooted to the spot, chewing on her nail in the middle of the room, eyes wide with what I *think* is apprehension.

With slow, deliberate movements, I close my book and place it on the bedside table. "Something on your mind, my beloved Veil Vulturine?"

"Hmm?" she says, her thumb still in her mouth, brows raised in alarm.

She seems to realize what she's been doing and rips her thumb out of her mouth. Laughing nervously, she rubs her nape, then folds one arm around her waist, curling her fingers around the opposite arm.

She's a blatant show of nerves, and for once, I'm stumped as to why.

"Are you going to tell me what's on your mind?" I press since she has yet to say a single word.

"It's my birthday tomorrow," she blurts out.

"Correct," I say slowly, my eyes narrowing.

I pat her side of the bed, but don't bother saying anything

further. Her shoulders slump, but she scurries over to her side and crawls under the covers beside me.

I turn to face her. "What's wrong?"

"Nothing," she says quickly.

My face drops as I eye her warily, conveying just how much I don't believe her.

She sighs and looks up at the ceiling before finally giving me *some* hint of what's troubling her. "I've been thinking," she starts as she stares at a spot on the duvet between us, "about how much has changed since my last birthday ... and how much will continue to change now that I'm turning twenty-six." She lifts her gaze, watery with unshed emotions. "I don't want to begin this important chapter without—" Her voice cracks, and she clears her throat, toying with her lips nervously. "Without telling you that I love you." She pushes out the end of her sentence in one hurried breath.

My heart drops. Then does multiple pirouettes in my chest before I find my voice again.

I reach for her face, trailing the back of my hand on her cheek. "Can you repeat that? Slower this time," I say, a hint of tease in my tone.

Her smile is shy, as if she exhausted all of her courage just to say it. "I love you."

Her finger feathers over my tattoo—*her* tattoo—and I slowly curl my palm over her hand, bringing it up to my lips. "I love you too."

"But ..."

She tries to take her hand away, but I tighten my grip, pulling her closer instead. She gives me a half-hearted eye roll, but doesn't resist or protest.

"But what?" I murmur into her fingers as I continue to press kisses into her palm.

The nerves return. She chews on her bottom lip, then swallows hard.

"I don't know if I trust you yet."

A vague sense of relief washes over me.

"That's a small matter, beloved."

She scoffs, but there's humor tucked in the echo of the sound. "Such arrogance," she says under her breath.

I know what she will say next, so I beat her to the punch. "Time," I reply.

Her eyes brighten in surprise, and she nods. "Yes. Time," she repeats slowly, then quirks a smile. "Loving you was out of my control."

I give her fingers a bite in protest, and she laughs.

"But I choose to trust you. It's *my* choice, and it might be the most important choice I'll ever make." She leans closer and kisses me tenderly, then pulls away to look into my eyes. "I didn't want to wake up tomorrow, a year older, without having made that choice."

My chest lights up as if someone had struck a match behind my rib cage. "Do you choose me, Veil Vulturine?" I ask with a warm smile, trailing my free hand over her beautiful face.

She smiles, her hand finding the crook of my waist, and it's the most radiant thing I've ever seen. "I choose you, Gemini Foley."

EPILOGUE
VEIL

$\mathcal{A}$ pair of hands grabs me from behind and tugs me into their hard chest. I shriek in surprise, although I know that the person walking us back into a more secluded corner of Mercy's garden is Gemini.

Now that spring is fully underway, she and Wolfgang invited the heirs to dine in her newly bloomed all-black garden. I still barely know Mercy, but even I was surprised by her sudden hospitality. But there's an inherent understanding between the families now. Times are changing, and strengthening ties between the ruling families is in all our best interests.

Or at least, for the next nineteen years until the next Lottery.

"I missed you, my beloved," he rasps into my ear as his hands rove over my summer dress, palming my stomach.

I'm only roughly ten weeks pregnant and still not showing, but Gemini doesn't care. He's always finding a reason to touch me, as if already sensing the growing life under his fingertips.

"I was gone for less than five minutes," I tease as I turn around to face him, my arms effortlessly circling his neck.

His back rests against the tree trunk as he pulls me closer, kissing me with lips curled into a grin. "Again, your maddening obsession with time," he says before pressing a kiss just under my jaw. "Time has no meaning in the affairs of the heart."

My laugh is breezy and full of ease. "You're the maddening one." I feel his chuckle vibrate against my skin, and I smile into a happy sigh.

Since my birthday, Gemini has been nothing but supportive, and the trust that I so begrudgingly gave him that fateful night has only been growing in strength since.

His support was especially meaningful during my first Tithe Season on the spring equinox, four weeks ago. It was my first Season as an heir of the city of Pravitia. Luckily, it wasn't as overwhelming as it could have been. For the servant to the god of thievery, collecting tithe is similar to Mercy's way—personal and much less attention-seeking.

However, since I now ruled over half of Gemini's territory, he insisted I attend his day of tithing and listen in on the countless secrets divulged to him that day.

"My secrets are your secrets, my beloved."

After all, trickery and thievery go hand in hand.

Just like us.

And thus, my walls continued to crumble brick by brick until there were no more stones to remove. I know Gemini would like to get married and that, ultimately, it will be expected from us. But I'm in no rush. I'm the one deciding our fate next, not Gemini.

"Come," I say breathlessly after kissing him one more time. Taking his hand, I lead him back onto the stone path. "We're missing the feast."

"HE CAN'T HELP HIMSELF, CAN HE?" BELLADONNA SIGHS BESIDE me while giving me a playful side-eye. Her red lips are pressed into a small pout, as if trying to conceal her mirth, but she can't hide the twinkle in her green eyes.

We finished dining about an hour ago, now stuffed full of every dish imaginable—from perfectly cooked steaks to buttery pastries that melted on my tongue with every bite.

As the long black-draped table was slowly getting cleared away by servants, Gemini took the opportunity to jump up onto the table and make a toast. His speech has been going on for the last five minutes, and Constantine is the only one who seems to be completely riveted by his words, Aleksandr faithfully by her side. Mercy and Wolfgang seem mildly entertained but are distracted, sharing some private words at the other end of the table.

Gemini's little performance can't help but remind me of that *other* fateful night, with a feast just as decadent as this one. But tonight, the apprehension isn't twisting my stomach into knots. Instead, I revel in being here among them.

I take a sip of water and smile at Belladonna, followed by a warm chuckle. "Any opportunity to put on a show."

She nods, returning my smile. I don't miss her eyes dipping down to my stomach before looking back up.

"Can you believe he's the father of your two heirs?" Her tone is in jest, but her words are anything but.

My heart skips a beat as my mouth drops open. "Are you — are you saying that I'm having ..."

Her gaze is twinkling as she nods, her smile growing even wider.

"Gemini!" I yelp across the table without thinking, cutting through the chatter.

He stops mid-speech, a coupe of half-drunk champagne lazily hanging from his fingers. "Yes, my beautiful future wife?"

Silence has fallen over the group and all eyes are now on

me. I feel nothing but elation and am equally ecstatic to share the good news with the others.

"We're having twins," I say softly yet loud enough for everyone to hear.

The reactions are simultaneous as I jump up from my seat, eager for an embrace from Gemini. Constantine lets out a shriek and starts clapping with glee while Gemini's eyes widen in shock. He takes a step back but fumbles over one of the centerpieces, loses his balance, and falls off the table, taking Wolfgang with him.

I hurry over to where he fell. Mercy and Aleksandr have already joined in to help both men off the ground.

"Mindless fool," Wolfgang barks as he gets back on his feet. He brushes off his suit, glaring at Gemini as if he committed the highest offense.

But Gemini ignores him, his full attention on me, beaming as brightly as if he'd collected entire galaxies of stars just for this moment. I jump into his open arms, my hands circling his neck as he spins us around, his laugh just as giddy as mine. When he sets me back on my feet, he peers into my eyes, and the love I find in his gaze is enough to keep me warm for eons to come.

"Twins," he whispers as if just for us. "How did I get so lucky?"

I kiss him before falling even deeper into his tender gaze. I know his question is rhetorical, but I still answer anyhow. My voice is just as low, keeping this small moment in time just for the two of us before we return to the festivities around us.

"Luck?" I tease. "Or fate?"

More from Naomi Loud

a line cook x
server romance

MORE FROM NAOMI LOUD

Don't miss out on the bestselling dark romance series "Was I Ever".

Sunny and Byzantine	Was I Ever Here
Lenix and Connor	Was I Ever Real
Lucy and Bastian	Was I Ever Free

If you don't want to miss out on any future book announcements make sure to follow me on Instagram and Tiktok at naomi.loud or subscribe to my newsletter! You can find the link on my website: www.naomiloud.com

You can also join my Patreon to receive exclusive behind the scenes updates, teasers, character art, giveaways and bonus content!

And if you loved Feast of Fools I'd be forever grateful if you could leave a positive review on Amazon. Your support is why indie authors can continue doing what we love. Thank you!

ACKNOWLEDGMENTS

Thank you to my dream team: Cait, Lotte, Shani, Bella, Meghan & Nouha. You are the best alpha team a girl could ask for. Thank you for giving up your precious personal time to help me birth book after book into existence. LOVE YOU SO MUCH.

Thank you to my bully—sorry *beta* team: Casadi, Jessy, Ada, Janine, Lo, Aly & Connie. Ya'll keep me humble lmao!

Thank you to my editor Jovana! And my OG editor Louise, look at us go!! And lastly, thank you to my cover designer Cat. I'm so obsessed with your brain and creativity, love you so much.

ABOUT THE AUTHOR

Naomi Loud is an author of angsty dark romance. While her first love are words—spirituality and magic are the lenses through which she experiences the world and this heavily influences her writing, especially in her debut series "Was I Ever". She lives in Montreal, Canada with her husband and three cats but secretly wishes she could live underwater.